FIVE STAR DETOUR

By Sherban Young

THE ENESCU FLEET SERIES

Fleeting Memory
Fleeting Glance
Fleeting Note
Fleeting Chance
Fleeting Promise

THE WARREN KINGSLEY SERIES

Five Star Detour
Double Cover
Double Talk

MORE BOOKS

Opportunity Slips
Dead Men Do Tell Tales

FIVE STAR DETOUR

SHERBAN YOUNG

Columbia, MD

New MysteryCaper edition published in 2019

Cover and illustrations by Katerina Vamvasaki

Editing services by Katherine Richards from *The Reading Panda*

ISBN-10: 0-9912324-0-2
EAN-13: 978-0-9912324-0-6

MysteryCaper Press
Columbia, Maryland

www.mysterycaper.com
www.sherbanyoung.com

Dedication

To Pelham Grenville

Part One

1 — The Errand

The maître d' looked up from his reservation list and stared disapprovingly. A tall young man wearing a sport coat and blue jeans had stepped across the threshold, flooding the Churchill Inn's tastefully lit foyer with afternoon sunshine. As the door shut behind him, the visitor paused, apparently contemplating the coat of arms displayed on the wall to his right. After a moment, he turned and noticed he had captured the host's attention.

"Oh, hello. Didn't see you there. Is this Latin?" he asked, nodding to the words below the shield. Detecting a lack of interest, he continued, "Well, it doesn't matter. Has a guy named Hathaway popped in yet?"

"Did you say Hathaway?"

"That's right. Gruff sort of geezer. Looks like a tyrant having a bad day."

"You don't mean *Congressman* Hathaway, do you?"

"Yes, that's the one. I usually just call him Uncle George."

The maître d' sniffed and without further comment conducted the guest to the Wellington Room.

John Hathaway knew his uncle wouldn't have invited him to lunch without an agenda. Even in their early days, back when Hathaway was a gangly bundle of energy and George, his guardian, still had a few hairs that had not turned white, the latter did not seek the former's company capriciously. During those years, Hathaway the Younger had gone one way and Hathaway the Older had gone the other. To this day, they only met up in the middle when financial and/or legal reasons dictated.

As usual, they exhausted the small talk over soup and spent the intervals between courses in silence. John Hathaway had fallen into a quiet reflection of his entrée when the congressman finally got down to the issue at hand.

"Johnny, you're a wastrel."

Hathaway took a bite of his fillet and weighed the remark. "I don't know. How are you defining 'wastrel,' Uncle George?"

Uncle George, who could have easily authored volumes on the subject, spoke broadly:

"I suppose I'd define a wastrel as someone who spends money faster than most people could burn it; as someone who constantly hits his uncle up for loans; as someone who doesn't work, has no prospects and has no interest in life but for the most pleasurable of pursuits."

"Well, if you put it that way …" Hathaway agreed, trailing off. "You know what Francis Bacon says about that, though? No, wait, maybe it's Shakespeare. Anyway, one of them says 'Riches are for spending.' "

"It's Bacon, and I'm sure he meant one's own riches. You see, Johnny, to be a wastrel you have to have some money to waste. And, as you will recall, you have now merged into the business of wasting my money."

In or out of a political forum, George Hathaway was acknowledged as a formidable orator and only needed the slightest encouragement to become long-winded. To reinforce his portrait of his nephew as a spendthrift, he began to reflect upon the pattern in Johnny's youth of borrowing a twenty here and a fifty there, this retrospective segueing to the time that he lost a small fortune in a craps game while at school.

As this tirade unfolded, John Hathaway let his attention wander. Not a formidable orator himself, he had turned from the argument to rest his eyes on a woman in a formfitting business suit seated by the window. It was perhaps two minutes later that something in the lecture brought him out of his trance.

"And tomorrow," his uncle was saying, "you can do something useful for a change. I have a little errand for you."

"But I have plans. I'm going to Foxwoods tomorrow, remember?"

"This won't interfere with your trip too drastically. I need you to deliver a parcel to an old friend of mine. His name's Roger Banbury. I think you met him once when you were away at boarding school."

"The Brit? Yeah, I met him. Big fellow, flamboyant mustache ... Wait, you're not saying I have to haul this thing all the way to England, are you?"

"Roger hasn't been in the UK for twenty years. He lives on a huge estate in Maine now, just a few dozen miles from civilization. Since you're heading up to that same area anyway, I thought you could handle this for me."

"Connecticut and Maine are not in the same area!"

"Nonsense. It's barely out of your way."

Hathaway prodded his potato defiantly. "Really, Uncle George. Can't you give this chore to some flunky?"

"I just did."

"Another flunky, then? I mean, why do you need me to deliver it?"

"You're a courier, aren't you?"

The younger Hathaway nodded sullenly.

In the two years since he had graduated college and begun his "career" as a freelance courier—"The courier you call when you're in a pinch"—he had made precisely four deliveries. It was not that he hated the work. He merely preferred to work when the feeling moved him, and in the last four months of his semiretirement, living off his savings account and the occasional advance from his uncle, the feeling had not moved him.

"Yes, but, I'm pretty selective about the work I take on."

"Work!" the uncle scoffed. "I'd hardly call it work. If it were a real job, you'd work more than twice a year and would actually make some money."

"And I'm sort of on vacation."

"Your life is a vacation."

"Nevertheless. Besides, I'm not the most experienced courier. I'm freelance—specialized. There are people who do this sort of thing all the time."

"I don't need experienced. All I need is someone I can trust who can get this item from Point A to Point B. I assume you can handle that?"

"Can't you mail it from Point A to Point B?"

"Too valuable."

"What is it?" the younger man asked.

"Not important. It's just a parcel. You can pick it up from my office before you leave tomorrow."

John Hathaway sipped his wine moodily.

At these times when he really wanted to tell his uncle to stuff it, he ground his teeth and reminded himself that any backchat could mean certain poverty. Thanks to some last-minute scribblings amending his grandfather's will, Hathaway was saddled with George as the trustee of his inheritance. It was not an enormous amount of money, but the trust paid the bills, and considering that the congressman had recently advanced him four years' worth of income from it, Hathaway knew better than to rub the geezer the wrong way.

This dependence on the relative grated on him, though. If he had a real job or even a plan, things would be different. Hathaway's only plan, however, was an idea to devise a plan at some point in the near future.

"Don't look so distressed," his uncle said, his manner lightening. "Banbury's place is like a five-star hotel. You'll love it."

*

John Hathaway, for good or ill, never let things bother him for long. Sure, the idea of lugging some parcel around New England had lowered his spirits initially, but it was only a momentary lowering. The attitude he adopted as he walked down Allegheny Avenue toward the Fairview Luxury Apartments was nothing short of cheerful. The sky was blue, the birds were chirping, and Brittany Landers and her new bathing suit awaited.

Hathaway had known Brittany for just over a month. They had met at a cocktail party at his uncle's house and from that point on had seen each other on a regular, although somewhat casual, basis. This weekend would be their first trip together, and it was one Hathaway had been planning for a while. His description of the vacation, when prompted for details by Brittany, had been sketchy, however, for it had occurred to him early in their relationship that they were not of like mind on hobbies. Where he preferred gambling, quiet evenings by the fire and lots of room service, she leaned more toward the great outdoors and the open excitement of skydiving, bungee jumping and white-water rafting. Convincing her that a weekend in a smoky casino would be as fun as hiking down the Appalachians was not going to be an easy task, but he figured his manly charm would see him through.

He arrived at Brittany's apartment at half past three and tapped on the door.

"Come in, please."

A careful listener would have detected a cool, almost calculated tone to these words, but Hathaway, in his enthusiasm to enter, let them pass unnoticed. He was therefore unprepared when he stepped within and something sailed from across the room and thumped him in the chest. Once he had identified this projectile as a hiking boot, he looked up and noticed Brittany. Standing by the window—a petite, energetic woman with flashing eyes—she had the appearance of someone who had just thrown footwear and could do it again.

"Was there a reason why you flung this boot at me, Brittany, or was it just a whim?"

Brittany spoke calmly, restraining her emotions. "You told me we were going white-water rafting and rock climbing this weekend."

"Right."

"You don't deny it?"

"Yes. I mean no," he said.

"So that's why we're going to Connecticut, then?"

Hathaway let the question breathe a moment before replying.

"Yes—" he replied, hesitating. "Of course, we may get up there and decide to change our plans. No one likes hurtling down savage rivers and dangling from jagged rocks more than I, you understand. But we may find, once we arrive, that river hurtling fails to fascinate or that rock dangling is, er, not much to write home about. Sort of a Plan B, in that case, might be to—"

"Go to Foxwoods?"

He stiffened. There had been a leak. "Foxwoods?" he asked.

"The casino in Connecticut."

Only now could Hathaway appreciate the full brunt of what he was up against. He attempted to backpedal with "There's a casino in

Connecticut?" but one look at Brittany's dark, glaring eyes told him it was no use. "How did you—I mean, who told you?"

"The travel agent called. She wanted to confirm our reservations at the hotel."

"She did, did she?" Hathaway held back his remark that travel agents should mind their own damn business.

"She said there are no mountains suitable for climbing or white-water rivers anywhere near the hotel."

"Wow, she really knew her stuff. It's good we have Plan B, then, huh?"

"When were you planning on telling me that we weren't rafting this weekend?"

It occurred to Hathaway that he had only really planned to form a plan to tell her. "I mean, casinos are a lot like rafting," he said. "Why are you shaking your head?"

"I want something adventurous. Danger, excitement. What's so adventurous about playing cards?"

"You obviously have never tried to draw to an inside straight."

The quip failed to mollify. "My father was right," she announced.

"Right about what?"

Brittany Landers was Governor Landers' daughter, a fact that always made Hathaway feel slightly uneasy, as if on their dates the National Guard had been dispatched to survey their every move. He had never met the man in person and found himself curious what the gov could have inferred purely from reputation.

"My father said you're a compulsive gambler, and he was right. Your uncle told him," she added. "He said you used to lose your text-book money playing craps in school."

Hathaway turned pale at this reminder of his misspent youth, the second mention of it that day. To clarify the facts, he only put down money earmarked for math textbooks, and in all fairness, he never did understand the game much anyway.

"I was young. Foolish."

"So why are we going to Connecticut?"

"To play poker. It's totally different. Look, I'm sorry about the rafting. We can still have a fun weekend, though. As it turns out, we have to make a brief stop-off in Maine—Roger Banbury's place. I understand he has quite a house up there, complete with a giant indoor pool. So what I say is bring your bathing suit, or better yet don't, and we'll forget all about this and take a few midnight swims."

The other boot, thrown by one no longer restraining her emotions, told him that Brittany and her new bathing suit were going to remain in the metropolitan area for the weekend.

Hathaway, seeing continued application of his manly charm useless, made his exit.

2 — A Guest List Overflows

At roughly the same moment that John Hathaway left the Fairview and began wandering the now dull streets back toward his home, some six hundred miles away, Lady Margaret Banbury, an attractive woman in her mid-fifties, stepped into the den of her husband, Sir Roger Banbury. She found him seated at his desk, gazing out at the acres of Maine landscape that made up their estate.

Profiled in *Life* magazine, Rangeley Manor had been called "a definitive tribute to the British Empire in America ... and a nostalgic look back at a bygone nobility." Indeed, as its owner's eyes rolled over the plush meadows and across the horizon to the stables, he could almost feel the years melting away. Even the weather lately seemed consistent with the English countryside: it rained constantly.

Hathaway might not have realized it at the time, but twenty years ago, when he met Roger Banbury, he was seeing the man on the brink of corporate stardom. A captain of industry at age fifty, Banbury would soon leave England as a tax exile and proceed to run amok in the world of electronics. He would continue to dominate the market for the next two decades, before finally, in his seventies, selling his business and retiring to the backwoods of Maine.

Today, as an elder man of affairs and a US citizen, he enjoyed living out his golden years in the country that made him his fortune. It was a good, quiet life. Even the Crown, showing a willingness to let bygones be bygones, had knighted him a few months back.

Lady Banbury—the designation one of the courtesies of Banbury's recognition and one she never tired of flaunting to her untitled friends—stood at the doorway, watching her husband. Clearing her throat twice before he registered her presence, she spoke softly but with a characteristic succinctness. "Roger, we have guests arriving the day after tomorrow."

Sir Roger failed to note how this related to him. "And?"

"We need to make preparations for them. Have you forgotten that Grace Bosworth is coming to stay?"

"I have not forgotten," said Sir Roger sharply. "I never knew it."

"I do wish you would listen to me, Roger. Miss Bosworth is a very important person."

"I don't care who she is. I'm tired of people treating this like some kind of country hotel."

"We have to play good hosts," Lady Banbury offered, appealing to her husband's social ambition, of which there was hardly a droplet.

The latter turned in his chair. He took a long breath, letting his chest puff with air before deflating it once again. "Do you remember why we built this place, Maggie?" he asked. "It was supposed to be the three of us. Me, you and Adrienne."

"And we're all here."

"Along with half the world's idle rich. I often wonder if these people have homes."

"High society has its burden, sweetheart. How would it look if we shut our doors to the upper crust?"

"Splendid. Just spectacular. I can think of nothing more enjoyable than sitting on my porch watching the upper crust file off into the distance, a sad and dejected mass."

"I'm afraid that's not going to happen, dear. If you wanted privacy, you shouldn't have made this place so big."

Sir Roger responded with a snort. "The least you could do is bring us someone stimulating."

Lady Banbury made no comment. "Assuming that's all settled," she went on, "I have a surprise for you. And you needn't give me that look—this is a good surprise. The nephew of a friend of yours is coming to stay."

"All my friends are dead."

"Not all of them. Congressman Hathaway is in reportedly good health."

Sir Roger looked up. A glimmer flickered in his eye. "George? Is he still a congressman?"

"Thanks to you," said Lady Banbury. She spoke coolly. "You did finance his campaign."

"I suppose I did," Sir Roger agreed. "Congressman Hathaway. Honestly, I never would have thought he had a shot in politics. Of course, standards here are very low. Good old George. My word. He once threw up on my shoes, you know?"

Lady Banbury raised an eyebrow. Though she admittedly found herself intrigued by the statement and couldn't help wondering what a member of Congress was doing throwing up on her husband's shoes, or anyone's shoes for that matter, she nonetheless had to insist that they stay on the subject.

"Roger, about Mr. Hathaway—"

"It was at Oxford. We had just finished off the vodka, and—you don't appear interested, my dear."

"Not at the moment, no."

"You used to love my anecdotes."

"I do, darling, but not when we have issues at hand. Now then, it appears that Mr. Hathaway is bringing a Miss Landers with him, daughter of Governor Landers. Then there's still Miss Bosworth."

"You say her name like I'm supposed to recognize it."

"The Bosworth family owns a newspaper in London."

"A newspaper, eh? I hope it's a good issue." A wry smile played over his lips. A pretty good comeback, he thought. Years ago, he used to make witty remarks like that all the time. Kept the board of directors in stitches.

Lady Banbury did not approve. Far from the audience of guffawing yes-men Sir Roger had grown accustomed to, she did not appreciate levity at her expense. She huffed impatiently and said, "I don't mean a single newspaper; I mean the publishing company. The Bosworths have been in publishing for nearly a century."

"And she's one of them, is she? Why's everyone sending us their blasted relatives? That's what I want to know. Can't we get any celebrities here themselves, or does Rangeley only have the lure to bring in their families?"

"I really couldn't say. Now then, in anticipation of our guests' arrival, I want to engage the Bath Chamber Orchestra. As you know, the orchestra is looking for a new conductor. With any luck, Kurt Richter will fill the post. He recently moved here from Austria and is entertaining offers. I'm hoping to snag him before Sylvia Wainwright, the head of the arts council in Boothbay, beats me to it. Richter is very much in demand."

Sir Roger stared. "Just how many people did you invite here this weekend anyway? We're not a symphony hall, you know?"

"I know we're not a symphony hall, Roger. A small ensemble is coming up from the coast to play for Mr. Richter, not the whole orchestra. Aside from them, there's Mr. Hathaway and his Miss Landers. And Miss Bosworth. And Dr. Powers. Let's see, I think we'll have sixteen in all. Oh dear. We're going to be quite full this weekend," she declared. Realizing that she would need to hire extra cooking staff, Lady Banbury departed.

No sooner had his wife left him than the door opened and Adrienne Banbury came in with a purposeful stride. Seeing his daughter and recognizing the look in her eye, Sir Roger slumped lower in his chair.

Sir Roger loved his family, but in small doses. No doubt Adrienne's arrival meant she was about to bring up the subject of her idiot fiancé—*Ditters-Dup-Something*—and Sir Roger, weakened from the news that his house would soon be opening its doors to sixteen strangers, some of whom would be tooting horns and other noisemakers, found himself emotionally unprepared for the conference.

At times like these, when he felt them coming at him from all sides, his urge was to lock himself in the basement among his many treasured collectibles. Since retiring, he had made collecting his obsession, and the basement was his sanctuary. There he could think. Knee-deep in trinkets and doodads from around the world, he was content. He asked himself: Did Indonesian statuettes ever nag? No. Had they ever filled his house with guests he didn't know? Never. Did his prized spears from Madagascar ever plant brainless fiancés on him? Not that he could recall.

Happy thoughts, but at the moment his daughter had begun to question his far-off stare.

"What?" he answered. "Yes, I'm listening, and I don't want to talk about this Dipperdorp, Adrienne."

"His last name's not Dipperdorp. He's been here over three weeks, and you still don't know his name. It's Dittersdorf, with an *f*."

"I know perfectly well what his name is."

"Then why do you insist on mocking him?"

"He looks like a Dipperdorp. What sort of name is Dittersdorf anyway? Sounds German."

"Father—"

"Adrienne," said Sir Roger, a thought occurring to him, "couldn't you find some nice, upright man? He doesn't even have to be a businessman. Just someone with half a brain—that's all I ask. Couldn't you find someone with half a brain?"

"I don't want someone with half a brain," Adrienne squeaked. "I want him!" Seeing that she had broken her reserve, she paused. Stepping back and assuming a rigid posture—a tall girl even when she slouched—she took a different approach. "Father, my fiancé is a wonderful, caring man, and you're just too pigheaded to see it. Of course, I'm not saying that he doesn't need any work. I have never said that. But you have to see past all that, as I do. Why can't you learn to overlook his flaws?"

"Overlook his flaws," said Sir Roger. "Overlook his flaws," he repeated, drawing himself up in his chair. "My dear, if I overlooked this Dipperdorp's flaws, the man would be invisible."

"Father, really!"

Just then, as if to bring a ceasefire to this family chaos, Jackson, the Banbury's butler, entered the room. "Lady Banbury is looking for you, Miss Banbury."

Adrienne submitted the servant to a chilly glare. Remarking to her father that the subject was far from closed, she turned and left in what amounted to a huff. Jackson followed, not at all in a huff, and once again Sir Roger was left to himself.

Completely rattled from the past two interviews, however, he found little solace in the landscape. His mind was reeling, and considering that Sir Roger's mind often reeled for hours once it got started, he decided to take advantage of the mental energy and settle another subject, also concerning a guest soon to arrive at the mansion.

Reaching for the intercom on his desk, he called for Randal, his executive secretary. After pounding the buzzer repeatedly and still finding himself Randal-less, Sir Roger rose and trotted across the room. A towering man in his late seventies, he moved with considerable swiftness. In his prime, one would have called him stately, perhaps imposing. Even today, Sir Roger's thick mustache and determined brow brought to mind a figure of well-aged virility. Bounding into his secretary's office, he began to shout Randal's name. Noticing Jackson, he attempted to solve the mystery of his employee's disappearance.

"Mr. Finch is in Washington, DC, sir, arriving home on the train the day after tomorrow."

"What the hell is he doing in Washington? Who told him he could go to Washington?"

"Lady Banbury sent Mr. Finch to meet Miss Bosworth and escort her here, sir."

"Oh blast!" Sir Roger stood staring at a vase.

In this modern era, it has no doubt occurred to all thinking men and women that the need for a butler has all but slipped into the past (especially in America, where the butler fad never really caught on). That was why Bertram Jackson prided himself on being an excellent butler. A less experienced manservant than he would have skipped off as soon as he observed the old guy's eyes glaze over. But Jackson knew his employer and understood that his mind was at times wont to stall, a quality not so much attributed to his years as it was simply a feature of Sir Roger's brand of intellect. As a businessman, he would frequently indulge in moments of far-off thought. His board of directors used to plan lunch around them.

The butler waited patiently. Perhaps thirty seconds later, Sir Roger spoke again.

"Listen, Jackson, you're going to have to handle this for me."

"Yes, sir."

"No good saying, 'Yes, sir'; you don't know what it is yet."

"Yes, sir."

"Tomorrow a guest is arriving—a well-known art dealer. His name's Konig."

"Konig," Jackson repeated.

"Yes, that's it: Konig. He has a first name, I'm sure, but I've forgotten it. Never mind that for now. The point is he's coming here, and my wife mustn't know why. She thinks he's coming to tour our gardens, but that's not why I invited him."

"No, sir?"

"No. Konig's bringing me something for my collection."

Jackson knew full well Lady Banbury's opinion of her husband's collection: somewhat along the lines of Sir Roger's opinion of Dittersdorf but without the same open-mindedness. The butler, therefore, asked no questions at this use of subterfuge.

"Very good, sir," he said.

*

Between the Fairview and Cardhu Towers, if you take Allegheny Avenue, you will come across Norman's Tavern. John Hathaway, directly after his argument with Brittany Landers, had strolled by this old hangout and gone inside. Propelled by matters of business more than of thirst, he had gone in to find Norman himself, owner of the tavern and world-renowned poker chump. It seemed Norman owed him $200 from the previous week's card game, and with this trip coming up and Uncle George threatening financial independence at every turn, Hathaway could use every cent he could get. Once he had sorted out the debt, he spent the bulk of the evening playing pool and thinking of Brittany.

He tried to look on the bright side. He figured that a weekend with Brittany Landers probably would have ended with him broken over rocks, drowned or torn to shreds by a bear, the last of which he could picture Brittany taunting with a pointy stick. Though these were sound arguments against her, he found little comfort in them. Largely on his mind were her flashing eyes, her flowing hair and her adventurous spirit.

This was the same adventurous spirit that made her speak her mind loudly, though, and once, he recalled, got him into a bar brawl with some local football rowdies. No, as he thought of that, and rubbed the spot where one of them had socked him below the eye, Hathaway consoled himself that perhaps she wasn't the right one. Some softer woman—that's what he needed. Fun, yes; dangerous, no.

He was still working this line of thought through, and considering himself a pretty lucky fellow to have freed himself of the Brittany entanglement so easily, when Colby Humner, his lanky neighbor from across the street, joined him at the pool table.

"Hey, Hath, you're here."

Hathaway agreed that he was.

"It's just that, lately, you've been spending all your time gallivanting about with the governor's daughter."

"That's all over now."

"Really?" Colby seemed invigorated by the news. "It's probably all for the best. Seriously, I'm surprised you didn't get yourself killed."

Hathaway didn't know how to respond to this. After all, his argument with Brittany might not have been pleasant, but he'd hardly have called it death defying. He prompted his friend to elaborate.

"I thought you knew? About her boyfriend?"

"Colby, I have no idea what you're talking about. I know nothing about any boyfriend."

"Oh. Well, I thought you knew."

"Yes, I think we've covered that. What's this about a boyfriend?"

"She has one—Brittany does. The guy's a complete lunatic. Apparently, she is stringing him along. You didn't know about this?"

"This is the first I've heard of it."

"According to him—the loon—she enjoys the danger of associating with him. He's not the sort of man she would ever tell her father about. I mean, he's done time: something about attempted murder, assault with a deadly weapon—"

"You sound like you've talked to him."

"Oh yeah. Nice guy. I mean, completely nuts, but, you know, friendly. He used to be a Green Beret—a sniper. They threw him out because of his temper, that and some papers of his they found outlining a plot to overthrow the government. I don't really know all the details. Anyway, he's extremely jealous—and confrontational. I've only talked to him a few times, and he always ends the conversation by ranting about someone who got under his skin and what he plans to do about it. That reminds me. He was in here asking about you."

"Me?"

"Yeah. He seemed to know all about you. You can handle him, though, right? I mean, you're always telling me about the rough element you run into at the casinos."

Hathaway gave a distracted nod. It was true; he'd had his share of run-ins with the underbelly of society. Very few churchgoing, wouldn't-hurt-a-fly-type people take a seat at a high-stakes poker game (which is one of the reasons why you never see the Amish dominating the tables in Vegas). Nevertheless, a trained killer is a trained killer, and Hathaway had always endeavored to avoid that particular brand of rough element.

"Actually, Colby, I just remembered I have a prior commitment."

In the years since Hathaway had been going to Norman's Tavern, he'd seldom left the premises before one in the morning. In light of these developments, he happily called it an evening at eight, changing his routine one step further by leaving the pub via the kitchen. If he hadn't been so determined to shield his face as he skulked across Allegheny Avenue to the Cardhu Towers Apartments, he might have observed the brown pickup truck parked in a nearby lot. He may have noted that the man inside was watching him. What he wouldn't have noticed was the photo on the back seat, which showed him with a big red circle around his head.

3 — Hathaway Gets a Crank

The next morning, Hathaway's cleaning woman came. Leaving her assailing the kitchen with bucket and mop, he headed out to run the last few errands before his trip. The instant his blue Land Rover pulled out from the underground garage, the brown pickup, waiting patiently since the night before, came alive and began to follow.

Hathaway became aware of the tail on his way home. It occurred to him, as he looked up and noticed it in the rearview mirror, that he had seen the same truck at the market: a nondescript Chevy idling in the far corner of the store's lot. Now, almost five miles later, it appeared to be maintaining a calculated distance several car lengths behind. Figuring all this talk of jealous boyfriends was just beginning to get to him, he shook his head and stepped on the gas.

When the pickup pursued his turn onto Kenilworth, Hathaway was amused. When it shadowed his last-minute turn onto Joppa Road, he was intrigued. When it mimicked his U-turn at the intersection of Joppa and York, he was concerned. Fortunately, a few blocks later, Hathaway saw an opportunity to speed through a red light—this time abandoning his entourage on the other side of the intersection.

Back home, Hathaway slammed the door shut and propped himself up against the archway, a look of unmistakable agitation on his face. As he stepped away, he noticed his cleaning woman, apparently unaffected by his sudden and chaotic entrance.

"You got message," she said, casually dusting his liquor cabinet.

"What?" asked Hathaway, still grasping around for his bearings.

"You got message. Message," she repeated, flapping a piece of paper vaguely in his direction.

Hathaway moved across the carpet, pausing on his way to look surreptitiously out the window. He took the scrap and puzzled over it.

"I don't understand, Maria. What does this mean?"

Maria slipped the duster under her arm and picked up the paper. A moment passed in silence, as both parties took a deep breath and prepared to communicate without the benefit of a translator.

Maria, who had a somewhat better grasp of English than Hathaway had of Spanish, began. "The *fun* ring," she said, pointing to the phone. "*¿Sí?*"

Hathaway nodded. So far, so good.

"Man on line say he know all about *treep*."

He stumbled over this one. *Treep?* He didn't think he had any treeps. "*Treep?* Oh, *trip*. You mean my trip to Connecticut?"

"*¿Qué?*"

"Or do you mean my trip to Maine?"

A spark of recognition lit in Maria's face.

"*Sí*, Maine. He say he know you go to Maine. He know all about that, he say."

"Who was it? Did he leave a name?"

"*Sí*, Wal-ter."

"Walter?"

"*Sí, sí.* He say he name Walter."

Hathaway paused over this one too. He didn't know any Walters. As far as he knew, he had never known a Walter. The name meant nothing. Turn it over and shake it: the folder marked "Walter" was empty.

"You sure he said 'Walter'?"

"*Sí.* He say he Walter. Walter say he know about *treep*."

"That's the whole message?"

"*¿Qué?*"

"Is there more?"

"*Sí.* He say he is going to *git* you."

This statement hit Hathaway like a sucker punch to the abdomen. "He's going to *get* me?"

"Sí," nodded Maria, pleased to find the young man on the same page with her.

"What did he mean? I mean, was he angry?"

"¿Qué?"

"Was he angry!" Hathaway shouted, demonstrating the effect. *"Mad?"*

"No, he no mad. He *git* you. He say you watch out, because he going to *git* you."

Feeling she had delivered the message adequately, Maria left her employer to stare blankly at the opposite wall.

As Maria was going out, Colby Humner entered. He strolled over to where Hathaway was standing and announced his presence with a hearty "Howdy, Hath!" Observing his friend's puzzled look, he remarked, "You said I could borrow your golf clubs, remember?"

Hathaway's mind, like Sir Roger's, reeled. Who was Walter? And, more importantly, how did he mean "git"? Was this "git" with a high-powered rifle?

"Colby, I think I just received a death threat."

"That sucks."

"I mean, I assume it was a death threat. He said his name was Walter."

"He left his name?"

"I thought it was strange too. Perhaps we're supposed to be familiar with his work."

Colby eyed a basket of muffins. Fondling one at the top, he decided on second thought that he didn't like blueberries.

Hathaway continued, "What did you say this Green Beret's name was? You know, Brittany's goon? Could it be Walter?"

"I don't know."

"You've talked to him, haven't you?"

"Sure. But now that I think about it, he never actually introduced himself. He was too busy talking about sucking chest wounds."

"Well, did he look like a Walter?" Met with no response to this, Hathaway dropped down on the sofa and sighed.

Colby removed a nine iron from the bag and examined it approvingly. "You know, I have a friend who can help you. His name's Kingsley. Warren Kingsley. He's the best bodyguard around."

"I've never heard of him."

"And how many bodyguards do you know? The funny thing is I hadn't spoken to this Warren guy for years. We knew each other when I lived in Boston. At any rate, I was at the golf club today, and there he was: the answer to your dilemma. We got to talking, and I told him about this situation. He said he could help." Colby took a test swing with the nine iron, missing Hathaway's television by inches. "He free-lances, sort of like you with the courier job. He's an executive body-guard. Execs like him because he blends in. You hardly know he's there."

"Hire a thug?" asked Hathaway, tensing as Colby connected with the coffee table and sent the remote control sailing into the dining room.

"Not a thug. An insurance policy. Besides, Warren doesn't come off that way. He's no goon. If you didn't know any better, you'd think he was a stockbroker or a lawyer or something. A lawyer with muscle."

"I hate lawyers, with or without muscle," said Hathaway. He paused. "What's your angle on this? What's made you the body-guard's advocate all of a sudden?"

"Nothing. I mean, you need a bodyguard anyway. And if you hire Warren, I, of course, would act as his agent, taking a small percent-age—"

"Ah!"

"It would still be cheaper than hiring someone from an agency."

"I thought this Kingsley was the best? How can he be cheaper?"

"He's affordable," Colby replied, explaining briefly how freelance bodyguards, because they get clients mostly by word of mouth, can afford to undercut agency prices. "Besides, he'll give you a good deal as a professional courtesy. You never know; you might need to use him with your courier business sometime. You should hire him, Hathaway. Maybe your uncle will foot the bill. I'm sure he'd hate for something to happen to his favorite nephew."

Hathaway, who could have pointed out that he was hardly George's favorite anything, did see a certain soundness in his friend's words. "Maybe I need to talk to Uncle George about this. If this Walter knows I'm going to Maine, then Maine's the last place I want to be."

*

Later that day, Hathaway took a quick trip to his uncle's office. To his great relief, he found the roads bare of suspicious brown pickups, at least those with homicidal driving patterns.

His manner was that much more relaxed, therefore, when he stepped off the elevator and plowed into Uncle George's secretary, the charming Susan Hamilton.

"I didn't break anything, did I?" he asked.

Susan Hamilton smiled and said no harm done. Picking up the papers she had dropped in the collision, she returned to her desk.

Hathaway had always liked Susan, sort of a Bond to Moneypenny relationship, if you can picture John Hathaway as 007. He could see why his uncle loved her too. She was beautiful and efficient—four parts assistant, one part leggy supermodel.

"Oh, I almost forgot, Johnny; you left this here last time." Opening a drawer, she produced a hat. "I guess you were in a rush to leave," she joked.

"I've been looking for this," he said, running his fingers along the brim. "Say, Susan, do you like gambling?"

"Not particularly."

"How about tall men with tons of money?"

"Tons of their uncle's money, you mean?"

"Something like that. So, what do you say? Up for a trip?"

"I'd love it, but your uncle and I are working on his speech for next Friday."

"Tell the old goat to stuff it."

"I can't."

"I've never been able to manage it either," Hathaway admitted. He placed the hat on his head and adjusted it. "Does the tyrant have a minute to see me?"

"You'll have to be brief. He has a fund-raiser in five minutes."

Hathaway thanked her and strolled across the hall to his uncle's office. He found the congressman inside, sitting at his desk behind a stack of committee reports.

"So you're here finally? The parcel's on the table."

Hathaway eyed the package: a thin, brown-papered wad, about the size of a hardback book.

His uncle continued, "Now, if you don't mind, I'm very busy."

Hathaway nodded. He stepped across the room and floated Maria's note onto the desk. "What do you make of this? Strange, huh?"

"You could say that."

"What do you think?"

"What do I think about what?"

"What do you think about this strange message?"

"I wouldn't give it much thought."

"You don't think it's a death threat, then?"

"How should I know?"

"Right. Well, this—well—dammit, Uncle George, is that all you have to say?"

"Johnny, I get so many death threats myself that I try not to notice them. Got one just the other day."

"I remember. So how is Aunt Eloise anyway?"

"Fine, just fine." A short silence. The uncle furrowed his brow. "What do you think you have on your head?" he asked.

"A hat," his nephew replied promptly. "A trilby hat, if you must know." Hathaway spoke without defensiveness. He had come to expect this attitude toward the thing.

"You look like a nitwit. Don't wear that hat when you meet Roger Banbury. He'll think I sent him some sort of escaped mental patient."

A quick description of the trilby might be in order here, especially for those who neglected to set *The Dictionary of Hats* by the reading chair or loaned the volume out to a friend. George Hathaway seemed to see the thing as a sort of monstrosity, but, to be fair, the trilby actually looked like any gentleman's felt hat; in the fedora family, but more Edwardian.

Hathaway loved it.

Sadly, though, ever since he connected with it, he had been putting up with endless snide comments, a popular one being that he looked like a displeasing blend of Indiana Jones and Norton from *The Honeymooners*. Yet, he had conditioned himself. You live with these things for style.

"Forget my hat," said Hathaway. "My hat does not concern us here. Stop evading the issue."

"What issue?"

"My death, that issue."

"Oh that."

Hathaway sniffed. He picked up a small brass replica of a Civil War cannon from his uncle's desk and frowned at it. "Can I have this?"

"No."

"Right. Anyway, I think in light of this evidence, a trip to Maine would be inadvisable."

"Look, Johnny, if you don't want to deliver this thing, I'll find someone else."

"Good."

"Someone with a little backbone."

"Right."

"As far as I'm concerned, though, if you can't complete this simple errand, you can forget about any more money from me."

Hathaway dropped the cannon. "Uncle George, you're not serious."

"I am."

"But it's my trust fund!"

"I know. And if you can live without the income you have spent in advance, then more power to you. But it might be a long five years."

"It's more like four, and I think this is very unreasonable. I mean, one might even call it extortion. Well, not extortion exactly, but something like extortion. It's unfair, that's all."

"Perhaps you should write your congressman."

Hathaway glared. "Is this what politicians do? Stick it to close relatives?"

"Among other things. Cheer up. Perhaps you can start borrowing from your friends. No, that probably wouldn't work. They're all deadbeats themselves."

Hathaway was a strong man, but he knew when someone else held the winning cards. "Oh, all right," he snarled.

"Pardon?"

"I said all right. I'll go."

"Good. If there's nothing else?"

"One thing. I want to take on a partner for this case. His name's Warren Kingsley. He's a security expert."

"A security expert?"

"A bodyguard."

"Bodyguard? Important people have bodyguards. For goodness' sake—you're only going to Maine, not Beirut."

"I think for the sake of the parcel, it would be advisable. This will double my fee, of course."

"For the sake of the parcel, huh? If it will shut you up, then fine. Just don't screw this up. I'm hoping to get another campaign contribution out of this. Ever since Banbury's name appeared on the Honors List, his wife seems to think the old boy's too good to back my cause. I'm hoping to butter him up so he'll slip me some funds without her knowing."

"Behind her back, huh? Explain to me why your marriage broke up again?"

"This isn't going to break up anyone's marriage. It's just politics. Speaking of which, don't be your typical driveling self with Governor Landers' daughter."

"Define driveling."

"Don't start. I know her father. I'd stay and talk to you about this further, but now you've made me late." Bundling up a wad of papers, the congressman stumbled out the door.

Hathaway followed. He made no attempt to explain that he had already been his typical driveling self with Brittany Landers. He knew, as one knows never to mix gin and wine, that if Uncle George found out that he had made the name Hathaway mud with the Landers family, a line that wove through the state and federal government like a cinnamon swirl in a Danish, the congressman would have screamed and frothed and jumped atop his desk, kicking brass replicas of Civil War cannons into distant corners. Taciturnity was Hathaway's best course of action. He could deny everything later.

*

Back at Rangeley Manor, the night's sleep had done nothing to ease Adrienne Banbury's frustration. The next morning, nearly eighteen hours after her argument with her father, she was still flushed with anger at his unreasonable attitude. Quite simply, her father had not given her betrothed a chance. Why shouldn't she marry him? He was amusing, kind, open to suggestions. Dittersdorf—with an *f*—was the man for her, she told herself.

Waking early, she spent the day in mild distraction, supervising the manor's staff. Like her mother, she took a great interest in these last-minute preparations before guests arrived. But, as she moved about the mansion, checklist in hand, telling the gardener that the violets clashed with the lilies, pointing out spots the window cleaners had missed and generally putting it across the servants to shape up, it occurred to Adrienne that her heart was not in it. She might have looked cool and collected while she criticized the table setting, but inside she was boiling about her father's stubbornness.

With this in mind, at precisely two thirty, she decided to have another go at the negotiations. Scouring the mansion for her father, she came up empty, however, for it had been the work of Sir Roger immediately after lunch to retire to the library and remain there, obscured in the dark, napping in a distant corner of the room. Outplayed, Adrienne eventually took her search outside, to find her fiancé. She spotted him over by the lake: a short, cheerful figure, mindlessly skipping rocks along the surface of the water. She moved swiftly across the lawn.

Walter Dittersdorf, "Ditters" to his friends, did not heed her approach. Like his fiancée, his manner was distracted. From a distance, he might have appeared to be skipping rocks with a childlike enthusiasm, but on his face there was a furrowed look of meditation. To be precise, at the moment Adrienne stepped up, he was wondering why rocks sink but wood floats. But, like all great thinkers, he had more than one thing on his mind. For the past half hour, he had been trying to figure out why his old school chum John Hathaway hadn't called him back.

Adrienne, again reminding us of her mother, spoke succinctly when she had issues to get off her chest. "Father's still being a problem," she said.

Ditters turned and blinked at his fiancée. He thought about asking her how long she had been standing there, but decided against it. It might have been quite a while, he reasoned, and he may have already missed part of the conversation.

"Problem? What about?"

"You."

"Oh right."

Adrienne looked down at the pile of flat stones by Ditters' feet and brushed back a few uncooperative strands of blond hair from her cheek. "What were you doing, Walter?"

"What? Oh, I was just skipping some rocks. Wanna try?"

"No. Listen, we need to talk about Father. There are quite a few guests arriving tomorrow, and things will get pretty chaotic. Besides Mother's symphony group, there will be Grace Bosworth and Congressman Hathaway's nephew, whom I hear is something of a bum."

"John Hathaway? Yeah, he's one of my closest friends."

Adrienne raised two attractive eyebrows. "Oh really?"

"Yup," said Ditters, skimming a rock a clear fifty feet. "We've been friends for years, since school. Imagine my surprise when I heard he's coming here, to the same house I'm staying at. Funny, huh?"

"Hilarious."

"I tried to reach him this morning, to tell him I was going to get him at the airport, but he wasn't in. I talked to his cleaning lady, I think. It was hard to tell; she had an accent, and you know my French isn't the best. I left a message, but I haven't heard from him."

"Well, we heard from his travel agent. She called to ask how close we were to the train station. He's probably coming in on the same train as Randal tomorrow."

"That works. The train station's closer. I'm sure if he got my message, Hath will be watching out for me when he gets here." He paused as the full scope of his fiancée's narrative sank in. "Randal Finch is coming back?"

"Of course Randal's coming back. He works here."

Ditters skipped another moody stone, bouncing this one off the dock. The biggest drawback to staying at Rangeley was definitely this Finch. Ditters knew Finch from school, at which time Finch had been the class bully and Ditters the bullied. "It's just, I thought he might have quit or something."

"Well, he didn't," said Adrienne, pausing a moment, her attention diverted. "Walter, why is there a jar of pickles floating in the lake?"

He turned and followed her gaze to the container bobbing several feet from the shore. "What? Oh, I dropped it in there by mistake a couple minutes ago."

"What were you doing with a whole jar of pickles out here?"

Ditters, too chagrined to admit that he had been feeding them to the ducks, said, "Um, nothing. Why?"

Adrienne looked askance at the jar again.

"Speaking of jars," said Ditters, "I wanted you to taste the new batch. I put less garlic in them this time." Grabbing a second jar from the ground, he opened the lid. "Don't worry; this one didn't fall in the lake."

"Walter, I hate pickles."

"Taste one; they're good."

"Walter, this is precisely the sort of stuff that makes Father think you're weird."

Ditters stepped back, wounded. Making pickles was his hobby—his dream—something he had learned at his mother's knee. "Adrienne, if I can get this recipe right, then I can get the grocery store to carry them."

Adrienne had no reply to this. "Speaking of Father," she said, turning to and fro to see if they were alone, "we need to discuss what we are going to do. Tomorrow all these guests arrive, so it's the perfect time for us to act. We'll try to talk to him again, but if Father's going to keep playing the villain we'll have to move on to Plan C."

"Plan C?"

"Yes. Plan C."

"What was Plan A again?"

"Getting Father's blessing and getting married!"

"Right," Ditters agreed. He thought that had been Plan A too. "You don't think your father's going to let you marry me?"

Adrienne drew herself up. "It's not a matter of what he'll let me do, Walter. I do as I please; don't forget that. It's a matter of getting his approval. Father could delay this wedding for months if he doesn't approve, and I'm tired of him acting like I'm ten years old and telling me what to do. So then, we go with Plan C, and tell him to stuff it."

"Right … what was Plan B?"

"We never had a Plan B. We left B open in case something more sensible than C came along. But it looks like Plan C is the one," said Adrienne, departing.

Ditters thought about asking her what Plan C was but, judging it unwise, returned to the business of skipping stones.

4 — Enter Hired Muscle

John Hathaway, tired and slightly harassed, pulled up at the train station at ten to five. For a man whose concerns seldom amounted to more than what he should have for lunch, the previous four hours of his day had been ripe with complications.

Trying to hire the bodyguard spelled the main hitch. Warren, it turned out, did not fly. Colby, who had arranged everything, explained Warren's preference for train travel over lunch. Hathaway wasn't clear what Warren had against planes exactly, only that Warren was a train man through and through. Initially, this development had distressed Hathaway, but fortunately his very efficient travel agent had sorted it out. It took some doing, but she managed to get them on the overnight train service, leaving at five.

According to Denise at "Travel Fun," it was only recently that the train service to Maine had started up again. Ground travel was fine with Hathaway. Taking trains always made him feel like a character in an Alfred Hitchcock movie. All he needed now was a mysterious lady socialite—beautiful, charming and on the run from the police for lifting the crown jewels of Madagascar.

A sudden rain shower had begun when he arrived, clearing the already scarcely populated platform. Hathaway opened an umbrella and reflected. His outlook as he stood there in his leather jacket and trilby—no more chipper than any man's mood when standing alone in the rain—was plunged somewhat deeper by heavy thoughts.

The parcel, tucked tightly in his suitcase, intrigued him. The death threat, folded and placed in his jacket pocket, distressed him. But it was the bodyguard, neither in his suitcase nor his jacket pocket, that disturbed him the most at the moment.

He tried to have a gracious mind about it. While he appreciated having a crack at the best bodyguard around, he couldn't help feeling less than overjoyed about the prospect of trooping about the place with a one-man regiment following on his heels—some big bouncer type who would collide into his back every time he stopped to pick up a magazine, or who would loom conspicuously in the near distance when he tried to meet mysterious lady socialites.

It will probably come as no surprise, then, that when a large bouncer-like man emerged from the other end of the station and began to tread heavily in Hathaway's direction, Hathaway did not wait to welcome this new addition with a warm embrace. Not that Warren would have let Hathaway welcome him with a warm embrace.

The first thing most people noticed about Warren Kingsley, bodyguard extraordinaire, was that he looked the part. Even at Hathaway's distance, he recognized Warren as someone you wouldn't want to tangle with. Yet, as Colby had pointed out, he was no simple thug. As the two men met, Hathaway noted that Warren wore a tailored suit. When he reached out and shook hands, the client detected the subtle glimmer of a Rolex.

"Mr. Hathaway?"

Hathaway took back his hand and nodded. "Warren Kingsley, I presume."

That out of the way, they stood facing each other blankly. As one untutored in the bodyguard game, Hathaway half expected Warren would want to secure the area before proceeding. This necessity did not appear to occur to Warren.

"Say," the bodyguard said, after an interim of about half a minute, "do you mind if we board the train now? This rain can't be doing my suit any good."

Hathaway nodded, and they moved off. Warren and Hathaway each had their own compartment with a bed and shower. After taking a glance of approval at his own accommodations, Hathaway shuffled down the hall to Warren's, finding the bodyguard in an involved search of his quarters.

"I know they're here somewhere ..." he was saying to no one in particular.

"Looking for bugs?" Hathaway offered.

"Bugs?" asked Warren. "Why in the world would I look for bugs? I hate bugs."

Hathaway, observing that his question had been misinterpreted, tried again. "No, I mean eavesdropping devices," he said to the other's dull expression. "You know, little electronic gizmos the criminal element uses to listen to what we're saying."

Warren looked thoughtful momentarily, as if this struck him as a weird thing for the criminal element to do, and then shook his head.

"No, I was looking for the towels. I want to dry my hair."

The debriefing, as such, was interrupted by the entrance of the conductor collecting tickets. "One thing," Hathaway remarked, before the conductor could leave. "I'd like to send a telegram."

The conductor decided he disliked this passenger. He slid his hand into his pocket and pondered the request. "A telegram?"

"Yup," said Hathaway, "you got it exactly."

"We have a tele-*phone*."

"I'm sure you do. So do I. But, you see, I don't want to talk to the guy."

The conductor scratched his ear. "I'm not sure we have telegrams."

"I guess telegrams aren't big these days," said Hathaway, mentioning that he had probably seen too many old movies. "Telegrams and their like have melted into the past," he observed. "The computer age, huh?"

The conductor, less of a ponderer of the ebb and flow of history than Hathaway, asked, "What about it?"

"Nothing. Let's see. How about a fax? You have a fax on board?"

The conductor nodded. They had a fax. "Couldn't you just email or text?" he asked, growing antsier by the millisecond.

Hathaway shook his head. "No good. He'd only respond." He took out a scrap of paper and began to scrawl out a note, reading it aloud: "CONGRESSMAN HATHAWAY—UNCLE GEORGE STOP." He paused. "I know what you're thinking: it's a fax machine, not Morse code. I think the 'stops' add a certain flavor, though, don't you? Anyway, where was I? Oh yes: 'UNCLE GEORGE.' Or better try: 'HEY UNCLE GEORGE DETOUR ENORMOUS HASSLE STOP. MUST TAKE TRAIN DAY OUT OF WAY STOP. WILL QUADRUPLE FEE STOP. REGARDS NEPHEW JOHNNY.' That should do the trick," he said, signing the bottom.

"You missed a 'stop,' " the conductor remarked, peering over his shoulder.

"You're right," Hathaway said, pausing. "No, we wouldn't want to overdo it," he decided, handing over the correspondence. "Send that when you get a chance, would you?"

The conductor nodded, grumbling something about his retirement on his way out.

*

Across the train, in a car that served as lounge and bar, Randal Finch—executive secretary to Roger Banbury—took a seat and opened a Maine newspaper. Grace Bosworth, the guest Lady Banbury had instructed him to meet and escort back to Rangeley Manor, had not shown. After waiting for her on the platform for almost an hour, he had come inside to dry off. Her absence disturbed him very little, for he was a man who preferred his solitude when he could get it, something he found in limited supply working at Rangeley Manor.

Seizing this solitude now, he ordered a beer and started to read an article on lobster fishing. Having read far enough to learn that the price of lobster per pound was down this year, Finch let his mind wander.

He began to think of Sir Roger's daughter, Adrienne. He admired Adrienne Banbury enormously. Ever since he had come to work for her father, he couldn't stop thinking about her. She was so different from other girls: strong, commanding. He esteemed Adrienne very highly and never failed to grind his jaw muscles when he thought of her engaged to Dittersdorf. He had gone to school with Dittersdorf, and during those days when he used to regularly push the twerp's face into the mud and throw his textbooks into the street, he never once imagined him having the sort of attraction that would appeal to a girl like Adrienne Banbury.

How long Finch would have gone on thinking of Adrienne Banbury, we can only speculate. Just as he had begun to dreamily picture her hair and her face and the way she would reprimand the cooking staff when lunch was served late, the door leading from the next car opened, and in walked another vision from the past. This vision was John Hathaway, someone whose textbooks Finch had also regularly flung into traffic when they were young.

The years had not changed either much. They stared at each other in silence, until the door slid shut behind Hathaway, stirring him to speak.

"Finch?" he said.

Finch peered up from his seat. He was a round, menacing man who looked like he would be best suited playing goalie for a professional hockey team. "Hathaway," he replied.

If Hathaway had stopped at some point to make a list of people he never wanted to run into—and Brittany's estranged boyfriend topped it—the name Finch would have come next. Hathaway could still recall hours spent with his friend Ditters Dittersdorf mapping and planning ways of avoiding this schoolyard hooligan between classes. The fact that they were now adults, Finch with a preposterous little goatee and Hathaway, though lacking facial hair, a tall and dignified figure, did little to lessen the jolt of the reunion.

At first, Hathaway couldn't fathom what Finch was doing there. Then he remembered: a few years back, Uncle George—a friend of Finch's father—had gotten Finch a position at Rangeley Manor. Hathaway hadn't thought much about the gesture at the time, his attitude having always been as charitable as the next, but then he never thought it would mean sharing a train with the thug.

Civilized men, they exchanged a few insincere *How-are-yous*—Hathaway replying fine and Finch all right. That concluded, Hathaway asked Finch if he was heading back to Rangeley. Finch responded that he was, and Hathaway said, "Ah." At the height of this joviality, a waiter appeared with a drink for Finch.

Hathaway took this as a perfect opportunity to make a dash for it. He moved to retreat, also with a view to finding a drink of his own, but in his haste he was not watching for obstacles. Backing up, he began by accidentally jabbing a second waiter in the jaw with his elbow. Spinning around full of apologies, he was just thinking, *Waiter,*

waiter, everywhere and not a drop to drink, when the train jostled and sent him stumbling back into the first waiter, spilling a tray full of these drinks onto Finch. Needless to say, this had not been the sort of graceful exit he had in mind.

The moment the drinks hit, Finch sprang to his feet, sending Waiters One and Two scattering in all directions. Covered in tea, wine, beer and a particularly dark fruit juice, he was still deciding which of Hathaway's vital organs to rip out first, when a commanding voice broke in on the party.

"Mr. Hathaway," it said.

Hathaway turned to behold the one and only Warren Kingsley.

"Mr. Hathaway. There you are. Is this the drink car?" he asked, ambling over. Reaching the pile of waiters, he looked across at Finch. "Who's this? Friend of yours?"

Finch stood in the bodyguard's shadow. He did not intimidate easily, but 220 pounds of Warren materializing in their midst definitely sidetracked him. "Ulp," he observed.

Hathaway, taking advantage of the newfound muscle, smiled and spoke casually. "Was there something else, Finch?"

Finch turned, at a loss for a reply. "No, Hathaway," he answered.

"Sure?"

"Yeah, I'm sure."

"Sorry about the drinks, old buddy."

"That's all right."

"Accident, you know?"

"Yeah."

"I'm glad you agree, Finch. Of course, you will send me your cleaning bill."

"Thanks."

Once Finch had stormed off, Hathaway turned and gave Warren a friendly nod. Perhaps the bodyguard was worth it.

A moment later, giving the Finch rampage ample time to clear the area, Hathaway left the lounge himself and headed for his room.

As he strolled back out into the hall, he froze. Something dazzling had caught his eye. A young woman with a tender face and a taut yet shapely figure stood as in a dream by the window, gripping the rail and shaking the moisture from an umbrella. She appeared unsettled.

Hathaway moved closer. Her brightly seductive eyes met his, and she smiled shyly.

"Could you help me?" she asked, hooking her brown hair behind her earlobe.

Hathaway detected a British accent to her speech. He also observed that, when she spoke, the words rolled off her lips like sweet nectar. It seemed he had found his lady socialite, after all. If he had been one who acted on impulses, he might have thrown himself at her feet.

"I hope I can help," he said, gazing back at her.

"That man," she continued, "the one who left grumbling obscenities under his breath? That wasn't Randal Finch, was it? The porter said I'd find him in the bar."

"The grumbling brute? Assortment of beverages across his front? Yeah, that was Finch. You don't know him, do you?"

"I was supposed to meet him. He's escorting me back to a mansion in Maine. Rangeley Manor."

Hathaway stifled a yippee. "Rangeley? That's where I'm headed. John Hathaway," he revealed.

"I'm Grace Bosworth. It's a pleasure to meet you, John. That's a very attractive hat, incidentally."

He followed her gaze. "Oh, you mean the trilby? Thank you. I'm glad to find someone who appreciates my fashion sense."

"Oh, I do. I love a man in a hat. They're coming back, you know? It's a good color for you too. Are you English?"

Hathaway made an indefinite gesture. "Call me semi-English. Born in the States, schooled in England."

"Oh, I see. You're certainly not like the other Americans I've met here. You're more dignified. Does it strike you that so many young people in your country behave as if they're mental?"

"Mental? Young people? Yes, I do notice that. Most of them are, I think."

"Perhaps they're just intoxicated?"

"Some are, I'm sure. Take that Finch you were supposed to meet. Wafting of the stuff. He's more of an angry drunk too. If I were you, I'd avoid this Finch. Tell you what. How about I escort you back to Rangeley? We're both headed there, after all."

"You're very kind. If you won't think me a bother?"

"I'll try not to. If you haven't eaten, I know this great little place. In fact, it's the only restaurant on the train."

*

An hour later, Warren Kingsley left his room and maneuvered down the hall. On the other side of Hathaway's compartment, the conductor and porter stood viewing an unoccupied cabin. Warren reached them in time to hear the conductor speaking.

"This one didn't show. Must have missed the train."

"Where do we leave this?" asked the porter. He was holding an envelope with the name "Harold Konig" printed across it.

"I don't know. Someone left it for him. Toss it on the seat."

The porter did so, and together he and the conductor left to continue their inspection of the train. Warren moved to let them by. Watching them exit, he slipped over to the empty Konig cabin. He had formed a pretty low opinion of his own compartment, finding it crowded and stuffy, and wanted to compare the accommodations afforded other guests.

In fact, the room was identical. With a sigh, he wandered back out into the hall.

On his way, he noticed the envelope. As a principle, Warren did not pry into other people's mail. He occasionally listened in on phone conversations, but letters were different—more official. Nevertheless, this note intrigued him. Curiosity got the better of him, and he reached for the letter.

No sooner had he secured it than a voice spoke, causing him to toss the note across the hall. The young woman Hathaway had met earlier stooped to retrieve it.

She was on her way to the dining car.

"I'm sorry to startle you like that," she said. "I was just wondering what time you made it. The battery on my mobile died, and I'm more or less lost without it."

Warren stared back at her, caught in the glow of her smile. "Erf."

"You dropped this, I think," she said, handing him the envelope.

"Erf," he agreed blankly, slipping the note into his pocket.

*

In the cabin next door, Hathaway dressed for dinner.

The passenger service, in the interest of tourism, had begun an experiment to restore the grand old days of train travel. This included offering inexpensive upgrades to first-class and overnight compartments, as well as requiring a dress code in the gourmet section of the dining car. Hathaway, who appreciated these grand old days as much as anybody, was in the finishing laps of tying his necktie when Warren entered.

"If you don't mind," he said, slightly distracted, "I'm going ahead to dinner."

"Go ahead," answered Hathaway cheerfully, straightening the knot. "Take the night off. Hopefully no assassins will set upon me while you're gone. Oh, incidentally, that was good work you did this afternoon. You know, with that Finch thug in the lounge."

"What? Oh right. Just part of the job."

Hathaway popped on the trilby to see how it completed the package. He admired himself in the mirror. "I think I'm going to enjoy this train ride. By the way, you never told me why you don't take planes. Security reasons?"

"No. I don't like planes."

"I guess they can be pretty noisy and uncomfortable."

"What they can be are deathtraps. Planes crash," said Warren Kingsley.

Hathaway had not expected this attitude, but let it pass. Who says you have to love flying to be a bodyguard? "Really fortunate you were available," he went on, changing the subject. "Colby tells me you recently finished up with your last client. I suppose a bodyguard of your standing has had some pretty impressive ones?"

"Clients? Oh sure. Last year I was in charge of the security for Edgar Roderick."

Hathaway was impressed. Edgar Roderick, the Canadian film producer. He remembered reading something about him in the paper a while back.

"Too bad about the accident," said Warren.

"Accident?"

"Car bomb got him. Shame too, he was a good client. Well, off to dinner."

5 — A Star Is Born

The conference with his bodyguard remained fresh in Hathaway's mind through dinner. No matter what angle he viewed it from, he couldn't figure out why Warren would bring up this blot on the Kingsley escutcheon. The thought process went as such: Say you are a bodyguard, and in the course of conversation you are put on the spot about your clientele. Would you mention your kudos, recalling with pride the time you took a bullet for Smith and threw yourself on a grenade for Nelson? Or would you talk about the one that got away? Of course you would mention Smith and Nelson, showing scars if you have them. Option B, he concluded, was just not the way to inspire confidence in new customers.

Still confounded by this peek at Warren's résumé, Hathaway decided to put it out of his head and return his attention to his date. Though he scarcely thought it possible, she appeared even more radiant than she had when he first met her. She was dressed to the nines and looked every bit the portrait of beauty and charm. She seemed a shade on the pensive side, though.

"Say, Grace, is something wrong?"

She came out of her reverie. "What? No," she replied, but not with any conviction.

Hathaway nodded and looked out the window. Watching the silhouettes of trees and rocks pour by, he reached for the wine.

"What?" she asked.

"I didn't say anything."

"Oh, I thought you did."

"Nope," he assured her, filling his glass. "An old friend of mine, Hutton, said a funny thing the other day—"

"John, do you see that man over there?" She was peering suspiciously at someone in the distance behind him.

"Who?"

"That man," she said, indicating a table to the back of the car. "I think he's watching us."

Hathaway turned in his seat. He observed a man wearing a black turtleneck and herringbone sport coat. Though it was difficult to tell from Hathaway's angle, the passenger seemed to be looking their way.

"I don't know. Probably just lost in the spell of your beauty. Which reminds me of the funny thing my friend Hutton said—"

"No," she interrupted again, making it clear that it was not in the cards for the public at large to learn what amusing thing his friend Hutton had said. "I saw him earlier."

"Small train."

"No, you don't understand, John. I think he's following me." She could tell Hathaway was puzzled by this. She would have to elaborate. "You don't mind if I'm rather personal with you?"

"Not at all."

"You're so nice. Well, to jump right to the point, I think people are after me."

Hathaway shook his head in astonishment. There must be something in the air.

"I know you can hardly credit it," she continued, "but for the past month I have noticed someone stalking me."

"You'd be surprised what I'd credit on that front, Grace. You think it's this guy?"

"Maybe. I don't know. I'm probably losing my mind."

That was something Hathaway would not credit. "Let's start at the beginning. What makes you think someone's after you?"

"Intuition mostly. I have seen men watching me. No, I don't mean like that. They're trailing me about."

Hathaway stared back at her, wide-eyed. "You're not carrying around the crown jewels of Madagascar, are you?"

"No. Why?"

"No reason. Just exploring every avenue." He paused thoughtfully. "You know what you need, Grace, is a bodyguard."

"Yes, but that's so drastic, isn't it? Do you even know any?"

"Actually, I was thinking of me."

"Oh, John, that's so sweet. Would you really do that for me?"

"In a heartbeat. I think I can manage to keep you out of harm's way." He refreshed her glass and thought of Warren. The irony did not escape him.

She smiled brightly at him. "You're a knight; you know that."

"One tries."

"I feel safer already."

"Good. Actually, I have some experience in this area. I think people are after me, as well. The other day this brown pickup almost ran me off the road."

"Is this something to do with your courier company?"

"Courier company?"

"You were telling me earlier that you work as a freelance courier—transporting diamonds, vital documents, that sort of thing. Is this something to do with that perhaps?"

Hathaway opened his mouth to speak and then caught himself. "Actually, yes. I mean, it might have something to do with it. You see, my uncle—the congressman—did give me this parcel to take up to Rangeley. See, in my line you have to avoid the criminal element. They're all over the place."

"And you agreed to make this delivery? Even though you knew the danger involved?"

"Well, you know, he relies heavily on me, my uncle does, and I didn't want to disappoint him. Shame to have a political crisis because I couldn't get his parcel through."

"Absolutely. Is it in a safe place?"

Hathaway looked puzzled again. "The parcel? Oh yes. It's in my cabin. Why?"

"Nothing. It's just that man, the one I pointed out to you, I saw him prowling about your cabin earlier. It's the one at the end of the train, right?"

Hathaway had picked up the steak knife and applied it to his fillet. Hearing this, he missed the fillet entirely and gouged the tablecloth. A waiter appeared at his elbow.

"Is there a problem with the fillet, sir?"

"What? No. No, it's fine." Hathaway turned to get another look at their observer. "Um, Grace, when you're done, I think we might want to take a walk."

*

Soon after the couple had left the dining car, the shady man in the corner carefully dabbed his mouth with a napkin and rose from the table. Straightening his sport coat, he followed them into the next car.

Across the aisle from where he had been sitting, another observer, muscle bound and bursting at the seams of his suit, shifted around in his seat. He faced a smaller, sharp-eyed man poring over a salmon fillet.

"They're gone," the first man observed.

"I can see that," the fish lover replied.

His companion seemed puzzled. "What's he doing with her?"

"Obviously, we have underestimated her. Now we wait."

*

Hathaway and his lovely "client" returned to his cabin and shut the door. Turning the lock, he glanced through a slit in the shade.

"Shouldn't we check on your parcel?" she asked.

Hathaway revolved around to face her. At the moment, his only thought was whether the man from the dining car was following them—and if so, was he after Hathaway or his date? He wished he had gotten a better look at him. "Sure. It's in the suitcase."

Nodding, she opened the case, dashing socks and shirts and a single mountain boot about the place (the last of which Hathaway had packed by mistake), before unearthing George Hathaway's parcel. "It's still here!" she rejoiced. "I wonder if that man was after this," she said, giving it to Hathaway.

"I don't know," said Hathaway.

"What is it?"

"I don't know."

"Do you think we should open it?"

"I don't know."

"You know what I think—"

Hathaway, whose next response was to be "I don't know," handed her back the parcel. She tore off the outer paper and creaked open the box inside, displaying its contents.

Ten seconds passed before anyone spoke.

"It's a dagger," Hathaway said at last. "It's a garish little dagger."

"It does look rather garish," she agreed.

The dagger, arguably garish, had a thin silver blade, with uniform rows of clear and red gems. In the center of the bronze hilt was a large, blue stone.

"Kind of gem studded for a dagger," she observed.

Hathaway frowned. Why would Sir Roger want an ornate whatsit? Then again, Hathaway considered, why wouldn't he? He closed the box. On the outside of the case he noticed the following words engraved in gold:

THE AZURE STAR

Decidedly un-star-shaped, it was an enigmatic name for an enigmatic trinket.

"Now what?" she asked idly. Before the question could be answered, a knock came at the door, startling them both. "Are you expecting anyone?"

Hathaway stood riveted to the spot. Maybe he was paranoid, but he suddenly regretted giving Warren the night off. Normally, as an amateur bodyguard, he would have enjoyed having the stage clear of pros, but at times like these, professionals have their place. "You better hide in the bathroom, Grace."

She nodded approvingly and slipped through the small door. Waiting for her to secure the latch, Hathaway attended to the pounding, which had grown more forceful now. He hardly had time to undo the locks before a gruff figure shoved past him and into the compartment. Spinning around, Hathaway perceived that this gruff figure was not the mysterious passenger from the dining car but was none other than Randal Finch.

"What are you … deaf? I have been knocking for ten minutes."

Hathaway brushed himself off. He spoke sharply.

"What is it, Finch? This is no time to reminisce."

"I'm not here to reminisce," said Finch, the idea revolting to him. "I'm looking for Grace."

"What do you want with Grace? I mean, Grace who?"

"Grace Bosworth. She's a passenger. I was supposed to meet her on the platform in Washington and escort her back to Rangeley Manor, but she never showed. I thought she missed the train."

"Maybe she did."

"Then how do you explain this?" Finch whipped out an envelope from his pocket. "It's a love letter."

"I don't want your love letter."

"It's not to you, you idiot. Some imbecile left it for her in her compartment. I found it on her dressing table."

"What were you doing looking through her dressing table?"

"Nothing. I mean, I was in her compartment looking for her, and I needed a tissue."

"Why did you need a tissue?"

"Stop asking so many questions!"

Hathaway took the letter and looked it over. Typical love letter stuff, a bit overdone in the parts about how she made the author's heart feel warm and squishy inside, but not, as a whole, stomach turning. Actually, the poem on the back was very good, Hathaway noticed.

"Yes, Finch. So?"

"So! This shows that she's on board. Why else would someone leave her a letter? There was luggage in her room too."

"Who sent the letter? Maybe he can help."

"I don't know who sent it. Look at the signature."

Hathaway found the bottom of the letter and read it aloud: " 'Your secret admirer, Snuggle Bear.' Yes, I can see how that would leave you in a spot. You can't go around the train asking people if they answer to the name 'Snuggle Bear.' "

"So you haven't seen her?"

"I have no idea where she is."

Finch gave his mustache a thoughtful stroke. "I think you do know."

"What?"

"I think you know Grace Bosworth. You're acting funny."

"I'm not acting funny. I always act this way. If I did know Grace Bosworth, I'd act completely differently, believe me."

"I think this is exactly how you would act."

"Well, you're wrong. Besides, why would I lie?"

"Because you're a sniveling little snot, that's why."

"Other than that. I mean, what would be my motivation?"

"Motivation?" As a man who went through life punching people in the face whenever the thought of punching people occurred to him, the idea of motivation seemed alien to Finch.

Hathaway went on, "I mean, you don't see her here, do you?"

"No."

"You don't think I actually stashed her in the bathroom or something, do you?"

"No."

"You can take a look if you like."

"No."

"No, I insist," said Hathaway, stepping back. "Examine my bathroom."

"I don't want to examine your bathroom, Hathaway. Look, if you do find her, tell her I'm looking for her. This is a picture of her." The oaf felt around in his pocket, eventually pulling out a scrap from a London society page.

Hathaway stared at the page. On it there was a shot of a rather pretty blonde at an estate auction. She was not the woman in the bathroom.

Finch leaned over his shoulder. "Pretty hot, huh?"

"Yeah …"

"Yeah." They stood ogling the hot blonde in the photo. "You better not be lying," Finch said. With that, he snatched back the paper and left in the same stormy manner in which he had arrived.

Grace, or possibly not Grace, stepped out from the bathroom. She had heard everything. "I'm sorry, John, I'm not Grace Bosworth."

"You could have fooled me. Do you mind telling me who you really are?"

"I'm Lesley Darlington. I'm a friend of Grace Bosworth's. Grace was concerned about me. When I told her someone was following me, she offered to let me come here instead of her. She didn't really want to go anyway. She was supposed to stay for a few weeks with some friends of friends, none of whom knew her. I was going in her place, to hide out until this thing blew over. I never thought they'd have a photo. Grace is on safari in the outback, and there's no way to get in touch with her. No one can verify who I really am. They'll think I'm some sort of freeloader or something."

Hathaway gazed at his renamed companion softly. She was beautiful when she was ruffled.

Lesley continued, "I would have told you my real name, John, but I liked being Grace. I enjoyed the opportunity to travel in circles I never would have before. You probably hate me," she said, dropping down to the bed with a heavy sigh.

He could not suppress a smile. "Grace, or that is, Lesley, you're adorable; you know that. Why would I care what your name is? Shakespeare had something to say about that. Involved roses. The point is I care about you, not your name."

"But the Bosworths are so rich and famous. I'm only an assistant fashion designer."

"Wealth and fame are overrated."

"Really?"

"Well, I wouldn't shove them away if someone offered them to me. But, returning to the subject of your safety, I think you should still come with me to Rangeley."

"You mean you're still going to help me?"

"Of course! We'll stop off at Rangeley, I'll deliver the parcel, and then, if you'd like, we can hit Foxwoods Casino."

"That sounds exciting," she said, perking up.

"Great. Now then," he went on, joining her on the bed, "it seems to me your problem is you picked a bad false name. You need a wiser choice. You will go as Brittany Landers, daughter to Governor Ernest Landers."

"How?"

"Easy—she was supposed to come with me, but she backed out. They're all expecting her up at Rangeley. None of them know her either."

"Brittany. It's a nice name."

"I've always liked it, but I think I like Lesley better, Lesley."

She leaned her head on his chest. He held her closer.

He was just thinking what to say next when he looked down and noticed she had dozed off in his arms. He smiled and rested against the pillow.

Since getting cornered into this errand, he had made no attempt to look for the silver lining, figuring that the lining in question had skulked away into some distant celestial corner and given strict instructions not to be disturbed. But now, looking at the woman breathing lightly on his neck, he could hardly imagine a more sparkling silver lining than Lesley Darlington.

Brushing her hair back from her face, he lay there watching her sleep until he nodded off himself.

Part Two

6 — A Bodyguard Comes in Handy

Hathaway rose early the next morning. Typically the Hathaway sleep plan involved remaining unconscious through lunch, and on most days he would have stayed in bed with the covers pulled tight up over his head until someone made a point of waking him or the train happened to derail. This morning, however, it only took the sun rising steadily over the horizon for Hathaway's eyes to pop open and dart rapidly about the cabin. Lesley, alias Brittany, had disappeared. He poured off the bed and stumbled out into the corridor.

Still half-dressed and thoroughly ruffled, he walked down the hall toward Warren's cabin. Spending the night waking at the slightest footstep or muffled conversation can take its toll on a man, and as Hathaway had awoken approximately forty-seven times during the past six hours, he was not at his mental best when he stepped within Warren's compartment and stood blinking at his surroundings. Eventually, it came to his sharp, discerning eye that something about these surroundings was amiss.

As a slob himself, to which his maid Maria could attest, John Hathaway was in no position to judge Warren's cleanliness. But as he looked around at the even spraying of trousers, shirts, overturned mattresses and torn-open luggage, it seemed to him that here was a room at which even Maria would have to look askance. Slowly, as the fog began to clear, a sick feeling crept up on him: this was the site of a scuffle.

Hathaway could picture a shadowy figure built like a Green Beret stealing into Warren's compartment the previous evening. Struggling ensues. There's a walloping noise as the GB lands a blackjack to Warren's temple. The next thing the poor lummox knows, he's hurtling from the train, bundled up in a gunnysack. Hathaway, who had been rocking back on his heels while he thought of this, quickly turned on these heels and went to finish dressing. It was not until he had thrown off the formal attire from the night before and grabbed some casual clothes that he noticed a note on the mirror:

> WENT TO BREAKFAST. DIDN'T WANT TO WAKE YOU.
>
> LOVE, ~~LES~~ BRITTANY
>
> P.S. PUT THE "PARCEL" IN YOUR JACKET FOR SAFEKEEPING

Hathaway sniffed thoughtfully and left for the dining car.

His intention had been to find the porter, or anyone else who might have noticed a large bodyguard-shaped object sailing by their window during the night. What he found instead was the bodyguard himself, helping himself to the breakfast buffet and with no detectable sign that he had spent the last few hours rolling around the countryside in a gunnysack.

"Warren!"

Warren Kingsley flinched. "Hathaway! Don't sneak up on me like that," he said, taking his seat.

"Warren, we need to talk."

"Sure. What's that?" He prodded Hathaway's jacket pocket.

Hathaway frowned. "What? Oh, nothing. Just some parcel I'm dropping off."

"Can I see it?"

"I guess. Actually, it's kind of heavy. Maybe you could hold on to it for me?"

"Sure." Warren took the package and peeled back the paper. He stared at the contents a moment before folding it back up. "What is it? A can opener?"

"I don't know. Never mind that for now."

"What's wrong, Hathaway? You seem agitated."

"I am. I thought someone knocked you off."

"Knocked me off what?"

"The train, to be technical about it. I thought you were for the long jump."

"I once twisted my ankle doing the long jump."

"I thought someone murdered you, Warren. It looks like they trashed your room. Didn't you notice?"

Warren stopped eating eggs long enough to picture his compartment. "It did look sort of messy when I came back last night."

"Did you mess it up?"

"No." He set down his fork. Warren disliked the idea of someone trashing his compartment.

"I'm not sure," whispered Hathaway, "but I think the guy who's after me may be on the train."

"Really? Why would he trash my room, then?"

"I don't know; he's insane. He probably thought your room was mine. They're both in my name."

"So this guy's pretty nuts?"

"He's deranged. We're lucky he just trashed your room. From what I've heard about him, I'm surprised we didn't find him balled up on the floor chewing the carpets."

"No kidding. What's his story?"

"His story is he's a goon. This is the guy who—guk!"

"The guy who guk?"

"That's the guy," Hathaway snapped, slumping down in his seat. He nodded to a table in the back where the solitary observer from the night before sat behind a morning paper. "That's the guy she saw snooping around my compartment."

Warren swiveled carefully to his left in the direction of Hathaway's glance. He turned back casually. "Oh, don't mind him."

"Don't let his appearance fool you," Hathaway replied, from beneath the table's edge. "I grant you, I would expect a Green Beret to dress a little more militantly. But look at his face—hard, determined. It's the face of a killer. No, really. Just because he's sitting there thoughtfully sipping from a teacup now doesn't mean he wouldn't stab this butter knife between your ribs if the circumstances were right."

"Nah. He's fine."

"Warren, I'm telling you there's something suspicious about this guy. I think he's Walter."

"Who's Walter?"

Hathaway was no longer listening. This fellow, could he be Walter? Did he look like a Walter? Hathaway concentrated. If someone happened to yell "Walter!" at the top of their lungs right now, would he be among those present who stepped forward and said, "You rang?"

"Who's Walter?" Warren repeated.

Hathaway, returning to earth, reached in his pocket and pulled out the death threat. "Walter is the guy after me." He slid the scrap across the table.

Warren took the paper. Examining it for no more than a minute, he nodded knowingly. "Yes, we're obviously dealing with a psychopath here," he said.

Hathaway's eyes widened. "Really?"

"Absolutely. Look at how they form their *n*'s, definitely a sign of anger and resentment."

"My maid copied this down."

"Oh, in that case, I don't know. Looks like this Walter is after you to me," he concluded, sliding the paper back. "Anyway, guess what? I met the most wonderful woman yesterday."

The disgruntled client looked up. "Warren, there's a guy sitting not twenty feet away who may want to kill me. This is no time for tales of your love life."

"She's gorgeous," Warren continued. "She didn't tell me her name yesterday, but luckily I bumped into her a little while ago. Her name is Brittany. Brittany Landers."

"Brittany?" Hathaway's face darkened. "Brown hair, pretty face?" he asked, filling in a quick description of Lesley.

"Yeah, that's the girl. We had breakfast together. It turns out she's some governor's daughter."

Hathaway took a thoughtful sip of coffee. It seemed that Lesley had warmed to her new pseudonym quickly. "I know *Brittany* too," he said, speaking carefully. "I also met her yesterday."

"Really? She's lovely. Doesn't it strike you that she has the most kissable lips?"

The other side of the table could offer no argument on this front.

"And her eyes," said Warren. It would have interested Warren to know that the real Brittany Landers had piercing eyes and lips that sneered. "What softness."

Both men nodded dreamily, until Hathaway shook out of it. "Hey!"

"I really like her," Warren went on. "Last night, after I met her, I had a few drinks and wrote her a love letter."

Hathaway, reaching for his cup again, sloshed the aisle with coffee.

Once again, a waiter appeared at his elbow. "Is there a problem with the coffee, sir?"

Hathaway paid him no heed. "You wrote her a love letter?"

"It was the only thing I could think to do. I didn't know her name at that point, so I described her to the porter, and he said he knew the girl I meant and delivered the note for me."

His client was speechless. Lunatics were stalking them, and his bodyguard, Warren Kingsley, was sending women love letters. Hathaway was doubly disturbed. He didn't like the idea that Warren and he had developed feelings for the same girl. But he also found it disquieting that Warren, when drunk, preferred to work under the pen name "Snuggle Bear."

"You should know," he informed his bodyguard sharply, "that Brittany is traveling back with us to Rangeley."

"I know. She told me at breakfast."

"Ah." Hathaway pondered the bottom of his coffee mug. For the sake of clarity, he probably should have told Warren that Brittany Landers was really Lesley Darlington. But, somehow, he preferred keeping Warren out of the loop. Hathaway liked being the only one who knew Lesley as Lesley. Nevertheless, should one keep secrets from one's bodyguard? Fortunately, Hathaway was spared the tough decision, as Warren broke in with a strikingly similar topic.

"By the way, Hathaway, I would prefer it if you would call me Harold from now on."

Hathaway digested this. With all the versions of names flying about lately, one more should not have seemed strange.

"What I mean is, pretend I'm Harold," Warren explained. "You see, Brittany thinks I'm Harold Konig."

"Why would she think you're Harold Konig? Who's Harold Konig?"

"Some passenger who missed the train. When Brittany and I met yesterday, she thought I was him because I was standing in his compartment, rifling his mail."

"Why were you rifling his mail?"

"I wasn't really rifling it. But that's not important. She saw the name on the envelope I was holding and asked if I was Harold Konig, the famous art expert. Apparently, she had heard of him. I already knew Konig wasn't on the train, so without missing a beat I said I was him. I didn't want to disappoint her."

"You told her you were an art expert?"

"Why not? People exaggerate all the time."

"Yes … but not to this degree, surely?"

"Just don't tell her who I am, okay?"

Hathaway found all this very trying. First, Lesley telling Warren she was Brittany, and now Warren with this Harold stuff. It was bad enough being in a love triangle, Hathaway reflected, without Sides B and C wanting to be known as F and K. "Did she tell you that people may be after her?" he asked, as the waiter refilled his cup.

"No. Are there people after her?"

"I don't know. She thinks so."

"That's no good. I know what it's like to have people after you, and it's no fun. People are always trying to kill me."

"You're a bodyguard, Warren."

"I know, but sometimes I think people are really out to get me."

Hathaway had paused with his mug raised to his lips. He was now regarding Warren with the curious stare of someone whose bodyguard has come unstrung and, for the safety of other passengers, should have all pointy implements removed from his reach.

He was about to speak, but it appeared that Warren was going to supply him with a *For instance.*

"For instance, when I was guarding Larry Mundsley, the late shipping honcho, someone put a tarantula in my slipper."

"What did they put in Mundsley's slipper?"

"Nothing. Someone shoved him off a cliff."

"What were you doing at the time?"

"Having my hair cut."

An uneasy feeling began to creep over Hathaway. He recalled Edgar Roderick—the film producer who had met up with the car bomb. He asked Warren if there was a pattern here.

"Roderick?" asked Warren. "That wasn't my fault. Studio politics."

Hathaway stifled a shudder. "You don't lose all your customers, do you? I mean, you would take a bullet for a client if you had to, right?"

"Take a bullet? Don't be ridiculous. If I took a bullet, it would probably kill me. Anyway, people don't usually shoot my clients."

"Usually? You talk as if it's a lot. How many have kicked the bucket?"

"It's difficult to say for sure. Quite a few … there was the one who was poisoned."

Hathaway slid his coffee mug to the edge of the table. "Poisoned?"

"Yes. At a tennis match in New York. If you want my advice, if you're in New York, avoid the orange juice. My client before last was Thomas Redding. Someone bludgeoned him with a golf putter. Speaking of golf, Colby says you play. Do you belong to the same club?"

"Warren!"

"What? Oh right. My most recent client was Dr. Oscar Port, the paleontologist. Shame about him. Stabbed with a sharpened femur bone. Pretty fortunate for you, though. Otherwise, you wouldn't have been able to hire me."

Hathaway tried to remain calm. "Warren, let's try this from a different angle. How many surviving clients do you have?"

Warren considered this. Math was not his strong suit. "Well, none really."

"None!" Hathaway launched out of his chair and smashed his head into the overhead lamp.

"People were out to get them," Warren explained. "You see, unlike me, my clients always insist on making themselves conspicuous. I try to blend in. But not them. Sure enough, I'll come back from dinner or from a movie or whatever, and find that the numskull I was guarding went outside, right in the middle of the street, and got run down by a black sedan with no license plate."

Hathaway shook his head. "What sort of bodyguard are you!"

"A living one. And I'd like to keep it that way."

"But you're supposed to be the best!"

"Yes, but how much can one man do? If it's your time, it's your time. That's why most guys in my line of work ask for their fee up front. Not me. Principle. I always collect from the estate."

Silence followed, as Warren finished his breakfast. The train went through a tunnel. By the time it had reached the other end, Warren had returned to the subject of golf but found himself speaking to an empty table. Hathaway had left to find Lesley.

* *

On Ridge Avenue in Baccup, Maine, there are perhaps four buildings that stand out as worth mentioning among the herd of dusty, run-down edifices that make up the downtown district. They are a police station, a gun store, a bakery and a post office.

It was to the store front of the second from the list that Ditters Dittersdorf was currently launching himself. He had come to town to mail a package, a jar of pickles he was sending to an uncle who owned a deli in New York, and it was with this parcel tucked snugly under his arm that he ambled into the shop.

The Travers Weapon Shoppe was old and musty inside, much like the little town it called its home. At the moment of Ditters' entrance, it was occupied by two men: a tall, grizzled customer in his fifties and a shorter, grizzled man in his seventies named J. Travers, the proprietor since 1969. The ambiance of the place did nothing to dampen Ditters' enthusiasm. It was not every day that he had an opportunity to browse through weapons from the Old West, and he enjoyed every second of it.

His gusto had begun to grate on those present in the shop, however, for Ditters was the type who enjoyed chatting with strangers, and

J. Travers and customer were not. He had just prodded the latter of the two in the ribs in order to point out a genuine Winchester Model 1873 on the wall, when J. Travers returned from the back room with an antique revolver and placed it on the counter.

"Hey!" Ditters exclaimed, setting his parcel down, "is that a Colt Peacemaker?"

J. Travers replied that it was.

"Are you buying it?" asked Ditters.

The customer said that he was.

"Pretty sharp," Ditters commented to both.

J. Travers wrapped the Colt up in brown paper and turned to finish his business with the customer at the cash register. Ditters had a few questions on prices, but the proprietor and customer had fallen into one of those discourses on shell casings that can take a while, so he decided to return at a time when J. Travers' attention was not divided. Picking up the package of pickles off the counter, noting vaguely that it had more heft to it than when he came in, Ditters glanced absent-mindedly at the archery equipment and left.

The next stop on the Dittersdorf schedule was the bakery. Exiting it with a cookie in one hand and the package in the other, he looked briefly down the street and noticed a disturbance outside the gun shop. The participants in the disturbance were J. Travers, the customer and one of the deputies from the station across the street. They were arguing back and forth, and for a moment Ditters thought perhaps the discourse on shell casings had become violent. Whatever the source of the disagreement, he figured it was not his concern. He popped the rest of the cookie in his mouth and began to stroll toward the post office. He had made it as far as the mailboxes when J. Travers spotted him and slapped the deputy on the back.

"That's the man," he yelled, pointing at Ditters.

Ditters was dumbfounded. Such was his shock that the parcel slipped from his hands and landed on the sidewalk with a clunk quite uncharacteristic of pickles. Scooping it up, he gasped as it spontaneously unwrapped to reveal the Colt revolver from the shop.

The deputy shouted, "Hold it right there!" and took off like a shot toward him.

Seeing this, Ditters' first urge, however unsound, was to panic and run. Ditters' father, currently under investigation for grand larceny, once told his son, "Never trust a cop," and it was these words that Ditters took to heart as he bounded down Ridge Avenue and skidded around the corner at Ridge and Main with a fleetness of foot that would have done any Dittersdorf proud.

* *

Following the illuminating discussion with the bodyguard, John Hathaway spent the next half hour walking up and down the train's corridors. On his fifth pass, he ran into Warren, who mentioned he was going to take a nap before they got to the station.

Hathaway returned to his compartment and retrieved a bottle of scotch from his suitcase. It was still pretty early to drink, but when your bodyguard is Warren Kingsley, early is never early enough.

His search for a glass was interrupted by a tap at the door. "Who is it?" he asked, hoping it wasn't Finch again.

"Train security. May we speak to you, sir?"

Hathaway had not seen any train security up until this point. He wondered where these guys were yesterday. He opened the door, and two foreign-looking men, one towering over the other, stepped within. The large one checked the door.

"What can I do for you?" Hathaway asked them.

The smaller man produced a semiautomatic pistol. "If Mr. Hathaway does not mind, we will take the Azure Star."

Hathaway frowned. "Mr. Hathaway damn well does mind," he said. "What is this?"

"I am sorry. Where are my manners? I am Nibu. My large friend is named Bu."

"Just Bu?"

"Just Bu. Now, if you please," said Nibu, prodding Hathaway in the stomach with the pistol, "the Star."

Hathaway stepped back, shocked. "You should know," he replied, taking a firm line, "I will be reporting this to your superiors immediately upon your withdrawal. You might as well forget about any Christmas bonuses."

Nibu grinned. "You labor, my friend, under a misinterpretation. We are not the security guards."

"Ah. Don't suppose filling out one of those customer-satisfaction cards will do much good, then, huh?"

"No, my friend. Perhaps my name did not register any bells with you. I will repeat it. Nibu Nibudar."

Hathaway looked blank.

"I am a very well-known assassin."

"Ah."

"I have killed many men."

"That's probably good for business," Hathaway agreed. "Wait. Walter didn't send you, did he?"

"The name is not one I know."

"Oh. Then what's this all about?"

"We are here for the Azure Star. And you would be best advised to try no funny stuff."

Hathaway couldn't believe it—someone really was after his parcel. "Let me get this straight," he said. "We're talking about the ornate letter opener, correct?"

"Yes. We have been looking far and thin for this treasure, and our patience is wearing wide, very wide."

Hathaway nodded. "I think you switched your thins and wides there," he remarked. "You'd call it a treasure?"

"Indeed."

"Your opinion, I suppose. So, you're the guys who have been following me? Did you ransack Warren's room?"

"I am sorry to say we mistook his room for yours."

Hathaway said it could happen to anybody. "So, which one of you was in the brown pickup?"

"That was Bu's cousin Larry. He was keeping tabs on you while we devoted our attentions elsewhere."

"Bu's cousin is named Larry?"

"Correct."

"Huh. And none of you know Walter?"

"No, Mr. Hathaway. I must ask, who is this Walter you keep speaking of?"

Hathaway told them it wasn't important. Nothing was now. "And, anyway, I don't have the Azure Star anymore, so I guess you guys are out of luck."

Nibu smiled. "May I ask where is Mr. Hathaway's attractive friend with the brown hair?"

"Lesley? She left."

"The train has not stopped."

"She's very impatient."

"Mr. Hathaway is a very funny man. No, my friend, we will find her."

"She doesn't have it. I gave it to Warren."

Nibu turned to his companion, who mumbled a response. "Then we will wait for Warren. He is the real security, is he not? He will be getting concerned about his client."

"I wouldn't bet on it," Hathaway grumbled.

The minutes clicked by, and Hathaway sat thoughtfully on the bed. He was just thinking that he needed a plan when the clickity-clack of train motion nudged the bottle of scotch off the table. Rolling across the floor, it came to rest a few feet from the bed.

Hathaway stood to retrieve it but was immediately jammed back down in his seat by Bu. Having demonstrated a limited vocabulary up until this point, he redefined this image by saying, "Sit!"

"I just wanted a drink," Hathaway explained, shifting around.

"Let my friend Mr. Hathaway have a drink," said Nibu, "and go check out in the hall for the one they call Warren."

Bu left, and Hathaway stood and retrieved the bottle.

Nibu, sighing quietly as his associate lumbered out into the hall, turned to look at the rain shower spraying the window. "Quite a fierce storm, would you say, Mr. Hathaway?"

Hathaway did not say. Currently, he was moving stealthily across the room, the bottle of scotch gripped tightly in his right hand. He had just raised this up to bring down on the back of Nibu's head, when someone behind him said, "Hey!" Bu, showing us once again that he knew the right thing to say at the right moment, had returned.

Hathaway stood frozen in his tracks, still holding the bottle up like a club. Nibu faced Hathaway. He looked back and forth between him and the bottle, and laughed.

"Mr. Hathaway is a very clever man," he said. "Look how he jumps at an opportunity. Very clever man. I suppose," he continued, cocking an eye at the bottle, "that was meant for bashing over Nibu's head?"

"That's about the size of it."

"Mr. Hathaway, you are very much a character. Very amusing man. Very much—" Whatever this last commentary of Nibu's was, we can only guess, because, after seeing his escape plan fizzle out before him, Hathaway decided to bash Nibu over the head with the bottle anyway.

Nibu hit the floor with a thud. Spinning around, Hathaway launched the unbroken bottle across the room, where it bounced off the other thug's larger, more rounded head.

This seemed to produce no effect on Bu. In his leisure time, he had often known a bottle or two to careen off his noggin.

There was a pause, while both men stood staring at each other. Simultaneously, they dove for the gun still grasped in the grip of the unconscious Nibu. Hathaway connected with the pistol first and fumbled for the trigger. Before he could fire, Bu grabbed him around the throat, and in the struggle Hathaway emptied the gun into the opposite wall. Losing their balance, they both spilled out into the corridor.

Crawling free, Hathaway had only time to jam his fist into his bodyguard's door and gurgle "Warren!" before Bu dragged him, arms flailing, back inside.

Choke hold reapplied, Bu waited until Hathaway dropped the gun. During this interval, Nibu stumbled to his feet and retrieved the weapon. He had managed to replace the magazine when the door opened, and in stepped the man Hathaway and Lesley had seen in the dining car the night before. The man Hathaway had spotted at breakfast.

He glanced about the cabin, his expression suggesting a calmness unbefitting the scene. Nibu whirled around to fire, but the new arrival wrenched the pistol from his hand and knocked him flat with a well-delivered blow to the chin. Bu, who appeared to object to this treatment of his employer, grabbed the man by the shirt. The last thing the gorilla would remember was pulling his fist back. In a blur, the passenger had directed four chops to his head and stomach and thrown him headfirst into the wall. Once the passenger had satisfied himself that the motionless forms no longer posed a threat, he walked over and helped Hathaway to his feet.

Hathaway thanked him warmly. "Where'd you learn to fight like that?" he wondered, still trying to breathe.

"Skills in hand-to-hand combat come in handy in my profession," replied the passenger, nodding politely.

"Who are you? Train security?"

"No, sir."

"You're not a Green Beret, are you?" Hathaway asked cautiously.

"No. My name is Borodin Mahrute. I am Warren Kingsley's bodyguard."

Hathaway stared. His bodyguard had a bodyguard?

Hathaway puzzled over this. He wanted to know why Warren Kingsley had hired someone to lurk in the shadows and follow them around the train. Any lurking or following was Warren's responsibility, as far as Hathaway was concerned. This Mahrute didn't even look like a bodyguard. For one thing, he was half Warren's size and had the cultured expression of a man attending the opening of an art gallery. The notion that he could have been Walter, the insane boyfriend, seemed ludicrous to Hathaway now—but no less ludicrous than Mahrute playing the role of Warren Kingsley's hired muscle.

Hathaway wanted an explanation.

In the midst of this confusion, a pounding could be heard coming from the next cabin. Warren's voice drifted through the wall:

"Would you mind keeping it down in there, Hathaway? I'm trying to sleep."

7 — The Makings of a Fine Pickle

The train approached the station. The conductor had been summoned, and Nibu and company were locked up in the storage room, all ready for the Baccup police.

Outside, the storm had dropped down to a drizzle, bringing a light mist of rain through Hathaway's recently ventilated cabin wall.

Warren, now well rested, emerged on the scene and stretched. "Hathaway? Hasn't this been an awesome trip?"

Hathaway stared at the bodyguard contemptuously. Warren continued:

"Oh, Hathaway, I was wondering if I could use you in a brochure? It's for a private security firm I'm starting, the Warren Kingsley Security Agency. Do you like the name? It's something I've been planning awhile. I was only going to put the big celebs in the brochure, but a surviving client is good publicity, even if you are unknown. Think it over and let me know."

The surviving client glared. His eyes searched the room for a blunt object.

"Gotta go, Hathaway," said Warren, steadying himself as the train slowed to a stop. "Brittany's meeting us on the platform."

Hathaway collected his luggage and filed out behind him. In the corridor, a man and woman were arguing with the conductor. Something about people riddling their suitcases with bullets while they were at breakfast. Hathaway didn't catch all of it. He milled past them, receiving, as he went, a sharp elbow in the ribs as the male half brought his arm back to make some dramatic point.

Outside on the platform, Hathaway didn't waste too much time viewing the station. Take a desolate platform and a handful of bumpkins to patrol it, and you had Baccup Central in a nutshell. The rain had stopped for now, but a dreariness remained. There was a glimmer of mountains to the north and a suggestion of a city to the southwest, but suffice it to say he was not sorry to skip the extended tour.

He ran across Mahrute by the reception area. "Where is everyone?"

Mahrute appeared perturbed. "Mr. Kingsley and the young lady have already found transportation. They are on their way to Rangeley Manor in a taxi."

"The young lady I was traveling with?"

"Yes. She seemed somewhat reluctant to leave without you, but Mr. Kingsley convinced her that you had business to attend to and would be along later."

Hathaway grumbled an obscenity under his breath. He had heard of the Ladies First rule, but Bodyguards First, unless they're deflecting sniper fire or checking for land mines, struck him as over the top. "The bastard left you too?"

"Indeed. There was no room left in the vehicle with all the young lady's luggage."

Hathaway noticed a hill of suitcases next to Mahrute. "Whose are all these, then?"

"Most of them are Mr. Kingsley's. As a safeguard, I stay with the luggage. The last time Mr. Kingsley was in charge of the bags, he inadvertently rolled our cases into the path of an incoming train. He was distracted by a female passenger."

This did not surprise Hathaway. He was glad to hear that it was only some luggage and not a client. "Seen any other cabs?"

As a small, simple town, Baccup had one notable flaw: a somewhat limited system of public transportation. Unlike your larger New York and Washington, DC, stations, Baccup did not have taxicabs coming and going from it every fifteen seconds. In fact, besides Harry M. Smith, the driver of Warren's cab, and Harry's brother Thomas, who was currently driving their sister to the supermarket, there were no other taxi drivers in Baccup to come or go.

This had begun to dawn on Hathaway and Mahrute, but before either could devise a strategy, they were joined by a serious-looking man in a trench coat and rain hat.

"Mr. Hathaway?" asked the serious-looking trench-coated man. "Mr. Hathaway, I'm Chief Adwick. I need to speak with you, if you don't mind. Step this way, please."

Hathaway frowned. He wouldn't have figured the town of Baccup big enough to have a police chief, and he was correct: it wasn't. Adwick was technically the sheriff, but after four terms, people really didn't care what he called himself. Nor did they concern themselves when he started wearing an inspector trench coat. If he wanted to pretend he was in Scotland Yard, let him, said the town.

Hathaway noticed the officer's arm was in a sling. "In the line of duty," he explained, looking down at the bandage.

The chief led Hathaway and Mahrute over to the train. He stopped at the spot where, even from the outside, they could see half a dozen bullet holes poking out from the side of the compartment. Chief Adwick, in his colorful way, called this "the scene of the crime."

Hathaway whistled as the chief made some notes. A few minutes spent in the officer's company was enough to tell him that the Baccup police frowned on the puncturing of their trains.

"I don't know," said Hathaway, viewing the damage. "I mean, it doesn't look so bad if you catch it from certain angles. You may want to try hanging a tapestry or something over it."

"A tapestry?" asked the chief, looking up.

"Or something. They're quite handy when you need them—tapestries, that is. I have an aunt who uses them all the time."

The chief nodded. "This is all very fascinating, Mr. Hathaway, but we're not interested in your decorating advice or your family traditions. You were involved in a brawl, and a very destructive brawl, at that. To begin with, I want to know about the two men you struggled with."

"What about them? You have them in custody, don't you?"

"Yes—"

"Locked up, key out of arm's length?"

"Yes—"

"Capable deputy on guard, a good prosecuting attorney standing by licking his chops?"

"Yes, Mr. Hathaway. If I could talk?"

"Go for it."

"We have reason to believe these two men were after a valuable object of some kind, possibly a stolen object. Unfortunately, that's all the information we have. Perhaps you could enlighten us further."

Hathaway laughed nervously. The subject of the valuable object known as the Azure Star had remained cloaked up until now. Considering that he had no idea how his uncle had gotten his hands on it, he had not planned on mentioning it.

The chief was contemplating him with a law enforcer's stare. "At the moment, we aren't charging you with anything, Mr. Hathaway, you being a guest of Sir Roger's and all, but unless we're convinced that you're cooperating fully, we may find it necessary to run you in."

Hathaway inhaled thoughtfully. "Sure. I mean, I can see you're doing your constabulary duty. It's really quite admirable. I know I will sleep easier tonight. But you have to understand I have nothing to do with all this."

"Surely—" That was all the chief got out. He was interrupted by a throat being cleared.

Mahrute, absent during the third degree, had now returned. "Mr. Hathaway, Sir Roger Banbury's assistant has arrived to drive us back to Rangeley Manor. Sir Roger is anxiously awaiting your arrival."

"He is? Oh right! Can't keep him waiting, can we? Sorry, Chief."

"We're not finished here, Mr. Hathaway. I may need to contact you. You can go for now."

Hathaway thanked him. After another brief decorating suggestion, this one involving pushing a bookcase in front of the holes in the cabin wall, he made his way off with Mahrute.

**

As they trotted down the platform, Hathaway decided to ask Mahrute to explain his role as the bodyguard's bodyguard. There was still much about the setup that mystified him.

"It is an awkward position, as you suggest," said Mahrute. "It has always been Mr. Kingsley's instruction that I do not make myself noticeable, especially to his clients. This one proviso was established because he felt my presence might hinder his image."

Hathaway snorted. "I'm glad you made an exception in my case. Let me ask you something, Mahrute. You appear to be a clever chap, good with your hands and all that. Assuming insanity doesn't run in your family, what are you doing working for Warren?"

"My association with Mr. Kingsley began a short time ago. It is a somewhat elaborate story, which I would not wish to bore you with."

"Try me. I mean, I'm curious how one bodyguard winds up hiring another bodyguard. How does he go about it?"

"Mr. Kingsley engaged my services several months ago because he believed his life was in danger."

"Warren's life was in danger? Who would be after Warren? I mean, I once saw a movie where an assassin was stalking a cop because the cop had foiled his plans to assassinate the president, but I can't believe Warren has ever foiled an assassin's plans in his life. Assassins probably send him a bonus."

"It was not exactly an assassin." It was clear from Mahrute's tone that he felt uncomfortable relating any more details of the case.

Hathaway could only shake his head. "And you have stayed with Warren ever since?"

Mahrute nodded.

"Is he always this hard to deal with? I mean, are you aware that he is telling people his name is Harold Konig?"

"It is one of Mr. Kingsley's traits that he will readily assume a false identity; it is his way of 'blending in,' as he likes to put it."

"You mean he does this often?"

"Mr. Kingsley seldom uses his real name. This helps to preserve his reputation and also throws off the people who may or may not be following him. As far as I know, this is the first time he has used the name of a real person."

"I can't believe this Konig will appreciate it. Does Warren really think people are after him?"

"Oh yes. In the last year especially, Mr. Kingsley has become rather obsessed with his own safety."

"How do you put up with him?"

"It is not bad work. Every once in a while, he has me taste his food before he will eat it, but other than that, he and I function as peers.

And Mr. Kingsley does have some fine qualities. For instance, he is a skilled cook and a competent poet."

Hathaway had seen the love letter. "You'd think you'd have better things to do than babysitting this menace."

"I suppose I have remained in Mr. Kingsley's employ as a personal obligation. I am not completely satisfied that he can make it by himself."

This admission did not instill a lot of confidence in Hathaway. A careless bodyguard is one thing, so long as he isn't helpless.

For the remainder of the conversation, Hathaway tried to argue to cut out Warren, the middleman, and hire Mahrute for himself. Mahrute stood strong on this point, however, as one who adhered to the position he had agreed to fulfill, and Hathaway did not press him long.

"Say," Hathaway remarked, once they had reached the end of the platform. "Where's this assistant you spoke of?"

"The gentleman told us to meet him here. He mentioned that he was hoping to avoid the chief."

"Seems sensible."

"He was very agitated. Evidently, he has been searching for you for the better part of an hour to no avail."

Hathaway found this strange. "Why would an assistant get himself all worked up over my arrival? You'd think that assistants to tycoons would have larger things on their minds."

"Actually, he mentioned that he was an old friend of yours."

"An old friend? That's curious." A sickening thought gripped Hathaway. "It's not that Finch, is it? Thickset guy with a goatee? Psychopathic manner about him?"

"He did not fit that description, no. He was a personable fellow. His name, I believe, was Walter."

For the most part, John Hathaway did not make a habit of letting stress show in his manner. Poker Face, people often called him. He wasn't poker-faced now. "Did you say Walter, Mahrute?"

Mahrute agreed that he had.

"The guy we're supposed to meet is named Walter? You sure you got the name right? Walter? It wasn't Daughter or Falter or something?"

"No."

"So what you're saying is the name you got was Walter?"

"Yes, Mr. Hathaway. Is there something wrong with the name Walter?"

Hathaway said no. As names went, Walter was fine. "Out of curiosity, Mahrute, if you were a mentally deranged Green Beret, you'd probably try to avoid the police, wouldn't you? Draw your victim over to some secluded area of the station? Yes, such was my thought. You see, I should explain that I have incurred the ire of someone named Walter. How I got under the skin of this Walter, I do not wish to go into at the moment, but rest assured I will bring it up during the next lull in the conversation. Meanwhile, the ire I mentioned remains. This Walter, it seems, left a threatening message with my maid yesterday promising to 'git me.' Just thought I'd throw this out to you, Mahrute, as a topic for discussion."

Mahrute had a dubious look on his face. He found it hard to believe that the cheerful man he had recently met could be capable of any calculated violence. For one thing, he was something of an unimposing young gentleman.

"Don't let his height fool you," said Hathaway. "Some of history's greatest murderers were short. It so happens that I can't think of any now. But if I could, I suspect they would all come to about here. Did you notice if he had a rifle with him?"

"Yes, sir. He did not."

"Doesn't really prove anything. Snipers always assemble their rifles from little suitcases. You know, I was just looking at that ridge. How would you feel about nipping over there and checking it out, while I step behind that rock?"

"If it would set your mind at ease. And for what am I looking?"

"Snipers. Well, one sniper in particular: this Walter. Of course, if there's some other sniper there who does not concern us, feel free to deal with him as you see fit. But, keep in mind, we all have to make a living somehow."

Mahrute moved off around the corner, and Hathaway took the opportunity to make for the rock referred to earlier in the exchange.

Reaching the boulder in question, he paused to survey the view. In the middle of his appraisal, something grabbed the back of his jacket and yanked him into the darkness.

"What are you trying to do?" asked an agitated voice. "Trying to get yourself spotted?"

Hathaway looked up from the ground and snatched a glance at a silhouette peering around the curve of the rock. If this was the infamous Walter, he disliked his greeting.

"Another second and Adwick would have seen you," continued the figure.

Hathaway stood and brushed himself off. He was about to explain how he hardly knew this Brittany Landers, when the figure turned, light fell on both their faces, and all, essentially, became clear. "Ditters? Is that you?"

"Of course it's me."

Ditters Dittersdorf had not changed much over the years. Same grin, same crazy look in his eyes, same mild scent of dill and vinegar wafting about him.

Before Hathaway could ask Ditters what he had been up to, or Ditters could ask Hath how's tricks, Mahrute returned with the news that all was quiet on the front.

"Mr. Hathaway," he said then, an element of surprise in his voice, "you found the gentleman?"

"You mean Ditters?" asked Hathaway, following the stare. "Do you know each other?"

"We were introduced earlier, at which time he identified himself as Walter."

"Walter? No, this is Ditters Dittersdorf. Why would Ditters want to 'git' me?"

Ditters spoke up. "Say, Hath, didn't you get my message? I called and spoke to your French maid."

Hathaway spun around. The fog was beginning to clear. "She's not French."

"Oh. Did you get the message?"

"Yeah, I damn well got your message! What on earth were you thinking?"

"Nothing. Why?"

"Why? Why? 'I'm going to get you.' What sort of screwed up message is that?"

"That's not what I said."

For the next few minutes, the two great minds set about puzzling through the muddle.

Ditters, who explained that he had merely called to offer to *get* Hathaway and drive him back to Sir Roger's mansion, could not fathom how the message could have gotten misconstrued.

"Couldn't you tell English was her second language?" Hathaway wondered.

"Yes, of course. You sure she's not French?" asked Ditters. "Anyway, I would have called back, but I was using the mansion phone, and it's long distance. They charge by the minute."

"Ditters, I thought it was a death threat. Why didn't you explain to Maria that you were an old school friend, that you were going to *drive me* back to the mansion, and repeat it a couple of times for her?"

"They charge by the minute, Hath."

"Besides, what's all this 'Walter' crap? Who's Walter? Your name's not Walter."

"Yes, it is."

Hathaway stared. It was as if Ditters had switched over to another language. Perhaps French. "What do you mean your name's Walter?"

"I mean my name's Walter."

"Since when?"

"Since always, I think."

"Why haven't I ever heard anyone call you Walter? Even the sternest, most by-the-book headmaster called you Ditters. No one calls you Walter."

"Oh, I know. I can't stand the name. Adrienne loves it, though, and she can't stand 'Ditters,' so that's that. Adrienne's my fiancée."

"Congratulations. But if you can't stand the name 'Walter,' why do you keep telling everyone it's your name? It's the name you gave Maria, not to mention Mahrute here."

Ditters looked perplexed. It seemed Adrienne's unswerving use of the name had made its mark on him. "Did I?"

Hathaway frowned. "I should tell you, Ditters, that thanks to your insane message I hired a bodyguard."

"Oh, Mahrute's your bodyguard?"

"No. Actually, Mahrute's my bodyguard's bodyguard."

"Hiya, Mahrute. 'The bodyguard's bodyguard,' " Ditters repeated thoughtfully.

"I thought someone was out to get me. Speaking of which," Hathaway continued, "what were you doing yanking me into the dust? You could have given me whiplash." The Hathaways could be patient with most things, but they resented being treated like the catch of the day, reeled in and left flopping around on the deck. The Hathaways were not haddock.

"Sorry about that. I didn't want the chief to spot you."

"So you've said. Why, aside from a generally sound practice, are you trying to avoid the chief?"

"Nothing, really."

Hathaway could see Ditters was only putting up a brave front, so he pressed him.

"Really, Hath, it's nothing. Really. Just some business to do with a warrant out for my arrest, that's all. I'd rather not talk about it."

* *

"Warrant for your arrest?" asked Hathaway, his manner softening. They had left the area behind the boulder and were walking along a gravel path to the parking area.

Ditters said yes. "They issue them shortly before hauling you off to jail."

For a moment, it appeared he was going to keep the sordid details sealed to the world. Then, after a few pensive strides, he began his tale.

"It all started with this parcel …"

"Don't tell me there was a gaudy little dagger in it?"

"No, there were pickles in it."

"Oh, okay," said Hathaway. "Bit strange, but okay."

"I was sending them to my uncle in New York so he could evaluate my current recipe. Why would I send him a gaudy little dagger?"

"No reason. Continue."

"Everything really centers around this antique pistol. I was in town, you see, to mail the parcel of pickles, and I had stopped in this shop to look around. This was about three hours ago. The owner was busy with another customer, and I was getting impatient, so—"

"You shot him?"

"No, I didn't shoot him! Are you going to let me tell this story or not?"

"Sorry. I was just trying to work in the antique-pistol motif."

"Well, don't. As I was saying, the owner was busy with this other customer. I was in a hurry, so after I looked around, I picked up my parcel and left. I had placed my parcel of pickles on the counter, you see."

"That doesn't sound so bad. Probably only a misdemeanor."

"I haven't told you the crime yet. You see, the parcel didn't have pickles in it."

Hathaway was no critic, but it seemed to him that Ditters' narrative was full of continuity errors. "But you just said there were pickles in it. Perhaps you should tell me the part about the parcel again."

"No, you see, I thought I picked up the parcel of pickles, but I didn't."

"You thought you picked up the parcel of pickles?"

"Exactly. I must've picked up the wrong parcel, though, the non-parcel of pickles. You know how it is, looking over old guns. Your mind wanders. What the parcel actually had in it was a Colt Peacemaker—a very nice revolver, by the way. I would have returned it, but by then the store owner had the cops on me. He called Adwick's deputy, and the deputy spotted me over at the bakery eating a cookie. Have you ever had a cop run full tilt at you?"

"Not that I can recall."

"The spectacle unnerves you. I made a dash for it. Actually, now that I think about it, I'm not sure I paid for that cookie. Anyway, I went around the corner and down a little side street. I took a detour through a furniture store and somehow wound up in the Baccup Hotel. The deputy was hot on my trail, so I dashed upstairs. That seemed like kind of a dumb idea, though, so I went out on the fire escape, and … Hath, you okay?"

"I'm fine, Ditters. Head's swimming a bit, that's all. Let me ask you something, before you continue. Did it occur to you, at any time, to stop and explain?"

"Not really. Why?"

"No reason."

"So, there I was—out on the fire escape. The ladder was stuck, so I had to jump from it. I had just hit the ground, when I realized that my landing was far from unobstructed. When I stood up to dust myself off, I noticed I had clobbered Chief Adwick, who, for some stupid reason, was skulking under the fire escape. We didn't have much to say to each other. I said sorry, or something like that, and he grunted. He was still on the ground at that point. Then his deputies, two of them now, came scooting around the corner. That's when I dashed down the alley, and they lost me in traffic. I would think the chief would remember me, wouldn't you? Fortunately, he has no clue who I am. You can imagine my agitation when I came here and saw you talking to him. Friend of yours?"

"Not really. He wanted to ask me about the bullet holes in my compartment."

Ditters frowned, perplexed again, and Hathaway said it was a long story and he would explain it all on the ride back to the mansion. "Couldn't you go to the shop owner and tell your side of the story?"

"I guess."

"Everything's jake, then?"

"For the shop owner maybe, but not for the police. They won't easily forget about the chase, or Chief Adwick's broken arm."

Hathaway hadn't realized there had been casualties. "You broke his arm?"

"I don't know. I see his arm's in a sling, but it could be for something else. Of course, I do remember the chief saying something like, 'You idiot, you broke my arm,' when I landed on him. But, you know, it could have been a figure of speech."

"So," Hathaway concluded, letting this all sink in, "besides gun running, what are you doing in Maine?"

"I work for Sir Roger."

This surprised Hathaway. "Are you really his assistant?" he asked.

He wouldn't have figured Ditters for assistant material. In fact, observing Ditters and noting his simple outlook on life, one imagines that on that day in the cosmos when most people were fitted with the goods for analytical and administrative tasks, Ditters was off somewhere pickling a cucumber.

"Assistant?" Ditters replied. "No, I'm engaged to his daughter Adrienne."

"Is that a job?"

"Not at all. You see, I'm going to marry Adrienne, so she convinced the old tycoon to let me work at the mansion. She's a beauty, Hath—Adrienne, that is, not the old tycoon."

Hathaway understood. He shook his head. He still couldn't believe Ditters worked in the same house as Randal Finch.

"Don't remind me," said Ditters.

"So he remembers you?"

"Of course he remembers me. If he hadn't remembered me, I never would have met Adrienne."

Hathaway wondered why, and Ditters said it was a funny story:

"About three months ago, we were all attending this political function in Maryland. Adrienne had to go to it, and Finch was escorting her."

"What were you doing there?"

"Free food. Anyway, I was wandering around, wishing I had brought a magazine, when I ran into Randal Finch. I have to give him credit, Hath, he was downright civil. He even introduced me to Adrienne. She and I got to talking, and we really hit it off. We made fun of the speeches. At the end of the evening, she gave me the name of their hotel. I thought Finch was going to have a fit. I saw her that weekend, and then I came up here, and then she—"

"Yes, yes, I think I get the idea."

"And that's how we got together. I always thought it ironic that Finch introduced us. Unfortunately, while we're living at the manor, I have to put up with him. He hasn't said anything, but I think he's jealous of me. Of course, we hate each other, and that doesn't help. I try to stay out of his way."

Hathaway thought this a sound policy. "You said you work for Banbury. What do you do?"

"Mostly I give him my opinion on something, and he tells me to stuff it. For a while, I worked as his chauffeur."

This seemed like the perfect opening to another topic Hathaway was interested in exploring—leaving Baccup station. "Where the hell is your car?"

"Car!" scoffed Ditters. "There's our ride," he said, pointing.

Hathaway stared at the object. It was over behind a tree, at the end of the lot.

"What is it?" he asked, as they approached it.

"It's a reconditioned army jeep. Like they used in WWII."

Hathaway looked it over. "Where's the top?"

"Doesn't have one."

"Where's the back seat?"

"Doesn't have one."

"No, really, Ditters, what are we taking back to the mansion?"

"Come on, Hath, this thing really gets around. You need a jeep in this area."

"You don't drive Banbury around in this, do you?"

Ditters threw the luggage in the back. "Oh, Banbury won't let me drive him anymore. I almost ran him over the other day."

Mahrute took the front seat. Hathaway, shaking his head, climbed in the back. He sat atop one of Warren's suitcases.

It was a bumpy ride at first, but Hathaway grew to like it. There was something exhilarating, he thought, about riding in a vehicle where you could potentially sail out of it on a sharp turn. Unrestricting, he would call it.

"May I ask," said Mahrute, over the sound of the engine, "where you purchased the vehicle?"

"The jeep?" Ditters shouted back. "Banbury knows this guy who hooked me up with a dealer. Banbury is quite a collector. Collects crap mostly, but when he wants something for his collection, this guy tracks it down for him. His name's Harold Konig."

Hathaway and Mahrute exchanged looks.

"Konig?" repeated Hathaway. "Was he supposed to be on the train with us?"

"I don't know. Why?"

"Oh, nothing. Friend of ours is impersonating him, that's all."

"Why would anyone want to impersonate an antique dealer?"

"He thinks it's fun. Does Sir Roger know him well?" Hathaway asked, anticipating the scene awaiting Warren at the mansion.

"Not really. As far as I know, they've never met in person. He usually sends the stuff."

"That's good. Perhaps Warren can pull it off, then."

Ditters still didn't get it. "This Warren sounds like a nut. Oh, that reminds me. Look in that toolbox behind you."

Hathaway opened a little trunk, and a thermos rolled out.

"Look inside," said Ditters.

Hathaway had an image of cocktails but was soon disappointed. A turn of the lid revealed a thermos full of pickles.

"That's a new batch," commented Ditters. "A new recipe and everything. Taste one."

"Ditters, I don't want a pickle."

"Taste one, Hath. They're delicious."

"I'm sure they are," Hathaway replied.

Since Hathaway had known him, Ditters had been on a quest: The creation of the perfect pickle. It had begun as a hobby. Whenever there was a picnic, Ditters would bring the homemade pickles. But then it grew into an obsession. He decided he wanted to sell them in supermarkets, aisles of jars with his face on them. This would have been a harmless dream too, but as the chef, Ditters could not always be objective about his creation. Man-on-the-street taste tests became necessary.

"Seriously, Hath, try one."

One would not have thought it possible, but Ditters somehow managed to reach over and snatch the thermos from Hathaway in the back.

With one hand on the wheel, he proceeded to distribute his pickles like a new father passing out cigars. In doing so, he ran over several bushes and, at one point, just about drove off the road.

"Really, Ditters. It will ruin my dinner."

"They're very light. Try one. I think I got a winner this time."

Hathaway and Mahrute, unwilling to bound from the vehicle and head for the hills, reluctantly munched down.

"Very refreshing," commented Mahrute.

Hathaway nodded dully. "Yes. Quite—picklish."

"Not too much garlic?"

Hathaway and Mahrute assured Ditters that he had done the seasoning justice.

"Good," he said, smiling. "Try another one."

8 — The Pickle Sours

Lady Banbury, concluding an afternoon of leisurely reading, stepped out from the library on the second floor of Rangeley Manor and noticed Randal Finch storming down the hall.

"Mr. Finch. I had not realized you had returned."

Finch stumbled in his tracks. His thoughts were preoccupied.

"What? Er, yes. I just got back. That imbecile Dittersdorf stranded me at the train station."

Lady Banbury frowned disapprovingly. "We mustn't call Mr. Dittersdorf an imbecile."

Finch wasn't so sure about that. "At any rate, he was supposed to pick me up. Adrienne—I mean, Miss Banbury—said she reminded him and everything. But he never showed. I was forced to get a lift with a farmer."

"That must have been very stressful for Miss Bosworth."

"She didn't show either. I think she was on the train, but she must have gotten off."

"Oh dear. Oh dear. We must look into this at once. Have the other guests arrived?"

"Hathaway's gang is here," he growled, and though he said "Hathaway's gang" his manner suggested that he would have been happier saying "Imbecile's gang."

"Oh really. You know Mr. Hathaway? How nice. Gang, you say?"

"Yeah, he's got this claque traveling with him. Besides the governor's daughter, there are two other guys: some guy with a weird name and someone named Harold Konig."

Lady Banbury arched an interested eyebrow. "Thank you, Mr. Finch," she said.

* *

While Lady Banbury made her way to her bedroom and Finch went to check in with Sir Roger, Ditters' jeep pulled up outside the mansion. A pouring rainstorm had begun.

Mahrute and Hathaway hurriedly retrieved their luggage.

"I better go park this thing in the garage," Ditters told them, the water filling up to his shoes.

Ditters tore off, and Hathaway and Mahrute dashed across the gravel to the covered porch. Reaching the marble steps, they could not help gazing up at the structure before them. From the towering pillars to the large oak door that Ditters could have driven his jeep through, Rangeley Manor impressed the weary travelers. Mahrute, typically a wealth of knowledge when it came to esoteric details, informed Hathaway that Sir Roger had built the manor to re-create the mood and atmosphere of the estate the Banbury family owned in England. Hathaway, nodding appreciatively, slammed the knocker against the door.

Received by Jackson, they entered a grand hall. The butler showed Mahrute upstairs with the luggage while Hathaway drifted behind them, gaping. He was still soaking in all the grandeur when the door knocker rattled once again. Looking up and down the corridor for a passing servant, he shrugged and attended to the knocking himself.

Several moments of fidgeting with knobs and latches revealed Baccup's foremost detective, Chief Adwick. Behind him was the shower of rain, another downpour in a weekend of heavy storms.

"Mr. Hathaway. Taken to butler duties, have we?" he said, spraying water from his coat.

"What? No. Everyone else seems to be off somewhere."

"That's just as well; my message is brief. I came to tell you not to try to leave town tomorrow."

Hathaway smiled wryly. "Chief, you yourself said that you weren't charging me with anything. So what's all this cop-to-suspect stuff?"

"Actually, the remark was not directed at you specifically, Mr. Hathaway. No one this side of town is going anywhere very easily. I had to close down the bridge. It's taken a beating the last few weeks with all these downpours, and it looks unsafe to me. I'm waiting for some experts to come up from Portland to have a look at it."

Hathaway, who had only heard of the authorities closing off bridges in bad horror movies, appeared skeptical. He was from the city, where bridges never got closed off, and even if they were, there were always sixteen other routes to take you where you wanted to go. He leaned against the doorframe and listened with the air of a man introduced to a new and startling concept as the chief explained that Rangeley Manor, along with an assortment of residences in the boonies, had only one road connecting it to town. Other than a trek through the surrounding forests, it was the only practical path back to civilization.

"It seemed fine twenty minutes ago," argued Hathaway.

The chief flicked some more water from his trench coat. "It isn't now. I would suggest that you all stay tight for the next day or so until we can get it repaired."

On that note, the chief trotted off to his car to visit the remaining residents in the area before the weather made the trails completely undrivable. The minute he stepped off the porch, his thoughts turned to the warm cottage waiting for him a few miles away. Though he never saw himself as a self-righteous man, he couldn't help thinking that lesser officers of the law would have knuckled under the storm: taking one quick look at the squall before retiring to the security of their cabins with a fifth of bourbon and the belief that the residents of the area could shift for themselves. His deputies belonged to this group, and he figured they were probably already at their respective homes, curled up in front of the woodstove.

He allowed himself to muse rudely on these poor excuses for police officers, breaking off these reflections when a gust of wind adeptly swept away his rain hat, compelling him to scurry after it in a sort of disoriented chase. Hathaway, unmoved by this display of man against nature, closed the door.

The foyer was still empty. With a sigh, he turned and climbed the arching staircase, his manner dismal, to match the weather. As he rounded the corner, the line of poetry "Stone walls do not a prison make" occurred to him. Although this was sound advice, he couldn't overcome the sense of being trapped, nor, for that matter, could he place the poet in question. Had he been asked for documentation, the name Richard Lovelace would have probably suggested itself eventually, but his first guess would have been Shakespeare or possibly Bacon.

At the top of the stairs, a maze of corridors presented itself. His search led him down the corridor on the right to a room that was softly filling the halls with the sounds of Beethoven. Popping his head in the doorway, Hathaway discovered Mahrute sitting meditatively next to a portable stereo. It occurred to Hathaway, noting the look of cool contemplation on the other's face, that Mahrute looked less like a bodyguard than he did a member of the British Royal Family relaxing after a particularly grueling polo match. He needed only a smoking jacket and pipe to complete the package.

"I'm not intruding, am I?"

Mahrute said not at all. Like Randal Finch, Mahrute valued his solitude, but unlike Finch, he also welcomed company, and in the days spent observing Hathaway on the train and speaking with him on their way to Rangeley Manor, he had come to view him as a sort of likable son figure, whose company he sometimes preferred over Warren Kingsley's.

The likable son figure, having relayed the chief's message, plunked down in a chair by the window and looked disquieted. Mahrute, who would not have looked disquieted if a meteor had struck the mansion, pondered the setup and remarked, "This is somewhat inconvenient."

Hathaway observed that it was damn inconvenient. At least he could spend time with Lesley, he realized, assuming Warren would give them a moment. "I guess we should find Banbury and tell him his residents are stranded here for the next couple of days." He stood and ambled toward the door. Hand on the knob, he turned back with a curious expression. "What's that you're listening to, by the way?"

"Beethoven, his *Fantasia* in C Minor."

"It's nice. I especially like the parts where the piano plays and then the orchestra repeats the same melody." The chorus chimed in now, and Hathaway listened to the refrain.

"It is in German," explained Mahrute.

"That would account for it. Damn hard to make out what they're saying."

"I particularly enjoy this performance. The conductor, Kurt Richter, is a guest of the manor."

"Be sure to give him the thumbs-up when you run into him. Any idea where I can find Banbury?"

"I would suggest locating Jackson, the Banburys' butler. If you would prefer, I could find him. Jackson informs me that the corridors here tend to wander and many of the guests get lost on their first visit to the mansion."

"I'm sure I can handle it," said Hathaway. He knew Mahrute was only trying to help, but he was in no mood. He had stayed in hundreds of hotels and never once needed a map to get around. The bellhops, in fact, often commented on his innate sense of direction.

He turned to leave, but Mahrute stopped him.

"Oh, before I forget, Mr. Hathaway, I took the liberty of securing this earlier on the train." Standing, he produced the Azure Star from beneath his suit jacket. "The rest of your luggage is in your room."

Hathaway accepted the dagger with a blank stare. "Did Warren give this to you?"

"Actually, I retrieved it from a table in the dining car. I noticed Mr. Kingsley forgot it after you had given it to him during breakfast this morning."

Hathaway thanked Mahrute for his thoroughness and shuffled off for the library, a site the latter had suggested was a likely area for butler spotting.

9 — Strange Behavior of a Waiter

The butler, as it turned out, was not in the library. Instead, he was on his way to the kitchen to retrieve a glass of grapefruit juice for Harold Konig (also known in some circles as Warren Kingsley). Warren, a big fan of vitamin C, always had a glass of fruit juice before dinner. Having made himself at home in a lounge overlooking the steady shower outside, he put up his feet and ordered the beverage right away, fresh squeezed if they had it. He had just kicked off his shoes and propped his head against a pillow (alleged to have once belonged to Napoleon), when the door opened to reveal not Jackson bearing refreshments, but Sir Roger Banbury bearing his checkbook. Warren nodded a greeting as his host took a seat beside him.

Sir Roger hesitated. Glancing back toward the hall, he leaned in and whispered slyly, "It's a pleasure to meet you at last, Mr. Konig. Did you get my note?"

Unaccustomed to being addressed as Mr. Konig, Warren looked around to see if Banbury was talking to him. Realizing that he was the only one in the room, he said, "Note?"

"On the train? You did get it, then? Splendid. As I said in my letter to you, we don't want to draw any suspicion to our business here."

"Business?"

"Correct. I didn't have a chance to tell you the last time we spoke, but I'll soon have something I want you to take a look at. I suspect you'll find it very interesting. But now's not the time." Sir Roger stood. "Here is a check for your fee. I believe you have an item for me, Mr. Konig?"

"Item?"

"You're right. It'll be better later. You may need it to compare. Remember, mum's the word."

Warren stared blankly. "Mum?" he asked the empty room.

* *

As Sir Roger emerged from the lounge and strode down the corridor to the east, Bertram Jackson came around the corner from the west.

Since arriving at the mansion, Warren Kingsley had wasted no time in dispatching Jackson to fulfill his various whims. This included sending the butler for dry socks, a toothbrush and several other toiletries he had forgotten to pack, while also—just before ordering the grapefruit juice—asking him if he wouldn't mind looking up all the European capitals that began with *K*, in order to settle a bet he had made with the cab driver.

It was the fruit juice whim that currently occupied Jackson. Carrying the pink beverage atop a tray, he turned the corner and moved smoothly down the hall. At the entranceway, he hesitated; something had sparked his curiosity. He rotated to his right and addressed a man somewhat unsuccessfully concealed behind a large fern.

The guest, who had been spying on the lounge for the last five minutes, jumped a foot and slammed himself up against the wall. He was a small, balding man with a shifty look. Even in a tuxedo he managed to look sleazy.

Jackson eyed him cautiously. The butler of a mansion, if he's a good one, views himself as a guard or bouncer, whose job it is to keep unsuitable guests off the premises. But he must also be careful not to overstep his bounds. Once a guest is within the stronghold, it is not the butler's place to loom up behind him demanding proper papers, just as it is seldom his right to grab a guest he does not like the look of and toss him out on the front lawn. This business of hiding behind ferns, however, he could definitely raise an eyebrow or two at.

"May I help you, sir?"

The man cleared his throat. "No." Perhaps feeling this hadn't covered it, he added, "No."

Jackson peered down at him. "Very good, sir," he replied, gliding into the lounge.

The guest was still a jangle of nerves. He adjusted his tuxedo, a garment he was not accustomed to wearing, and backed off. Though, on the surface, it would appear that he had nothing better to do than hide behind ferns all day spying on other guests, he actually had a very full schedule. He made his way across the mansion to a dimly lit hall that led to Sir Roger's private office. He listened carefully at the tycoon's door. Once he had determined that the perimeter was secure, he stole into the room.

Moving swiftly to Sir Roger's desk, he pulled open a drawer and began flipping through the papers. Turning to rifle the contents of the filing cabinet, the ransacker abruptly paused. There had been a tap at the door. He bounded across the room like a scalded kangaroo.

Three seconds after he had made his exit, the door opened and John Hathaway popped his head in. Somewhere between the kitchen and what appeared to be a wine cellar, he had gotten hopelessly lost and at present had a look of begrudging respect for the butler Jackson, or anyone else who could navigate this maze successfully.

"Hello?" he said, but the room did not answer back. Inhaling thoughtfully, he moved across to an open pair of French doors and walked aimlessly out onto the covered porch.

At the same moment, a heated discussion entered the room.

"Father," the Adrienne half was saying, "what do you have against Walter? Out with it."

Sir Roger traipsed into the room. Immediately after his conference with Warren, he had run into his daughter and soon found himself in the thick of her favorite argument. "Adrienne," he said, trying a more heartfelt approach, "you're my only child. I want you to have the best."

"Walter is the best!"

"He's a menace, Adrienne. I don't understand what you see in him. I sometimes think you got engaged to him simply to score off me."

Hathaway peered into the office. Piecing together their identities from the conversation, he stood quietly in the doorway thinking what to do next. He didn't like this loose talk about old Ditters. Ditters may have had his faults, but Hathaway felt classifying him as a menace went too far. He decided to keep his two cents to himself, however. He couldn't very well pop out from the shadows defending the name of Dittersdorf. Not with any sort of credibility.

At least he'd have to introduce himself first. Before he could even clear his throat, Adrienne shouted, "Daddy, I'm not a kid anymore!" and such was the force of her words that Hathaway shot back, as if he had found the doorframe electrified. Still startled from the jolt, he stumbled backward and caught his calves on some mysterious object in the night—the mysterious object replying "Oof!" as he kicked it.

Unable to compensate, Hathaway careened over the object and landed in a supine sprawl on the lawn. He goggled up at the stars, the rain pouring down on him.

He pulled himself up out of the muck. Across from him, he saw a small, bald man in a tuxedo lurking in the corner of the porch. The guest, having learned from his mistake with the fern, was now hiding behind a large cement pot: the site of their collision. Hathaway stared at him. Before he could speak, although one wonders what he would have said, the French doors flung wide open and Adrienne Banbury appeared in the entryway, roused by the racket.

She contemplated Hathaway with a cheesy stare. "Some man is lying out here" was her remark. It was not said with a lot of warmth. Of course, new guests found lolling across the back lawn, even those who seem amiable, cannot expect the same gracious reception afforded those who use the front door.

It is difficult to know what to say in these situations. Hathaway said, "Oh hello." He considered mentioning something about the weather but decided, on second thought, to skip it.

From within, Sir Roger had become aware of the developments.

"What's all that chatter out there, Adrienne? Who are you talking to? Who's that?" he wondered, stepping out onto the porch. "Who are you?" he asked.

"John Hathaway."

"George Hathaway's nephew? Splendid!"

Hathaway returned to the dryness of the porch and met the glare of Adrienne, the love of Ditters' life. He had a better view of her now. She was a tall girl—as tall as he was. He imagined Ditters came about to her neck. All in all, not an unattractive woman. Striking really, with her golden hair and chiseled features. These same features, however, also gave her a rather formidable look. Quite a difference from her father who, though large, conveyed a less forbidding appearance, especially with his big, broad face and harassed expression. Hathaway could see how she could get the old guy on the ropes in an argument.

The three, one wetter than the other two, stepped back inside. Sir Roger took his seat.

"Mr. Hathaway," he asked, hoping to break the awkwardness of the moment, "do you know my daughter Adrienne?"

Adrienne nodded in forced acknowledgment. "Father," she said, turning from her stare, "Mr. Hathaway was lying on our lawn."

"I noticed," replied Sir Roger, unconcerned. "Why is that, I wonder?"

"I don't know," said Adrienne.

"Seems strange, doesn't it?"

"Yes, it is strange," agreed his daughter.

"Probably just dizzy spells. A friend of mine, Harry Farmer, used to get those. He's dead now." Sir Roger looked across at their guest. "Was that it, Mr. Hathaway? Do you get dizzy spells?"

"No. I mean, not that I know of. You see, actually, I tripped over this waiter …"

"I knew there had to be a reasonable explanation."

"I didn't see anyone out there," Adrienne frowned. "Did you say a waiter?"

Hathaway attempted to clarify. "He seemed to be hiding. He's still out there."

Adrienne and Sir Roger exchanged glances. "I guess we had better check it out, then," said the latter, in a cheerful, humoring tone—the sort of tone he expected Adrienne would use one day when she came to tell him that she had enrolled him in a good nursing home.

The three returned to the porch, now completely waiterless.

Sir Roger consoled his guest. "Don't worry, Mr. Hathaway. Harry used to have episodes like this all the time. Blackouts, his doctor called them."

"But he was here a second ago."

"Harry? No, he's been dead for years. Went when he was only eighty-five. Cut off in his prime."

"No, the waiter."

"Oh right, the waiter. You were saying something about him?"

"Yes, he was—"

A disembodied voice drifted out to them from the office. It informed Sir Roger that he was needed in the library.

"Yes, yes, I'm coming," the duffer grumbled, apologizing for the interruption.

Adrienne followed her father down the hall, peering back at the soaked, confused figure of Hathaway as she went.

The soaked, confused figure came back into the office. To fill the empty moments alone, he began to stroll about, glancing at the various doodads of which Sir Roger had plenty. He had just picked up a statue of a scantily dressed maiden in mid-tiptoe—for scantily dressed maidens are something you can appreciate better up close—when an item by his foot captured his attention.

Apparently, the tuxedo-wearing guest, during his wild antics with Sir Roger's desk, had unearthed an old newspaper article. Hathaway noticed only part of the caption:

THE AZURE STAR AT THE HOME OF

It was enough to pique Hathaway's interest. He knelt under the desk. Unfortunately, the drawer that housed the scrap was stuck. He wrenched at it, trying to realign the bearings, if we can correctly assume that it was some kind of bearing issue, but the more he wrenched, the less it moved. It was at some point in this struggle that Hathaway heard a shuffling noise from across the room, then a muffled grumbling, and the next thing he knew, Sir Roger and Adrienne had returned, back on the familiar subject of the many facets of Ditters Dittersdorf.

"Walter is not a nincompoop, Father. He is the man I am going to marry!"

"Can't we discuss this later? In a few years perhaps?"

"Father, either give me your blessing now, or—"

"I will not have an idiot as a son-in-law," said Sir Roger firmly, and, put in that mind, continued with, "Oh, I say, I wonder where Mr. Hathaway got off to …"

As if on cue, the statue Hathaway was holding slipped from his fingertips and landed on the hardwood. Aside from doing the sculpture no bit of good, the thump with which it hit was enough to answer Sir Roger's question like a cry of "I am here!" sounding from the corner.

Hathaway bounded up from behind the desk.

"Oh, there you are. We were just talking about you, Mr. Hathaway."

"He was under the desk," whispered Adrienne.

Sir Roger could see that. "So, Mr. Hathaway, what do you think of our little cottage here?"

Hathaway looked around the room and nodded appreciatively. "It's quite a place," he said. He noticed Adrienne was staring at him again. In reality, she was peering across at the pedestal behind him.

"Father, where's your Pollaiuolo?" She indicated the spot where the statuette had rested.

"My Pollaiuolo?"

"Yes, your Pollaiuolo, the statuette that usually sits on that pedestal behind your desk."

"Oh, my Pollaiuolo? Yes, it does usually sit over there, doesn't it?"

"Well, where is it?"

Realizing that they were talking about the scantily dressed maiden, Hathaway interjected, "I have her over here."

"You have the statuette?" she asked, with no small amount of accusation in her voice.

"Yeah, sorry about that." He hadn't meant to pull a Dittersdorf with the thing. He nipped under the desk to retrieve it.

While Adrienne examined the piece for any evidence that it had been dropped and kicked across the floor, Sir Roger regaled Hathaway with the story behind the Pollaiuolo and how he had brilliantly outbid a competing collector for it.

Hathaway nodded with interest as the story unfolded.

Adrienne, replacing the statuette on its pedestal, left the room mumbling something about mental institutions. It was not clear for which of the two men she was suggesting the need.

Sir Roger led Hathaway out of his office. He had immediately warmed to their young guest. The man was clearly insane, but at least he had gotten Adrienne off his back for now.

"Have you seen my museum, Mr. Hathaway?" he asked cheerfully.

* *

About an eighth of a mile away, the figure of a small man in a tuxedo prowled across the moist grounds. After being chased from his task at Sir Roger's study by some officious twit he would have liked to have punched in the nose, the guest had left the arena of the mansion in order to regroup in the dry solitude of the greenhouse.

Upon arriving at the glass shack, he did indeed find it dry, but he did not find it empty. He had hardly stepped within the arboretum and taken a seat on a pile of soil, alone with his thoughts, when a clang sounded from the far corner.

Another disheveled character stepped out. The tuxedoed guest jumped to his feet, and both men stood staring at each other. The other man, soaked himself and for reasons unknown wearing a train porter's outfit, was Nibu Nibudar.

"Hello there, my friend. Terribly sorry to startle you."

"Who are you?"

"Me?" Nibu blinked. "I am the gardener."

The other occupant of the greenhouse was smarter than that. "You're not the gardener. Gardeners don't wear train-porter outfits. You're the guy they arrested at the train."

"You were at the station, my friend?"

"I was there. So … you escape or something?"

"You have a sharp mind. I did, as you say, escape. I am Nibu Nibudar, the famous assassin."

Most people, confronted by an escaped convict in a greenhouse on a rainy night would have found the situation uneasy, but the slick little man in the tuxedo betrayed no such emotion. To him, the criminal life was nothing to look down on. From time to time, in his line of work, he had found it necessary to run from the police himself. In fact, had Ditters Dittersdorf wandered along just then, the three of them could have swapped stories.

"What are you doing here? The cops are looking for you, aren't they?"

Nibu straightened his outfit. "Yes, they are. I have business to attend to here, however." He carried a small satchel with him, which he now dropped by his foot. "I am at a disadvantage in that you know who I am, but I do not know who you are."

"I'm Barnet."

"And my friend Barnet, what are you doing here, if I may ask?"

"I have business here," said Barnet, liking Nibu's explanation.

Nibu smiled again. Just as Barnet had pierced his guise, Nibu saw through this artful dodge. Criminals know each other. "Illegal business, perhaps?"

Barnet shifted his feet in some spilt soil and scratched his bald head, still damp from his dash across the landscape. He saw no reason to remain cryptic with this known fugitive. "I'm here to steal something, but I wouldn't call it illegal."

"Ah, I, too, am here to purloin a valuable object."

"I thought you said you were an assassin?"

"Sometimes we must take what we can get. Speaking of which, perhaps you can help me. As two men who are chiseled off the same block, so to speak, you could provide me a way inside the mansion."

Barnet hesitated. Chiseled off the same block or not, he didn't like helping the competition. However, this character appeared a more dangerous, professional sort of criminal, very much opposed to his own type of illegal activities. "I'm posing as a member of the Bath Chamber Orchestra," he said. "That's why I was at the station. We all just arrived. You could say you're one of us."

"Wouldn't the conductor question my presence?"

"We don't have a conductor. The orchestra was supposed to audition a new one this weekend, but he canceled because of the weather. We're here to play for the other guests now."

"What was this man's name? The conductor?"

"Richter, I think. Why?"

"This is extremely helpful. I will try what you suggest. Perhaps our paths will meet again."

"Perhaps," replied Barnet, leaving Thief #2 as he said it.

10 — A Parcel Arrives

Once he had changed into dry clothes and enjoyed a restorative shower, Hathaway was permitted the treat of touring the area known by collectors everywhere as "the mother lode." Sir Roger's need to collect went beyond the occasional ornate dagger. In the grand, spanning basement he called a museum, he had paintings, sculptures and rare books, though the bulk of his collection was devoted to ancient weapons. By the time they had shuffled through every inch of the place, Hathaway's head was swimming to such an extent that he had forgotten all about the uncomfortable scene in the old guy's office.

The museum occupied the entire distance under the mansion and took a while to walk. There was one main corridor lined with glass cases stretching from the entrance to the back wall and then several small corridors weaving out from it like a rat's maze. The main hall had a series of catwalks that ran above it and housed bookshelves of musty texts and a few odd displays. There was a certain organization to it all, which Sir Roger tediously detailed for Hathaway as they strolled, but a casual onlooker would hardly have noticed. It would appear to most that the Banbury System involved throwing the junk wherever the tycoon happened to have room.

About forty minutes into the tour, around the time Sir Roger had cornered Hathaway in order to demonstrate the proper use of a *bhuj*—a battle ax from nineteenth-century India—Adrienne emerged on the scene to announce that dinner had commenced.

Hathaway waited as Sir Roger went to put away his hatchet. He noticed Adrienne had an inquisitive look on her face. "You're the same John Hathaway who burned down the Sheraton in Baltimore, aren't you?"

The question startled him. The reference was to a party he had attended on his uncle's behalf a few weeks back, and to a small mishap with a tray of brandy-laced cherries.

"I understand you started some kind of riot? Something about you hitting on a diplomat's wife?"

Hathaway sniffed. "You have been misinformed, Miss Banbury. I wasn't the one who knocked the candles over, chasing an innocent guest around the table."

"Oh no?"

"No. And it was the Chesterton not the Sheraton."

"I stand corrected. I understand you have brought security with you this weekend? I hope you are not expecting more trouble. We don't want any riots or conflagrations here."

"I'll keep that in mind," said Hathaway.

Adrienne gave him a frigid smile. After commenting "Well," reflectively, she withdrew.

At this point, Sir Roger appeared from behind the display case. "You mustn't mind Adrienne," he said, over the sound of a door slamming in the distance. "She's in one of her snits—that's all. She's still angry at me about her fiancé. I don't know what the girl sees in this Dipperdorp."

"Dittersdorf," corrected Hathaway.

Despite his problems with strange parcels and skulking waiters and girls who thought he'd come to their homes to set them ablaze, he was still ready to push all this aside to help a chum with his prospective in-law.

"What did you say, Mr. Hathaway?"

"Dittersdorf, the man your daughter Adrienne's going to marry—that's the name, you know."

"I know my daughter's named Adrienne."

"No, the other one—Ditters. His name's Dittersdorf."

"It's all the same to me, Mr. Hathaway. I just enjoy calling him Dipperdorp. Adrienne hates it. You know this menace, then?"

"Oh yes."

"Have you ever had a daughter engaged to him?"

"No."

"Then you're very fortunate. He's a menace."

"Ditters? He's a bit on the peculiar side, perhaps. I've known Ditters many years, and I've always said he's a complex sort: toy enthusiast, nature lover, man in search of the world's perfect pickle—"

"He's an idiot."

"Sometimes you take the good with the bad."

"He's a real thorn in the side, Mr. Hathaway."

"I suppose he's not for everyone," the other agreed.

"I've even spoken to your uncle George about him."

"And what does Uncle George say?"

"He says we all have thorns in our sides."

"Sounds like Uncle George. Cheered you up, though, I suspect?"

Sir Roger nodded solemnly.

They walked out into a hall. Hathaway led the way up another flight of stairs. He noticed Sir Roger hesitating at the bottom.

"Mr. Hathaway, am I to understand from what my daughter said that you've hired a bodyguard?"

Hathaway explained that he was giving the bodyguard a trial run.

"Yes, I see. Trial run, yes," said Sir Roger, feeling trial runs were okay.

"Sort of an extra set of eyes to watch for dangerous lunatics."

"Yes, I just hired one."

"A dangerous lunatic?"

"A bodyguard," said Sir Roger. "Otto Pincher," he added, with a sneer. "I don't care for him. Never gives me a moment's peace. He's always following me around, making sure no one blows my head off. He's a big nuisance."

The bodyguard was new, hired on Lady Banbury's insistence. Even though Sir Roger was worth about a zillion dollars, which made him a target to certain undesirables, he had always felt that bodyguards simply got in the way. He couldn't even abide security to guard the mansion, which was also valued in the zillion-dollar range. "My father never had a bodyguard," he pointed out. "But enough about that. Speaking of this parcel, I suppose you brought it?"

Hathaway nodded. He was happy to unload it.

"It's something for my collection. It's very nice of you to go out of your way to deliver it. My secretary, Randal, tells me you'll only be here until tomorrow."

"Actually, the bridge is out. We're all stuck here for a while."

Sir Roger stared off into the distance, apparently captivated by this statement. "Splendid," he said.

It wasn't what Hathaway expected. It wasn't even "splendid" with a trace of remorse. It was a breezy, contented "splendid": cheerful, as if Hathaway had told him that all broad-chested billionaires with gray hair and thick mustaches received a complimentary cocktail.

"According to Chief Adwick, the storm has mucked things up."

"Splendid," repeated Sir Roger. It occurred to him that this would give him more time for his meeting with Harold Konig. Already he'd had to cut their time to a minimum, what with attending to all his wife's blasted guests. Yes, this would work out perfectly. He might even have this Konig look over his museum, assuming they could continue to keep his real presence here secret from his wife. "Do you have the, uh, item?" he asked.

Reaching into his jacket pocket, Hathaway handed over the Azure Star.

"Ah yes," Sir Roger commented, poring over the dagger like a child with the latest from the toy shop. "You know the story behind this thing, don't you?"

Hathaway looked up with unguarded interest. Sir Roger, realizing that he had come upon an uninitiated pupil, organized his thoughts.

"It's the ultimate warrior's weapon," he said, strolling a few steps down the passageway and then back again. "At least that's what the books say about it. It dates back to the early Middle Ages. I've had the hardest time locating the thing."

"Why's that?"

"Why? Because there are so many copies."

"Copies?"

"Duplicates," said Sir Roger, pausing at the stairwell. "I hope yours is the genuine one."

Before they could continue on this subject, there was a thud at the top of the stairs. Sir Roger's bodyguard, Otto, had opened the door and was now peering down the steps at client and guest. Hathaway could barely see him from his angle.

"Sir Roger, Lady Banbury wants you. She says you are neglecting your guests."

Sir Roger turned back and puffed. "Are you married, Mr. Hathaway?" he asked.

"No."

"Good for you."

* *

In the interest of avoiding awkward encounters before supper, it was fortunate that Hathaway decided to go straight to the banquet hall. Had he continued around the corner to his room after climbing the stairs, he inevitably would have run into Barnet. Instead, their paths did not cross. Just as Hathaway ambled into the dining area, Barnet, that bold and brash freelance burglar, slipped across the front foyer. Slowly traversing the flight of regal steps, he paused, as something atop a nearby table caught his eye.

The item that had captured his attention was a parcel. His eyes, though shifty, were sharp, and even from the seventh step he could clearly read the return address:

HAROLD KONIG
1414 CHUFFLE FLATS
BERWALD ISLAND, CT 06801

So far in the sequence of events, much of the spotlight has fallen on the name Harold Konig, but not much of this fanfare have we afforded Harold Konig the man. This is a shame, for among the art cognoscenti he is a fascinating character. To attempt to atone for this, a brief sketch of his activities up until this point follows.

After missing his train in Baltimore because an auction ran long, Harold Konig had not made himself idle. Realizing that his plans to visit Sir Roger had come a bust, he opted to take a train to Atlanta for an estate sale, an extravaganza he had assumed he would have to miss.

He recognized that popping off to Atlanta did Banbury no good, however, and as a matter of fact, he had been planning to bring the tycoon a parcel: an antique his client had been pestering him to locate for the past few months. To rectify his absence, he proceeded at once across the street and hired a bonded express service to deliver the package. It occurred to him that Rangeley would regret not having the great Harold Konig to stimulate dinner conversation over the weekend, but at least it would have one of his impressive finds. He thought about calling, but as is so often the case with men who spread themselves thin, he had forgotten his phone. He figured the politely worded note within the parcel would be explanation enough.

So closes the epic of Konig. The express service, a reputable firm, had delivered the parcel the next day—a few hours before Adwick had closed the bridge. Signed for by an upstairs maid, the package had remained in the manor's foyer undisturbed until it had so sharply piqued Barnet's interest.

The crook eyed it carefully. Not an inquisitive sort, Barnet only paused to speculate for a minute why Harold Konig would be sending packages if he was already on the premises.

These distinctions do not interest thieves long. Like a cat stalking his prey, he moved to pounce on the parcel.

Inches from his prize, he froze. Jackson had appeared in his midst, and Barnet readjusted his pounce to scratch his back.

Jackson picked up the parcel. Glancing at the label, he cocked his eyebrow and proceeded downstairs. Barnet, reapplying his cat imitation, followed. He crept carefully down the steps behind the servant. When the butler went to his room and closed the door, Barnet placed his eyeball to the thin sliver between the door and the frame and observed Jackson seated at his desk, poring over the package.

Jackson, too, wondered about the parcel, considering that he had just brought a pair of silk pajamas to the room of the man purporting to be Harold Konig.

It was not his place to question these things. He had strict orders to disguise Sir Roger's purchases the best he could from Lady Banbury. (In her words, she felt her husband wasted far too much time and money on pointless antiques.) The butler had also been instructed by Sir Roger to shield her from any transactions with Harold Konig, the supplier of these pointless antiques. So without question, Jackson did so.

The butler glanced down at the parcel with interest, however. Curiosity compelled him. If he were to truly handle the Konig situation for Sir Roger, it would help to know what it was he was handling. He reached for a letter opener and applied it to the wrapper.

And so, an unusual parallel existence was thus created. At the same moment that Sir Roger was moving about the dinner party with a sparkling dagger (known as the Azure Star) in his jacket pocket, Bertram Jackson was sitting downstairs flourishing another glimmering dagger, also identified for him by the enclosed note as the Azure Star.

Part Three

11 — Hathaway Chivvies a Guest

To accommodate all the guests at Rangeley Manor, dinner was served in the banquet room. Within that magnificent hall, a dozen elegantly attired visitors milled about snagging appetizers off trays and helping themselves to entrées from the generous buffet. The grandeur, all set to the sounds of the Bath Chamber Orchestra, made quite an impression on Hathaway, who paused at the door, surveying the spectacle.

Unfamiliar with most of the inmates, Hathaway did recognize a familiar bulk standing in the buffet line. He strode over to give this familiar bulk his two cents.

"Warren," he said to the man's back.

"Eh!" the bodyguard started, flipping his plate into the marinara. "Don't sneak up on me like that! Oh, Hathaway, there you are," he announced, as if he had given odds against it.

"Yes, I'm here. No thanks to you, I might add."

"I was worried about you," said Warren, watching his meal gurgle and sink without a trace to the depths of the sauce bowl.

"That's reassuring."

"I couldn't figure where you were. You just wandered off."

"You left me at the train station!"

"Yes, but that was hours ago."

"That's what happens when you leave people at train stations, Warren: they're stuck there for hours."

"Yeah, well, I can't do you any good as your bodyguard if you're not around. Besides, I've already called my printer about those brochures we discussed."

"What brochures?"

"You know, the brochures for the Warren Kingsley Security Agency. You can imagine how awkward it would be for me if you disappeared."

"I don't remember discussing any brochures," said Hathaway, whose mind had been otherwise occupied when the bodyguard had brought up the subject on the train. "By the way, why didn't you tell me you had a bodyguard? And what are you doing with a bodyguard anyway? Whoever heard of a bodyguard hiring a bodyguard?"

"I deserve protection as much as the next guy," answered Warren promptly. "Brittany doesn't seem to think it strange that I have a bodyguard."

The statement mystified Hathaway, until it dawned on him that Warren meant Lesley. "Brittany doesn't think you're a bodyguard!"

"I know. She thinks I'm an art expert. Isn't Brittany wonderful, Hathaway? You're not going to tell her I'm not Harold Konig, are you?"

"I gave you my word, didn't I?"

"I'm only asking. Sorry, I guess I can trust you."

Hathaway sneered. "Speaking of honor, I didn't appreciate you running off with her like that."

"What do you mean? At the station? I didn't 'run off with her.' "

"Oh really? You could have fooled me. I'm surprised you didn't club her over the head and drag her here in a gunnysack."

"What's that supposed to mean? Where would I get a gunnysack?"

"That's not the point. I'm interested in Brittany, and frankly I don't like you spending time with her."

"Well, if you were so interested," said Warren, "you could have gotten yourself out of the train a little quicker, couldn't you?"

His rival hesitated, exercising restraint. "Never mind that now. We have to discuss your bodyguarding, Warren." He took a deep breath. It's never easy handing someone the pink slip, but with no death threats looming on the horizon, Nibu in jail, and the jealous

Green Beret nowhere to be found, Hathaway had decided he no longer required Warren's brand of expertise.

"Bodyguarding?" asked the expert.

"You *are* a bodyguard, remember?"

"Oh yeah. Yeah, of course ..." This seemed to remind Warren of something. He submitted his new plate of food to a thoughtful glare. "You don't know where Mahrute is, do you?"

"No, I don't."

"It occurs to me that this food is right out in the open. Right where anyone could have gotten to it."

"So what?"

"So what? Someone could have poisoned it—that's so what. I usually wait until after Mahrute tries the food, just to be sure."

"Warren, no one is trying to kill you."

"That's your opinion. Say, Hathaway, you wouldn't mind—"

"Warren!"

"I mean, just to check—"

"Forget it! I'm not your royal food taster. I'm your client, remember? Actually, that's what I wanted to talk to you about—"

"I know you're my client, Hathaway. I just thought since Mahrute—never mind. Have you seen Brittany around here?"

"You're not having Brittany taste your food!"

"No, no. I only wanted to talk to her."

"Yes, well, Brittany or no Brittany," said Hathaway, and was about to conclude things pretty decisively, explaining to Warren that, while his presence had definitely made the trip more lively, his services were not at present a reasonable expenditure. But unfortunately, this speech, which could have been riveting, was held up by a new addition to the conversation.

"Mr. Hathaway?" asked this new addition.

"I'm Hathaway," he said, turning to meet the elegant gaze of Lady Banbury.

She gave a regal nod. "I wanted to welcome you to our home, Mr. Hathaway. I heard you had a bit of trouble at the train station?"

Hathaway turned to shoot Warren a glare, but the bodyguard had already slipped quietly away.

"Everything worked out fine. I got a lift from Ditters."

"Oh yes—Mr. Dittersdorf. Strange boy. Roger doesn't care for him much. Actually, Mr. Hathaway, the trouble at the train station to which I am alluding has to do with a call I received from a Chief Adwick before you arrived."

"Chief Adwick?"

"His call greatly perturbed me," she said, sweeping back her platinum hair.

Hathaway could see why. "You can't take Chief Adwick too personally. He's rather brusque with everyone."

"It was not his manner to which I am alluding. It was the subject of the call. He told me about a scrap you had with hoodlums. He wanted to confirm that you were really a guest of Rangeley Manor."

"I see. You set him straight?"

"Yes, I did—"

"That's good. And I wouldn't worry about the chief. He came by later to discuss the hurricane, and he and I couldn't have been on chummier terms. That is, as chief-citizen relationships go."

"Hurricane?" asked Lady Banbury—listening selectively, Hathaway noticed, but he didn't mention it.

"If you can call it a hurricane. Looks like it's calming down out there, actually. Didn't you know—it knocked out the bridge earlier today."

Lady Banbury stepped back. "My goodness, that's what Roger meant. He mumbled something about bridges earlier, but I paid him no heed. This is most disturbing. Oh dear. Excuse me, Mr. Hathaway. I must make an announcement."

Lady Banbury, still retaining her aplomb, darted off.

As if to fill the void, Lesley sauntered over. Hathaway greeted her cheerfully. It seemed like ages since he had seen her charming face. "Well, hello, *Brittany*."

Lesley beamed. "Hello, John. Splendid place, isn't it?"

His answer would have to wait for Lady Banbury's announcement.

Tapping her glass to hush up the crowd, she gave the room the run of the facts. After she had resigned the stage back to the musicians, Hathaway addressed the question. "Depends how you're defining 'splendid.' "

Lesley regarded him with wide eyes. "This is a bit of a rub, isn't it? How long do you think we'll be stuck here?"

"Hard to say."

"I don't know how well I can continue to pull off this Brittany ruse. Already some people have questioned my accent. I told them I was educated abroad."

"Good thinking."

They walked toward the terrace.

Before they could reach the door, Adrienne blocked their path. Her manner had shifted from its customary cool reserve to a more agitated state. "I must see Walter immediately," she informed the couple. "Have you seen Walter?"

"Not since this afternoon," said Hathaway.

"Well, I must find him," she argued. Though she did not disclose it to these non-allies, the recent developments with the bridge had altered Plan C. "Well!" she said again, and left them.

"An old friend of mine is going to marry her, you know," he muttered, watching her weave through the room.

"That's a shame," said Lesley. "Say, John, you haven't seen Harold around, have you?"

Hathaway frowned. He was beginning to feel like the official Rangeley switchboard, expected to keep tabs on everyone. "Why?"

"I wanted to thank him for escorting me back from the train. He's a remarkable man."

"Oh yeah?"

"Yes. I mean, most of these art experts really let themselves go. But Harold's so fit. And handsome! What's wrong? Don't you like him?"

"Harold? Yeah, he's fine. I mean, I wouldn't entrust the care of any beloved grandmothers to him, but other than that—"

"Are you saying he's irresponsible?"

"Only slightly. He has a tendency to allow people to fall off cliffs without lifting a finger, that's all."

"I'm sure I don't know what you're talking about, but I'm certain you're exaggerating. By the way, did you really think I wouldn't find out about your stalker?"

"My what?"

"You told me you thought people were after you because of your uncle's parcel."

"People *were* after me because of my uncle's parcel."

"I know they were, but you led me to believe you suspected it all the time. Harold informs me that you thought a lunatic husband was after you."

Hathaway spouted angrily. "She wasn't married!"

"But it was a jealous lunatic?"

"Uh, yes –" Hathaway backtracked. "But I *am* a courier, you know. Not quite as lofty as I made it seem, perhaps, but I—what else has *Harold* been telling you?" he asked.

"Nothing," she replied, as they stepped out onto the terrace.

Outside felt crisp and pleasant compared to the heat of the day. At first, they spent a thoughtful moment alone with the crickets, before Ditters Dittersdorf came bounding up the porch steps and broke the silence by tripping over a cart of dishes.

"Hath," he said, as he and his obstacles crashed to concrete. "I've been looking for you," he continued, stumbling over to where they were standing.

Hathaway turned and regarded the approaching third wheel. Although he could have done without Ditters' company in his current mood, he introduced him to Lesley and asked if all was well on the pickle front.

"Yes, quite well, and I'm glad you asked. Here, try one," he said, whipping out a little container. "New batch, less garlic."

"Actually, Ditters, I'm rather stuffed from dinner."

"I didn't notice you eating anything," said Lesley.

Hathaway frowned at her. "You know, Ditters, perhaps *Lesley* would like one?"

"Oh yeah?"

Lesley smiled. Arching her eyebrows in good nature, she accepted the pickle. While she munched, her brow remained raised, but in her eyes Hathaway perceived great pain. Finally, she finished it.

"Have another," offered Ditters.

John Hathaway could only see a woman go through so much before his chivalrous nature kicked in. "Maybe you should let her savor it awhile, Ditters."

Ditters nodded. "Oh, I almost forgot." Reaching into his coat pocket, he pulled out a revolver.

Lesley gasped. What with people stalking her and breaking into her residence back home, she had begun to view the world around her with a suspicious eye. While she had never really considered this cheerful little pickle fellow a threat, it crossed her mind that anyone could be an assassin in disguise.

She leapt behind Hathaway, who in turn glared at his friend. The drama of the maneuver shocked him as well. He had known Ditters since they were tykes, and though Ditters had always been eccentric in his views on vegetable preservation, Hathaway had never thought him the sort of man who packed heat to a dinner party. Perhaps he had snapped.

"Steady, Ditters; I'll have a pickle if it means that much to you."

"Huh? Oh, the pistol. No, no, it's that antique. I wanted to show it to you."

"You mean this is the pistol? The one you swiped?"

"Of course it's the one I swiped. How many antique pistols do you think I have?"

"I thought you said you would take care of it?"

"I wanted to talk to you about that. Would you mind dropping it off at the gun shop tomorrow?"

Hathaway goggled at his friend. The latter had not spoken gibberish like this since they were tykes. "And spend a few nights in jail while I'm at it?"

"You won't spend any nights in jail. The shop owner won't think you stole it. I'm the one he saw, remember?"

"He might think I'm your accomplice."

"He won't. All you have to say is you found it somewhere and thought you'd return it. Easy." He paused to polish the barrel, which was covered in mud from when he had dropped it earlier in the day.

Hathaway deliberated on his friend's request.

During his pondering, he shifted his glance to the lake, where a flash of movement caught his eye. He maneuvered to the rail and saw it again, a bobbing between the trees: the outline of someone wearing a tuxedo. Remembering the prowler in formal attire hiding on Sir Roger's porch, Hathaway eased down the steps.

Ditters asked where he was going.

"I'll be right back."

Striding across the damp grounds, he caught up with the man at the lake. "Hey you! Hey!" he uttered, poking him in the rib cage.

Before he could continue, the man whirled around, and Hathaway saw he had made a slight boo-boo.

This tuxedo wearer was an older, large-bellied gentleman with a gray beard: not at all the man he had seen skulking around Sir Roger's office. He looked, in fact, like an old headmaster of Hathaway's. Replace the tuxedo with a worn tweed jacket and exchange the look of mild surprise with a disgruntled stare of contempt, and it was Headmaster Hodges in person.

A few feet away, in the background, a tall man with a close-cropped haircut stood surveying the scene. Observing Hathaway accost the guest, he jumped into action and set upon this rib-prodding threat immediately. Hathaway had already stepped back apologetically when the observer grabbed him around the neck and yanked him backward into the darkness, Hathaway's heels dragging along the turf.

Before he could be completely hauled off, Sir Roger popped onto the scene. He addressed the bearded man first. "I'm sorry about abandoning you like that, Maestro. I had something to attend to. Oh, I see you've met Mr. Hathaway."

The thug applying the choke hold mumbled something in response to this. Though it was not entirely decipherable, the words clearly reflected a certain disapproval of Mr. Hathaway.

In the scheme of things, Sir Roger probably would have stepped in before Otto had a chance to snap Hathaway's neck. And had his bodyguard gotten ahead of himself in this department, Sir Roger no doubt would have had something to say about it.

But fortunately for all involved, the man referred to earlier in the exchange as "Maestro" interceded. "Herr Banbury, your bodyguard oversteps his bounds, I think."

Sir Roger blinked at Otto, the latter of whom was currently lifting Hathaway a foot off the ground.

Otto stared back. "He assaulted him, Sir Roger!"

Sir Roger rolled his eyes and waved a dismissive hand. Otto (somewhat reluctantly) let Hathaway drop unsnapped to earth.

The bearded guest smiled and peered down at the thin man struggling for oxygen. "You must be Hathaway. I have heard much about you, Hathaway. I am Kurt Richter, the conductor."

Hathaway stood wobbly and shook hands.

Sir Roger explained, "Mr. Richter just arrived, Mr. Hathaway. We thought he wasn't coming because his secretary called and canceled, but apparently he made it here, after all."

Anyone with a sharp ear would have detected a lack of excitement in Sir Roger's voice, for it mattered to him very little whether any of the guests showed or not. Yet, he had to play the host.

Hathaway smiled uncomfortably, trying to decide on the right moment to slink away. Besides reaching his quota of making an ass of himself twice in one day, the presence of Otto Pincher looming behind him gave him the heebie-jeebies. Laughing nervously, he turned to the conductor and made an idle comment about the weather.

The man nodded, a smug grin concealed beneath a thick beard.

Nibu Nibudar commended himself on a successful costume. Using the supplies he had in his case, Nibu had demonstrated what made him a master of disguise. A false beard, a padded stomach and a heavy German accent. Not even a man who had spoken with him four hours earlier could spot him.

"Well, I guess I'll return to dinner," Hathaway declared. He glanced back at the potbellied conductor. "Nice to have met you," he said. Trotting off, he could hear Sir Roger asking his new guest if he would like to see his museum.

* * *

Hathaway found Ditters where he had left him on the porch. Lesley, apparently, had retired for the evening.

Ditters held up the Colt for inspection. "I think I got the mud out of the chamber."

Hathaway murmured a response. "Where's Lesley?"

"Went to bed. By the way, she told me all about this Brittany ruse. So, if I got this straight, the other guy, Warren, is pretending to be Harold Konig, but Lesley doesn't know it. Meanwhile, Lesley's Brittany, and Warren is none the wiser. Do all your friends travel under aliases?"

"Only some. My more colorful friends ask me to return stolen goods."

Ditters followed the other's stare to the revolver. "Hath, you have to return this," he pleaded, pushing it forward. "Do you want me to go to jail?"

"I don't know," said Hathaway, sliding the barrel away from his rib cage. "You might enjoy it there. They'd call you the Pickleman of Alcatraz. You could trade jars for cigarettes."

"I don't smoke. Come on, how many favors do I ask you for?"

His friend huffed with exasperation. "Oh, all right!"

"You're a buddy, Hath. Wanna hold it?"

"Not right now. Maybe later. It is a handsome piece, though. You couldn't have chosen a better one to swipe."

"That's what I thought. It's one of those old six-shooters, you know—a Colt. Circa 1873, I believe," he said, scrutinizing the piece. "I can't find the date."

"I doubt they stamp it inside the barrel, Ditters. Don't take this the wrong way, but you might want to be a bit more careful about where you point that thing."

"It's all right. It won't shoot without the hammer cocked. This little whatsit," he said, pointing to the back of the pistol; "you have to cock the hammer before you shoot. That's why they call it single action."

"I didn't know that. I thought cocking the hammer was a matter of personal preference."

"No. See, the hammer's up, and the trigger won't fire," said Ditters, demonstrating the effect. "See, now the hammer's cocked. Whoops!"

The moment after the shot rang out, the gun authority adjusted the hammer properly.

"And that's how you fire it," he said meekly. Looking beyond Hathaway (currently attempting to clear his right ear), he observed Jackson standing in the doorway. "Say, Jackson, where did you come from?"

"Manchester, sir."

"No, I mean just now." Ditters stepped closer. "Jackson, are you bleeding!"

"Yes, sir. A bullet from your pistol grazed my left shoulder."

During Ditters' Billy the Kid routine, Jackson had been the only one in the vicinity who had not dived for cover. It would not have befitted his dignity.

"My God! Jackson, are you saying I shot you!"

"Winged me, sir."

"I'm awfully sorry!"

"It is only a flesh wound," the butler replied indifferently.

Ditters—always one to do right by anyone he happened to maim—insisted on taking Jackson to Dr. Powers, a physician staying at the mansion for the weekend. The butler was at first willful, but Ditters persisted, mentioning that he needed to go that way anyway to pick up some preserve jars from the kitchen.

Butler hanging on guest, the Jackson-Ditters machine maneuvered toward the door. Three-quarters of the way across the porch, something occurred to the Jackson half. "Excuse me, Mr. Hathaway. Before I forget, sir, Mr. Konig was asking for you. He is in the library."

Ditters and Jackson disappeared around the corner. Hathaway, moving to follow, paused at the entranceway. Someone was shouting his name. Turning and scanning the grounds, he observed the approaching figure of Chief Adwick. Hathaway was astonished. Normally the police get nothing but complaints about their response to a crime; the general idea being that, by the time they arrive, all that is left to do is draw a few chalk outlines and file the paperwork. But here, Hathaway couldn't think of an officer responding any quicker.

In fact, the chief had not heard the shot, nor would he have had any energy to do anything about it had he heard it. He reached the foot of the stairs, and Hathaway could see he was in more ragged condition than he had appeared from a distance. Besides the arm sling, he had added to the general presentation a torn trench coat and ripped trousers, giving the impression that he had been through some kind of shredding machine. He was also soaked from head to toe and made a wet, squeaking noise when he walked.

"Evening, Chief."

The chief shook off, spraying moisture on several guests. Most students of science know that a substantial amount of the body is made up of water, but anyone observing Chief Adwick now would have assumed he was trying to up his total by applying the stuff externally.

He made no reply to Hathaway's remark, except to huff in the other's general direction. Waddling across the porch, he fell into a chair.

"Out tangling with the thugs of the underworld, and decide to stop and have a breather?" Hathaway inquired.

The second party in the conversation finally spoke. "Mr. Hathaway—"

Hathaway agreed it was he.

"I was in the woods," said the chief.

"Ah. I wouldn't have advised that. You might have gotten lost."

"I did get lost!" snapped Adwick. "I tried to take a shortcut to my cabin, but my car got stuck in the mud. I've been wandering out there for hours."

Hathaway understood. Ditters was right: you did need a jeep to get around in this area. There was still one point that puzzled him, though. "Didn't it stop raining an hour ago?"

The chief didn't follow. "Oh, why am I all wet? I fell in the lake on my way onto the grounds."

Hathaway nodded amusedly, able to see a humor in the retelling that the officer did not.

"They need lights out there!" he said. "I could have drowned. Fortunately, it washed some of the mud off me. Speaking of which, you'll have to excuse me. I'm going to ask Mr. Banbury if I can stay here tonight. I'll try to get the car out in the morning."

"I'm not sure you want to do that," said Hathaway. He spoke guardedly. He was thinking of Ditters. Very few wanted felons jump at the chance to have a member of the force sleeping down the hall (especially those members with a particular gripe against them). "The mansion's a rotten place to stay. If I had my druthers, I'd probably beat it for the great open spaces. Find a comfortable pine tree and curl up."

"Mr. Hathaway, I've spent four hours in the woods. I am going inside, and I am asking for a room."

Hathaway had in mind adding "Have it your own way" or "To each his own," but Adwick had already lumbered into the cocktail area.

* * *

If Nibu Nibudar had ever considered giving up his life of crime, it was during the tour of Sir Roger Banbury's museum. After filing through what seemed like miles of useless objets d'art, each with a delightful anecdote behind it, a temptation rankled at him to tear off his disguise and proclaim, "It is I, Nibu, wanted assassin! Take me away!"

"You're falling behind, Maestro," Sir Roger would remark, as Nibu trailed listlessly a few feet off.

It didn't help that Banbury's thug, Otto, had tagged along. Upon adopting the Richter persona, Nibu had assumed he would have to work hardest to avoid Lady Banbury, who had already cornered him on three separate occasions to talk shop. But Nibu saw now that tap-dancing around his limited knowledge of the world of orchestral music was a walk in the park compared to falling under the scrutiny of this Pincher punk. Otto had a way of disrupting anyone's reserve, looming and glaring the way that he did.

And, of course, Otto Pincher had to be German, making Nibu's impersonation of an Austrian conductor all the more difficult. (Nibu's German was barely passable to those who did not know it as their mother tongue.)

Yet, you should always watch out for the silver lining, or in this case the Azure lining. Up on the catwalks, he leaned against a railing and sighed. Turning to subject the cases along the wall to a cursory glance, his beady eyes focused. Four feet in front of him, he noticed a display case, within which rested a particular ornate dagger.

Nibu sprang forward. He stared in astonishment. Stepping back, he blinked. Finally, he rotated around and peered hurriedly over the railing for his host.

Sir Roger's on-running lecture on the Bronze Age, a twenty-minute dissertation that had begun at the broadsword section, was now echoing into the marble distance. Satisfied that master and bodyguard were sufficiently out of range, Nibu returned to the case. There was no label to the dagger, but he would know it anywhere.

Hathaway must have delivered the goods on arrival, Nibu decided, staring at it, his face pressed to the glass. Nibu's criminal mind raced. He reached for the latch, only to freeze again as a colossal paw fell on his shoulder.

"Sir Roger thought you might have gotten lost," said Otto, withdrawing his grip.

Nibu spun around, goggling at the security officer. "No! I mean, not at all, my large friend. In fact, I would be very much obliged if you would tell him I had retired. I have a bit of a headache, I am afraid."

The bodyguard folded his arms. "You have *Zahnschmerzen*, do you?"

Nibu looked blank. *Zahnschmerzen?* He supposed he could have *Zahnschmerzen*. "Yes, yes, as you say, my friend. You will give Herr Banbury my regards?"

Otto betrayed a slight smile. "I will."

Nibu strolled off and down the steps, still puzzling over that *Zahnschmerzen* remark.

Seconds later, Sir Roger bounced onto the scene, coming up from the other staircase. "Where's Richter? I didn't get to show him my throwing axes."

"Richter is gone. At least the man purporting to be Richer is."

"What are you talking about, Otto?"

"That man, he is no German."

"Of course he's not. I think he's Australian."

"Austrian. He's supposed to be Austrian, and no man from that country would speak such poor German. I asked him if he had *Zahnschmerzen*, a toothache, and he agreed."

"Why would you ask him if he had a toothache?"

"To see if he knew the word. *Kopfschmerzen* is for headache. He didn't realize."

"Well, maybe he had a toothache too. I do wish you wouldn't pester the guests like this, Otto."

"I do not pester! He was looking at this case, Sir Roger. I found the *Schwein* trying the locks."

Sir Roger turned to the case. "That case? The one with my Azure Star?"

"Yes!"

"It doesn't matter anyway. That's not the piece Mr. Hathaway gave me. I already had this one; it's a counterfeit."

Sir Roger shook his head and ambled off, leaving Otto to stare broodingly through the glass at Azure Star #3.

12 — Plan C

Warren Kingsley paced the library impatiently. He had the appearance of a man pulled in all directions. Beginning with Roger Banbury, everyone seemed to want a piece of this Harold Konig. A couple minutes earlier, a little old man stopped him in the hall and asked if he would come to his estate sometime and appraise his El Greco. Warren didn't know what an El Greco was and told him so. It was as if these people were speaking a different language.

Hoping to escape his public, he ensconced himself in the Modern History section. On his sixth lap around England 1840–1990, Hathaway joined him.

"Jackson said you wanted to see me."

"That's because I told him to say that," Warren replied, hesitating. "Did I hear gunplay on the porch earlier?"

"Just a friend of mine amusing the residents." Hathaway took a seat on a wooden chair and began to flip idly through a copy of Churchill's memoirs. "What is it, Warren? You look jumpy."

The bodyguard glanced around to see if they were alone. "Being Harold Konig isn't easy. People keep accosting me. They seem to think I'm some kind of art expert."

"You're the one who started this, Warren."

"To impress Brittany, not to be the stupid center of attention."

Hathaway wondered what other kind of center of attention Warren thought he could be.

"About Brittany—" Warren began.

"Yes?"

"Brittany says you said I want to push her grandmother in front of a bus."

Hathaway frowned. Slowly, his conversation with Lesley at dinner came back to him. "Actually, I think it was off a cliff."

"Yeah, that's it. Why did you say that, Hathaway?"

"I didn't literally say you'd push her grandmother off a cliff; it was sort of implied."

Warren did not appear consoled. In fact, he did not appear like Warren at all. He was jealous, resentful. The lovable bodyguard had vanished, and in his place was this green-eyed beefcake.

"I can see how you would take it the wrong way," Hathaway went on, "but you're getting it out of context."

"Am I?"

"Sure. I mean, you had to be there." A moment passed in silence. "You were saying something about becoming the center of attention?" he said, hoping to steer the subject away from grandmothers.

"Oh yeah." Warren was Warren again. "I am the center of attention. The thing is, I'm trying to blend in here. How can I blend if people keep pouncing on me? I mean, this Harold Konig is even more famous than I am as a bodyguard."

"Surely not."

"Well, maybe not that famous, but his reputation as an expert is known far and wide. Everyone here has snagged me to talk art. Sir Roger even tried to give me a check."

Hathaway was amazed. He had only met Sir Roger briefly, but he would not have put him down as the type to give people like Warren Kingsley checks.

"Evidently, he's the one who left me the note on the train."

"You mean he left Konig the note?"

"Yes."

"What did it say?"

"How should I know? I lost it. At any rate, Banbury has been at me since I got here. First in the lounge—before I even had a chance to unwind—and then on the grounds after dinner. He started babbling about the Middle Ages and something about the warrior's ultimate women."

"You sure he didn't say 'ultimate weapon'?"

"Maybe. That does make more sense. At any rate, he just kept rambling. Finally, he gave me this." Warren whipped out the familiar dagger and stabbed it into the desk.

Springing back, Hathaway and chair crashed to tile.

"Dammit, Warren! You just about ran me through." He peered over at the object, still trembling from the impact. "Why'd he give the Azure Star to you after I gave it to him?"

"He said he wants me to authenticate it."

"Of all the nerve! He doesn't think it's genuine?"

"How should I know? He said, 'Compare it to yours, Konig.' What does that mean? Does he think all his guests have Azure Stars?"

"You sure he said to compare it to yours?"

"That's what I thought he said. Who cares?" Warren contemplated the floorboards. "Oh, and get this. Jackson tells me that Banbury is expecting Konig to review his art collection tomorrow, sniff out the forgeries. I have no idea how to do that. But Konig already agreed to it, the bastard!"

Hathaway looked perplexed. "Warren, you're not referring to yourself in the third person, are you?"

"Huh? No. Konig told Sir Roger he'd do it before he came here, or rather I came here."

"Gotcha. Thought you had a split personality there for a minute. I know! Why not just explain to everyone that you're not Konig?"

"Oh sure, that's just what the assassins would want: for me to reveal my identity. My name carries a certain weight, remember? Besides, Brittany might have heard of me, and I don't want her to know I'm a bodyguard. She's delicate, Hathaway—tender. I like her thinking I'm this cultured art expert. She wouldn't understand the life I live."

"I'm not certain any right-thinking person would."

"Jackson said Sir Roger is going to assemble a small audience to observe me tomorrow. I'm supposed to make a speech. I hate making speeches."

Hathaway nodded in agreement. He, too, had spent most of his scholastic career avoiding public speaking.

"Hathaway, what am I going to do?"

Hathaway shrugged, and Warren frowned. During this thinkfest, Ditters arrived.

Still deep in thought, Warren yanked the dagger out from the splintered wood. Wielding it moodily, he left the library.

Ditters watched him go. "Neat knife," he remarked. "So Jackson's all patched up. Lucky for him, the doctor had her bag with her. Jackson covered for me too. He said he dropped one of Sir Roger's guns and it went off. Fortunately the bullet only nicked him."

"That's good."

"Yeah, Jackson's swell."

"Oh, before I forget," said Hathaway, remembering someone who was anything but swell, "Adrienne was looking for you."

"Yup, she found me. We had to cancel Plan C."

Hathaway, unfamiliar with the inner workings of the Dittersdorf-Banbury romance, asked, "What Plan C?"

"I had forgotten too," Ditters admitted, fiddling with a row of DVD documentaries. "Plan C was our elopement. Adrienne and I were going to take off tomorrow. It's Sir Roger. Adrienne and I have concluded that he will never approve our marriage. Even though he tacitly accepted our engagement, that's as far as it will go, Adrienne and I think. But we had to cancel the stratagem because of the storm. They closed the bridge, you know."

"I know." Hathaway paused. In all the excitement he had forgotten an important point. "By the way, Ditters, watch out for Adwick."

His friend could only stand and stare.

Hathaway elaborated: "Chief Adwick. He showed up a little while ago. He's staying at the mansion tonight."

To the general dismay of those guests trying to sleep down the hall, Rangeley Manor's library suddenly filled with the sound of a large shelf of DVDs crashing to the floor.

Ditters stood frozen on the spot, gibbering. "Hath!" he said, finally becoming coherent, "this is horrible!"

"I know."

"Hath, you don't understand; this is horrible!"

"Yes, I know. Stop saying it's horrible."

"But, Hath, you don't understand."

"And stop saying I don't understand."

Ditters began to get antsier.

"Ditters, take it easy. Just stay in your room tomorrow. Adwick will leave in the morning."

"That's no good; he'll find me there. He's closing in. There's nothing else for it; we gotta elope now."

"What about the bridge?"

"We'll go around it. I know a shortcut through the woods, actually a long cut. I didn't mention it to Adrienne because I thought we had the luxury to wait for the main road. But now we can't wait. Thanks for the info. See ya, Hath!"

Hathaway tried to stop him, but Ditters had already spun around. Skidding on a DVD of Early Aviators, he launched from the room.

It had been one of those days. Hathaway looked forward to getting some sleep. Returning to his room, he crawled into bed and was out within moments.

* * *

"Hath, wake up."

He had been asleep no more than thirty minutes when he felt some lunatic shaking him. "Hath, wake up," the lunatic repeated. A blurry-eyed image cleared to reveal a grinning Dittersdorf, holding a pickle toward him.

Hathaway was appalled. It wasn't bad enough that his friend constantly foisted pickles off on people during the day; he had now resorted to these nocturnal sieges.

"Hath, wake up. I need you to taste this."

"Ditters," he mumbled, "my interest in pickles at three in the morning is tepid at best."

"It's only eleven thirty. I've had a pickle breakthrough!"

"Ditters, one does not have breakthroughs in pickles; in medicine, yes; in science, perhaps. But never in pickles."

He dozed off again. "Gug!" he coughed. "Ditters! Don't you know never to shove pickles into a sleeping man's mouth!"

"I've never heard that, no."

"It's one of those unspoken rules. My God, I could have choked! And your stupid pickles would be to blame!"

"You really must try them. I've outdone myself."

"Thanks anyway. I thought you were eloping?"

"I wanted you to try this new batch before I went."

Hathaway was impressed. Not even the threat of police chiefs looming in could pause Ditters from his duty of distributing pickled cucumbers to the public.

"Besides," continued the deranged chef, "there's a snag: Otto. Sir Roger has him patrolling the hall. He has orders to snap me in two if I go near Adrienne's bedroom. Sir Roger says until we're married I can stay in my own wing."

"Is this new?"

"Nah, it's always been that way. Otto never sleeps. I tried to sneak by, but he caught me."

"Did he snap you in two?"

"No, worse. He took my gun off me."

"The Colt? Why?"

"Because he saw me with it, and I couldn't explain it. He asked me if I always carry around antique revolvers. What was I supposed to tell him? He thought I stole it out of Sir Roger's collection. He took it to Sir Roger's office and said we'd work it out in the morning. It was exactly like Mrs. Bainer with my kazoo. Remember? She confiscated it because I was playing 'Old MacDonald' during long-division class. She said she would return it at the end of the year. You know, I don't think I ever got it back from her."

Ditters had paused to ponder where Mrs. Bainer might be keeping herself these days when a look from Hathaway indicated that he should move it along.

"Anyway, I've been in my pickle shop thinking about this for the last forty-five minutes. Otto will tell Sir Roger about the gun, Sir Roger will tell the chief who I am, and then I'll never be able to escape the long arm of the law."

"The long, broken arm of the law, you mean," said Hathaway. He scrolled back through the narration. "You have a pickle shop?"

"Little shack on the estate, used to be a boathouse. Betty helped me set it up."

"Betty?"

"Girl from the neighborhood, lives in a little cottage across the lake. I met her one day while I was skipping stones. She saves me jars so I can make my pickles. She's the first person I always ask to taste a new batch. She loves them. Gives me support too. She's a peach."

"She sounds like one," said Hathaway. "Anyway, let me think. Seriously, if you had simply gone to bed, the chief would have left tomorrow, and you would have been a free man."

Ditters bit into a pickle. "You sure you don't want one?" he asked, munching on it.

"No." Hathaway sat up and rubbed his face and hair. "Where'd you say Pincher put the gun?"

"Sir Roger's office. I need to get it back before Sir Roger sees it. I was wondering if you would help me liberate it."

Hathaway gave Ditters a dubious look. "Really, you're like a brother to me, but come on. We can't break into Sir Roger's office. I mean ... what sort of world would it be if people went around ..." A long pause. "Oh, all right, toss me my robe!"

After adopting a more suitable outfit than his bright-green pajamas, Hathaway followed Ditters through the dark mansion to Sir Roger's office. Ditters peered inside to see if the coast was clear.

"The coast is clear, Hath."

"Are you sure Sir Roger won't come back?"

"I told you he always goes to bed at nine. It's almost twelve."

"You better go to it, then. I'll stand guard."

"Okay, but we'll have to work the thing with Swiss-clockwork precision. Can't miss a beat. Every moment counts. Each second—"

"Yes, I think I get the idea."

"Okeydoke." Ditters advanced inside.

Hathaway peered anxiously up and down the dusky corridor. After what seemed like an hour, he heard a sound like a pickleman whispering "Hath, Hath" proceeding from within the darkened office. Looking inside, he saw Ditters waving his arms.

"What is it?" Hathaway whispered.

"I can't find it," Ditters whispered back.

"What do you mean you can't find it?" whispered Hathaway, not missing a beat.

"I mean I can't find it. I need your help."

Hathaway crept slowly inside. If for no other good reason, at least now he could raise his whisper to a more appropriate pitch. "Where do you think he put it?"

"Probably here," said Ditters in a clear voice. Seeing Hathaway cringe at the racket, he repeated, "Probably here," this time in a low murmur, as if it made a difference at that point.

"In the desk?"

"Yes. I'll check again," he said, switching on a small table lamp.

Hathaway glanced around uneasily. He couldn't help expecting Adwick or Otto to come bursting in, shouting, "Everybody freeze! We've got the place surrounded."

Ditters burrowed through a large drawer. It was during this mad ransacking that Hathaway noticed an article among the paperwork, the same piece he had spotted earlier. Someone had been highlighting sections of it.

He snatched the page and read the caption:

THE AZURE STAR
AT THE HOME OF BORIS PEFFERU

"It's not in here," said Ditters, speaking from beneath the desk.

Hathaway wasn't listening. He unfolded the paper and gaped at the headline:

PRICELESS ART TREASURE STOLEN
FROM GOVERNMENT PALACE

Hathaway emitted a strangled gurgle.

"What?" asked Ditters, from beneath the mahogany.

Before Hathaway could complete the thought, the lights around them flipped on, and Randal Finch shouted "HATHAWAY!"

Like any good cat burglar who knows never to get caught with the evidence in hand, Hathaway sprayed the stack of papers across the room. Ditters, not holding anything he could toss about at the time, bumped the back of his head against the bottom of the desk.

Finch marched over and shoved Hathaway in the chest. From his angle, he didn't notice Ditters ensconced under the table. "Hathaway!

What do you think you're doing? You were going through Sir Roger's desk!"

"Finch! Didn't expect to see you again so soon. This is quite a surprise. What are you doing here?"

"What am I doing here? *What am I doing here?* I work here, Hathaway!" he snapped, kicking a letter by his foot.

"Yes, I know. So, what is it that you do?"

"I'm Sir Roger's executive assistant!"

Hathaway rolled his eyes. Of all the people to make one's executive assistant! "You're 'Randal,' then. Sir Roger mentioned you. So your first name's Randal? I never knew that."

"You were going through Sir Roger's desk!" Once Finch got on to a subject, it was difficult to get him off it.

"No, no, Finch, it's not what it looks like."

"Oh yeah?"

"No, not at all. You got it all wrong, Finch. You see, I was just passing by and thought I'd pop in on Sir Roger."

"Pop in? You thought you'd just pop in on Sir Roger?"

"Yes, that's it. You have a real way of cutting to the heart of the matter. Yes, I just thought I'd pop in."

"And that's when you decided to ransack his desk!"

"No, no, you're jumping ahead. You see, I had just popped in, and, well, you can probably guess the upshot: Sir Roger was nowhere to be found; my popping had no effect. So, anyway, I was about to leave when I saw some papers on the floor, and, well, picked them up." Hathaway concluded his narrative with a that's-my-story-and-I'm-sticking-to-it nod of the head.

"You picked up Sir Roger's papers?"

"Yes, that's it. You got it exactly."

Hathaway could tell Finch was working this over in his crude mind. A few moments passed as he stared at Hathaway with giant bug eyes, a trait of his when pondering a supposition. Hathaway wondered if Sir Roger, another great starer, had picked it up from him.

"Sir Roger's asleep," Finch spoke at last.

"That's probably why he's not here," Hathaway agreed.

The two men continued in silence.

"So you're Sir Roger's assistant?" Hathaway asked.

"Yeah? So?"

"Nothing. Nothing. I mean, that's great."

Actually, it was quite a step up in the world for Finch, whose destiny as a young man seemed to lie along a more blue-collar path. Hathaway wouldn't have known it by looking at him, but Finch had gone to great lengths for his work. Even though his father had technically gotten him the job, it was Randal who had kept it. Since moving to Maine, he had started dressing better, talking better and, whenever possible, thinking better.

There was very little left to say here. Finch, having had his fill of chatting, whirled around to leave. Hathaway said he'd be calling it an evening too, and the pair of them made their way over to the door. The Azure Star article was lying on the threshold.

Finch had just stooped to reach for it, when Hathaway lunged in ahead of him.

Normally when two men collide, one weighing twice as much as the other, the lighter man reflects off the heavier man like a racquetball. But we must never forget that timing is everything, and approximately one second after Hathaway had hurled against him, Finch hit the floor.

"What the—"

Hathaway leaned over to help him up, giving Finch an excellent opportunity to grab him around the collar. "Don't ever shove me," he growled. "You understand?"

"Right," Hathaway gasped in agreement.

Finch let go, and Hathaway fell straight backward. The executive secretary marched out of the room, pausing on his way to lock a cabinet by the door.

Once the door had shut again, Hathaway picked up the article and trousered it. Before he could call to Ditters that the coast was clear, the latter had popped out from the desk, smacking his head against the wood again. "Ouch! Wow, that was close. Did he lock something?"

Hathaway pointed.

"That's just perfect," said Ditters, shaking his head while also rubbing it. "If the Colt wasn't in the desk, then it's probably in there." He ceased his shaking-rubbing trick. "That's it; if we can't get the gun, then I'm in deep tomorrow. Come on."

"Where are we going?"

"Back to Plan C."

* * *

Ditters and Hathaway had reached their destination: the back lawn. There was a trace of fog and a definite chill in the air.

"Ditters, what are we looking at?" They were positioned at the back of the house. Ditters had directed the other's attention to a third-story balcony.

"That's Adrienne's room."

"Charming."

"Adrienne and I must elope now, right?"

"I don't know that you *must.*"

"I *must*, Hath. If we had the gun, I might have had a chance lying low. But now Adwick has evidence. All it takes is Sir Roger blabbing to him, and I'm sunk."

"I see your point."

"And this is the only way to bypass Otto. Do you see that drainpipe?"

Hathaway stepped back. "Oh no," he responded, moving off.

Ditters grabbed his shirt. "Hath, it'll be a cinch," he said, pulled along the turf by the strength of the other's desire to vacate the premises.

"Super! Then go to it. You don't need me."

"But I do. Adrienne and I have been practicing when no one is around. My arms aren't long enough to help her over to the drainpipe."

Hathaway shook his head. It was always about arms with his friend Ditters.

"We both need to be up there, Hath. Adrienne says she thinks she can jump to it alone, but I think she's crazy. If you're there, then everything will be jake."

Hathaway had no energy left to argue. "This really sucks."

"It'll be swell. Just like in an old movie. I'll climb up to her balcony and wake her with a kiss on the forehead. It'll be pretty romantic." He paused. "Actually, why don't you go first? You're a better climber than I am. Do you think you should wake her so she can start getting ready?"

Hathaway didn't. "I have no desire to creep up on Adrienne in her sleep and have her respond to the sudden sight of me leaning over her bed by socking me in the eye. Add the forehead kiss to it, and you might as well forget it. I think, in this case, it would be best if betrothed woke betrothed."

"Okay, wait on the balcony for me, then. Watch the pipe. I think it's loose."

Hathaway stood at the foot of the drainpipe, rubbing his hands together.

People in old movies make drainpipe climbing look easy, but Hathaway figured it must be done with mirrors. As he began to shinny up the monstrosity, it creaked and shuddered with his weight. Forty feet above ground, he knew he had made a mistake. He had almost reached the balcony when the pipe gave out on him. By then it was too late—he grabbed on to it with all his might just as it yanked out from the wall, sending him plunging backward.

He had fallen back a good ten yards when the lower bolts buckled under the strain. A shudder ran up through the metal, and after a moment of attempting to shake him, the drainpipe resigned itself to the fact that he was there to stay and with a groan swung around, bringing him with a startling force back toward the building. Finally, he crashed into the wall, and everything went black.

When consciousness dawned again he dusted himself off and surveyed the scene. Apparently, the drainpipe had slung him onto a balcony at the other corner of the mansion. He looked down at Ditters, looking up at him from the back lawn. Ditters shrugged and shook his head. It was definitely better in old movies.

Hathaway sniffed rudely. With no other safe passage back to the lawn, he crept quietly into the bedroom behind Door #2. These entrances have to be done discreetly, however. Creeping through the darkened room, he observed two indistinct figures curled up under the covers, just a stone's throw away—not that he was going to throw a stone at them. To his great relief, the figures continued to rest soundly, unconcerned with the issue of noisy balconies or scraping drainpipes.

There's a funny thing about creeping through darkened rooms: unless you're a cat burglar, there's this amazing and inexplicable tendency to search out the object in the room calculated to make the most racket and, once found, to give it a swift kick. The object Hathaway met with sounded like the complete complement of a nine-piece marching band.

The figures shot bolt upright in bed. Before Hathaway could make a break for it, the light flipped on, and a high-pitched shriek filled the room. The shriek belonged to Lady Margaret Banbury. Sitting next to her was the now awoken figure of Sir Roger Banbury. The scream sent Hathaway leaping back, both apologetic and startled, thus freeing his ankle from the bear trap, which turned out to be the remnants of a floor lamp.

Sir Roger spoke for the both of them. "Is that Mr. Hathaway? Dear, it's Mr. Hathaway. I believe you two met at dinner."

There's very little to be said in situations like these, so after pausing to wave briefly, Hathaway removed himself. Rushing down the hall, he could hear movement and concern emanating from behind the closed doors. These doors soon burst open, and interested parties began to emerge into the hall. Just as Hathaway took the corner, Otto Pincher bounded onto the scene at the other end of the corridor.

Back at his room, Hathaway had only enough time to throw on a robe over his clothes when the pounding on the door started. He moved to answer it, figuring it was only a matter of moments before Otto got it into his head to kick it down.

The manor bodyguard was not a big proponent of discreet entrances. He stormed into the room. "Lady Banbury told me you broke into her bedroom."

Met with this, it was hard for Hathaway to keep up the old suavity, but he did his best. "What," he yawned. "Did I? My word, I must have wandered into the wrong room."

"You're claiming you went to the wrong room?"

"Yes." Stepping over to his luggage, he removed a bottle of scotch. "I was tired."

"So you're claiming you went to the wrong room, then?"

"That's what I'm claiming."

"Finch informs me you were in Sir Roger's office earlier. What do you have to say now?"

"Another wrong room." Hathaway poured his drink.

Otto was intrigued. "Is that some kind of scotch you have there?"

"Single malt. Macallan."

"You are kidding me. I have not had good single malt scotch in years. They do not sell it here in the backwoods of Maine."

"I thought Germans liked schnapps."

"Not all Germans like schnapps," Otto retorted.

Hathaway looked down at the bottle. "Would you like a shot?"

"I really should not."

Hathaway poured.

"I really should talk to Lady Banbury. Of course, I see now that you merely went into the wrong room," said Otto, taking the glass. "Yes, I would say this case is closed." He swallowed his first shot in one motion. Hathaway had hardly refreshed his second when Otto swallowed that too.

For the next five minutes, the mood lightened. Rather than the cold relationship of the past, Pincher and Hathaway were on "Otto" and "Johnny" terms now. They began to talk shop. Hathaway, feeling Otto would appreciate a good yarn, told the bodyguard about his experience with Nibu and Bu. Otto listened with a dreamlike expression.

"I envy you, Johnny. I never have trips like that."

"They're less fun than they appear on the surface."

"Not to me. I cannot think of the last time I had a good brawl. I tell you, Johnny, there is nothing I like better than pounding the stuffing out of a couple of fellows."

"I prefer cards myself, but interests differ."

"Single malt scotch and brawling: they're my reasons for living."

"Right. Well, drink up."

Otto drank up. "Why did you bring a bodyguard with you? Because of the thugs?"

"Partly. I hired one when I got this death threat. But that's a long story. Another drink?"

Otto had paused reflectively. "No—no, I must get back to my post now. If Sir Banbury knew I spent all this time drinking, I would be in for it."

From what Hathaway had gathered, Sir Roger might have preferred a drunken Otto to a vigilant one. "Speaking of your post, when do you sleep?"

"Not often. I have trained myself to sleep only three hours a day."

"Wow. People like you balance out the world for people like me. I'm not whole unless I get nine or ten." He corked the bottle. "Here, you can keep the rest."

"I couldn't."

"I insist. You might need a glass … or you could just swig it from the bottle."

"This is good stuff," Otto said, wiping his mouth. Nodding to his host, he left.

Several minutes later, Hathaway heard a tapping at the door more consistent with a Dittersdorf than a Pincher. Ditters stepped in. "Hey, sorry about the drainpipe scheme. But guess what? Otto's gone."

"I know. He's been in here grilling me. I bought him off with hooch. Where's Adrienne?"

"Still in her room."

Hathaway slapped his forehead. She had ten minutes to escape! "What's she still doing in her room?"

"Packing suitcases."

"Suitcases?"

"You can't elope without a suitcase, can you?"

"I've never really tried."

"Well, take my word for it. Adrienne packs about nine bags to go on a picnic. Come on; you can distract Otto if he comes back."

They arrived at Adrienne's door—still Otto-free—and Ditters proceeded inside. After a minute or two, muffled whispers could be heard approaching the door, and soon the happy couple emerged, Ditters carrying three suitcases and Adrienne looking as sullen as ever.

They had moved all of four steps when Adrienne asked, "Walter, where is the brown one?"

"Huh?"

"Really, Walter, I told you to get it. It was on the bed."

"Sorry, honey. I'll go get it."

"I'll get it," Hathaway interjected. "Take what you've got to the jeep, and I'll bring the bag out to you."

Ditters and Adrienne disappeared around the corner, and Hathaway nipped inside the room. He snatched the bag off the bed, turned and found Adrienne standing at the open door. She startled the bejeebers out of him.

"I wanted to make sure you got the right one," she said.

"I hardly think I could have missed it."

"I don't know; it didn't seem like that much of a stretch to me."

"Yes, well, as fun as this is, I think we'd better run before Otto returns."

"Let me make sure I have everything, if you don't mind? I think I forgot to pack a scarf."

What she would need with a scarf in the middle of summer was beyond Hathaway's comprehension, but she seemed pretty sure she had to have one. For a brief moment, while he stood there like some sort of lackey, he thought of poor Ditters marrying a gal like this Adrienne. His mind reeled.

"Why did you just quiver like that?" she asked, holding another valise.

"Oh nothing, a shiver ran down my spine. That's all."

"What spine?"

After a few more pleasantries, they trotted off. Along the way, an icy silence prevailed. Hathaway decided to chitchat.

"You're getting quite a guy in Ditters, you know."

"I know."

"Right, well, he's quite a guy. This way's faster," he said, pointing down the hall.

"No, it's not."

"You sure?"

"It's my house, jerk."

"If you say so" was Hathaway's response.

Adrienne turned a corner up ahead of him and, having done so, suddenly came trotting back.

"Say, Johnny, there you are. This is damn good scotch!"

The comment was not Adrienne's, who wasn't likely to bring up the subject of booze out of the clear blue sky. Otto Pincher had appeared from around the corner, holding the Macallan.

"I'm glad you like it," said Hathaway. He heard Adrienne enter a room behind him.

"Say, Johnny, was there a girl here?"

"Girl? No, no girl."

"A girl with luggage?"

"No."

"I really thought I saw a girl. Say, Johnny, this is good scotch." Waving happily, Otto maneuvered down the hall. Hathaway waited for the inebriated bodyguard to plod unsteadily around the corner before he left to find Adrienne. Stepping within the nearby room, he discovered her frozen in her path a foot from a snoring Chief Adwick.

Hathaway's eyes widened. Reluctant to trespass, he motioned to leave, but Adrienne, an obstinate eloper, had other ideas.

The exchange, performed completely with body language, ran as follows:

RELUCTANT TRESPASSER
(craning his neck toward hall)

OBSTINATE ELOPER
(shaking her head)

RELUCTANT TRESPASSER
(nodding to the bed, censuring frown)

OBSTINATE ELOPER
(returning frown with obscene gesture)

RELUCTANT TRESPASSER
(speechless)

OBSTINATE ELOPER
(craning her neck)

RELUCTANT TRESPASSER
(frowning, puzzled)

OBSTINATE ELOPER
(pointing to the balcony)

RELUCTANT TRESPASSER
(shaking head decisively)

OBSTINATE ELOPER
(nodding, threatening to fling valise at R. TRESPASSER)

RELUCTANT TRESPASSER
(reluctantly sneaking past SLEEPING OFFICER)

"Now that wasn't so hard, was it?" she asked, as Hathaway tiptoed out onto the balcony.

"Now what?"

"You climb down and catch me," she said, pitching her luggage over the side.

Hathaway demurred. "Listen, I've had my fill of this climbing stuff. I've tried it, and as a cat burglar I'm a washout."

"It's only one story, wimp."

Hathaway sighed.

Climbing over the side of the rail, with Adrienne whispering at him to hurry up, he bounded over the edge. Once back on firm earth, he called up to her that he was ready.

Hathaway didn't like to criticize, but for someone who had supposedly practiced, he thought Adrienne could have worked on her technique.

Untangling herself from the railing, she sprang down and dropped into his arms. He was just staggering back from this and preparing to set her down, when Sir Roger's office doors burst open, and there was the tycoon, wild-eyed and more imposing than usual, holding the *bhuj* instrument from his museum.

13 — Hard Luck for a Fiancé

"Ha!"

"Father!" gasped Adrienne. "Father, I can explain." Squirming around, she instructed Hathaway to put her down.

Once vertical again, Adrienne began preparing their defense. Before she could voice any of it, the tycoon bounded out into the night, waving the ax. Hardly the warmth Hathaway had come to expect from the man.

"Ha! Got you, Dipperdorp! Thought you could elope with my daughter, did you! I say there, you're not Dipperdorp."

"No," said Hathaway, backing off from the hatchet.

"But, I only assumed. I mean, who'd have thought?"

"I know this must look pretty odd," Hathaway began, paving the way for what would be a long explanation.

"Eh?" asked the tycoon, distracted. "Oh no. No, no, no. I thought you were Dipperdorp."

"Dittersdorf," Hathaway corrected. "You thought I was Ditters?"

"Yes. I mean, I could only assume. Otto said Adrienne was not in her room. You see, after you came into our room and woke me, Otto came in. I couldn't get back to sleep after that. That's what happens when you scamps wake me; I can't get back to sleep. The only thing that helps," he explained, leaning on the *bhuj*, "is a cup of cocoa, preferably with marshmallows, although on this I'm flexible. So, I went to get my cocoa—with marshmallows, if we had them—and in the kitchen I ran across Otto again. He seemed considerably more cheerful than usual. We started chatting, and he mentioned he saw Dittersdorf near Adrienne's room earlier; then he said he thought he saw Adrienne walking around with a suitcase. I figured the man had been hallucinating, but then he told me he checked on her, and she was not in her room. Well, I mean to say, I put two and two together. They must be eloping. So I grabbed the *bhuj*, and here I am. I was all prepared to chop this Dipperdorp into little pieces, but now I see I would have wronged the poor fellow."

"Really?"

"Yes, Mr. Hathaway. Because, quite obviously, it wasn't him at all."

"It wasn't?"

"No, it was only you," said the duffer. "Now then, what are you two young people doing out here so late? I'm pretty tired, so make it a quick explanation."

Adrienne cleared her throat. She had been standing offstage, her mind swirling through various scenarios. Latching on to one of them now, she stepped forward and announced, "Father, John and I were trying to elope."

Hathaway spun around. He gurgled. Sir Roger, not quite gurgling himself, appeared thoroughly stunned. "What are you talking about, Adrienne?"

"I'm afraid I haven't been very honest with you, Father. John and I actually met last year. You remember my trip to Washington?"

"I remember you going," replied Sir Roger cautiously.

"That's where we met. We fell in love."

Hathaway tried to speak, but like one of those nightmares where you try to run but find yourself stuck in place, the words did not come.

"A little while back we had a fight. I was actually only seeing Walter to make John jealous. But now, we've sorted everything out."

"I'm astounded," said Sir Roger. "And now you're eloping?"

"It's a whirlwind romance. We didn't think you'd approve."

"Approve? Next to that Dittersdorf menace, I'd approve your marriage to anyone." Sir Roger shook his head. Part of him still couldn't believe it, but it was late, and he liked the sound of all this.

"Really, Mr. Hathaway, you should have been up-front, instead of trying to elope."

"But—"

"I never would have guessed it. To look at you two yesterday, you'd think you hated each other."

"I—"

Sir Roger rolled over him: "Don't elope, you two. I certainly approve. We'll talk about this more in the morning, when I have my senses about me better. I'm going inside. All this business and I almost forgot about my cocoa; it must be ice-cold by now."

Hathaway gave it one more try. "But—"

It went unanswered.

As quickly as he had appeared, the tycoon had disappeared back into the mansion.

"Well!" observed Adrienne, which hardly seemed to cover it.

"What was all that about whirlwind romances?" asked Hathaway. "We're not having a whirlwind romance."

Adrienne was looking into the distance beyond him.

"We have to set him straight," he said.

"We'll do nothing of the sort."

The statement astounded him. "We won't?"

"No."

"Don't take this the wrong way, but I don't want to marry you."

"I don't want to marry you either."

"Don't take it personally. I just like my women softer. What did you say?"

"I don't want to marry you either."

He paused for a sigh of relief. Making sure he had heard right, he asked, "You don't?"

"No."

"On this we are in agreement, then?"

"Yes, but you're still not going to tell Father."

"Aha. You see, there you lose me."

"Don't you see? If Father finds out that his suspicions were right and Walter and I were eloping, he'll knife him while he sleeps."

"I don't know about that. Ditters really doesn't have a violent bone in his body."

"No, Walter wouldn't knife Father. Don't you see? Father would knife Walter."

"Ah. The old Macbeth routine," said Hathaway.

"Old *what* routine?"

"Macbeth. Your father would be like Macbeth. You know, going around knifing people in their sleep and all that. I mean, you can't gut the guests of your mansion and not expect clever observers to draw parallels."

Adrienne stared at him.

"Granted," he continued, "Macbeth didn't have any pickle-fanatic sons-in-law that Shakespeare makes mention of, although one can never be sure what the man's editor cut out."

Adrienne was wearing that burning glare she wore so well. "You're giving me a headache! The point is I don't want Father skulking in dark corners with a view to sticking a dagger blade between Walter's ribs."

"A very understandable objection. Nor do I."

"Good. Then, you agree we'll function behind this facade until tomorrow night, when Walter and I can elope properly."

It seemed to Hathaway that Adrienne was overlooking the obvious. "Why wait?" he asked. "I mean, no time like the present. Why not elope now?"

"That's why," she said. She pointed past him to the spot she had been surveying earlier. "All that clatter roused Otto."

She was right. There, flecking the horizon at the garage, was the good security officer. He was standing by Ditters, who flecked the horizon considerably less.

There was obviously some sort of debate being held. Otto was roaming back and forth, and Ditters, no doubt trying to explain what he was doing out at three thirty in the morning with luggage, was, for his part, scratching his head and, as far as Hathaway could tell, kicking at the dust.

"See?" said Adrienne. "By the time Otto clears out, if he does at all, it'll almost be morning. It would be no good eloping then. Everyone will be awake."

Hathaway absorbed this. "Yes, I suppose you have something there."

"Of course I have something. All you have to do is play along. For some reason, Father seems to like you. Why, I'll never know. This will distract him from his dislike of Walter." She turned and viewed the horizon again. "I can't wait around all night. When you see Walter tomorrow, explain everything, will you?" On that note, she strode off.

After taking another glance at the Rangeley Inquisition, Hathaway followed her inside.

* * *

The next day hardly seemed a new thing to Hathaway, the two of them having been thoroughly acquainted back in the early hours. When he finally did awake to it around noon, it would be misleading to say that he greeted it with a whole lot of joy.

Wandering down to lunch, he plunked down in his chair and stared blankly at the residents. Eventually, the smell of food worked to revive him, and once he had gotten into the coffee and was polishing off the last bit of dessert, he began to feel the old spirit coming back.

He had been to jollier meals, however. Between mouthfuls, he couldn't help noticing that Ditters, Finch, Adrienne and Warren were hardly eating. For the better part of the meal, they sat there, still and cheerless. As diners, you'd have thought they had been served a plate of floor wax and, through some fluky lack of culinary variety, had already had floor wax for breakfast.

The only other person at the table who welcomed the entrées as vigorously as Hathaway was Roger Banbury, who was snarfing down his meal with the distinct vigor of a man recently freed of the threat of a Dittersdorf joining the family.

The only time he paused from feeding was to comment on the mysterious fact that a drainpipe had been found strewn across his wife's rose garden this morning and how, in their opinion, this was not at all a pleasing addition to the arrangement.

Once Hathaway had finished off the last of the courses and compliments had been passed along to the chef, he went for a stroll on the grounds. He was stretching his legs by the lake, trilby hat atop his head, when Ditters ambled over to share his views on the surroundings.

"Hey, Hath. Rotten day, isn't it?"

"Hey, Ditters. I don't know; seems no more rotten than the rest."

"You would say that," responded his chum.

In the pause that followed, it occurred to Hathaway that the depressive Dittersdorf was trying to work up to something that was weighing heavily on his mind. Hathaway had a pretty good notion what that lofty heaviness was.

"Hath—"

"Ditters, say no more. I know what this is about."

"You do?"

"It's about Adrienne. You heard she and I are engaged, and it has ticked you off. Well, let me soothe your savage thoughts. The engagement is a sham. It was just a big misunderstanding. So you can tread the ground with a jaunty step once again. Adrienne and I are not engaged."

"I know that already. Adrienne told me."

"Oh. I just wanted you to be sure."

"I am."

"Good, then all's right with the world." They had another spell of brooding silence. It occurred to Hathaway that Ditters appeared far from right with the world.

"Hath—"

"Yes, old buddy."

"Adrienne's a wonderful girl."

"Adrienne? Yes, right."

"I'm uneasy."

"Really? Why?"

"It's Adrienne. I think she's growing tired of me."

"Come on."

"No. And now that you and she are together—just pretending, I know—I can't help thinking that, I don't know, maybe she wouldn't rather be with someone like you. I know all the guys we meet want her."

"Do they?"

"Sure. You should have seen the way Finch glared at me when Adrienne announced we were getting married."

"You can't go by that. Finch glares at everyone. He spent semesters glaring at us through school."

"I'm just uneasy."

Hathaway took a deep breath. "Let me put your mind at ease, then. For one thing, she dislikes me intensely. No, she does. She refers to me as a jerk and a wimp, and, beyond that, seems to suspect I have come to the mansion in order to dynamite the foundation."

"Still, I can't believe you feel the same toward her."

Hathaway hesitated.

"I mean, surely you find her irresistible?" asked Ditters.

"Suffice it to say I could resist."

"Really?"

"Four strong men couldn't make me succumb to her charms."

"That's good. You don't find her wonderful?"

"Wonderful? Well, you know, one man's wonderful is another man's hardened thug of the underworld. Believe me, I do not under any circumstances want your Adrienne."

"Then I feel better, thanks. You don't have to speak about the prospect like she's the plague, you know."

"Plague? No, not the plague. Touch of gangrene, perhaps, but definitely not the plague."

This seemed to clear things up, and for the first time that afternoon not an ounce of tension could be detected between them.

"You keep looking at her," said Ditters.

Hathaway pulled out of his meditations. For a fleeting moment, he thought they had returned to the Adrienne motif.

Ditters clarified. "Your friend." He indicated the distant figure of Lesley strolling by the lake next to Warren. "I noticed you watching her at lunch."

Hathaway continued to stare. A few minutes before, he had been dwelling on being stuck at the manor, the fact that he had no real source of income, and on all the other little annoying thoughts rolling around his head. And then all at once there was the image of Lesley, all sweet and lovely, and the mind wandered from these petty nuisances, and he was concentrating on her aspect, the way she moved, all of her.

"Hath, are you listening to me?"

"What?"

"Come back to earth, man. Are you two going to get together?"

Hathaway shrugged. "If I can manage to pry her away from Warren."

"I wouldn't worry about Warren. When we were on the porch last night, all she could talk about was you. She's crazy about you."

"Really? How crazy?"

He never got an answer. Chief Adwick had clomped over to join the conversation.

Sneaking up on them, he failed to connect the cheerful, rounded face behind Hathaway with the infamous Travers Gun Shop Bandit. "Excuse me, sir."

Hathaway turned. "Chief, didn't see you there. This is a pleasant surprise."

Ditters emitted no jolly greeting of his own. Instead, he remained anchored to the spot. Petrified.

"I've been meaning to talk to you, Mr. Hathaway. Now that we're stuck here together, I was wondering if I could ask you a few more questions. Specifically, I'm concerned about those suspects we have in custody."

"Suspects? Oh right, the guys from the train. I wouldn't be too concerned about them. I'm sure they're awaiting trial comfortably. Criminals condition themselves for these things."

"It's not their comfort, Mr. Hathaway. I want to know why they attacked you."

"Oh right. Damn confusing, I'd say. Like to know what it was all about myself. But, you know, sometimes these things are a mystery wrapped in an enigma inside a something or other—and, well, are simply not for us to know. It was probably just a whim on their part."

"It was no whim," maintained the officer, stepping within a foot of Ditters. "These guys are professionals. The one guy, Nibu Nibudar, is wanted over in England, not to mention Russia, *Bangladersh*, and in a whole slew of other countries. These guys had to be after something."

"Nothing I know of."

"Whatever they were after leads here."

Hathaway looked around at the spot. "Do you mean Rangeley Manor?"

"This is where all the indicators point. There is something crooked around here. Mr. and Mrs. Banbury, of course, are beyond reproach, but I'm not discounting anyone else. Someone in the area is circulating stolen goods, and I'm going to find out who."

"Right. Good luck with that."

There was a short pause, and then the chief let him have it with both barrels. "You wouldn't happen to know anything about a thing called the Azure Star, would you?"

Up until now, Ditters had been the only one among them stiff as a board. After this comment, Hathaway could feel his own nerves tightening. "Azure Star?"

"We got a tip about it. I looked into it, and apparently it's a stolen art treasure. I think someone brought it here, and these guys were after it. Now that I'm a guest, I'm going to keep an eye out for it, just in case one of the other guests smuggled it in."

"Why the—! I mean, why would anyone bring it here?"

"Oh, lots of reasons. If you couldn't unload it anywhere else, for instance."

"You mean 'you' in general, I assume?"

"What's that? Oh sure. Someone may be planning to offer this thing to Sir Roger, knowing he's a collector, maybe even coerce him into buying it. I see all sorts of things in my business."

Hathaway mused a moment on the chief's business.

"I don't suppose you think the guy with the Azure Star is some innocent bystander wrapped up in all the intrigue—the 'mild-mannered man framed for a crime he didn't commit' sort of stuff? No," he replied, noticing the unmoved audience, "didn't think so. Just thought I'd throw that out to you, Chief."

The chief nodded and stomped off, allowing Ditters to find movement again. "Did you hear him?"

"Of course I heard him. He was standing right here."

"He was toying with me. He knew who I was the whole time."

"I doubt it."

"You heard what he said about stolen goods?"

"He wasn't talking about you. He was talking about me."

"You? What did you steal?"

"Nothing. I was crazy enough to listen to my uncle—that's all. You see, he blackmailed me into delivering this parcel, which turned out to contain a stolen artifact. Some guys on the train wanted to take it home as a souvenir."

"What did the chief call it? The Azure Star?"

"Yes, and if it weren't for Mahrute, I'd be one of the landmarks along the railroad right now. Warren has the parcel now. I better tell him to give it back to Sir Roger before the chief snoops onto it."

Hathaway trailed off. He was thinking of PRICELESS ART TREASURE STOLEN FROM GOVERNMENT PALACE.

Why would Sir Roger want a hot trinket belonging to someone named Boris Pefferu? Ditters broke in on his reflections.

"Enough about stolen art treasures, Hath. The guy has me dead to rights. While he's sniffing around for your Azure Star, he might bump into the Colt."

Hathaway acknowledged this.

For another couple minutes, the two outlaws stood pensively by the lake, brooding in silence. Suddenly, a brilliant notion struck Hathaway, and such was his enthusiasm that he slapped Ditters on the back and almost sent him sailing headfirst into the water.

"Ditters, I got it! You need to hide the Colt somewhere the chief couldn't find it with a pack of bloodhounds. Well, the answer's right in front of us. No, not in the lake; try to follow along. You need to give it to Sir Roger."

"Give him my pistol?"

"Of course. A nifty old pistol is probably just the thing the tycoon needs for his collection. Fill that empty feeling he's always had but could never quite express. The Colt will be plunged deep into the man's collection and lost to all but that small sect of the world that Sir Roger manages to ambush and drag around his museum. And even if the chief happens to see it there, he'll notice nothing strange about an antique pistol. He already said that Sir Roger is beyond reproach. What safer place is there for stolen goods than a tycoon's collection?"

"Wouldn't it be easier to throw it in the lake?"

"If we had it, perhaps. But now that we have to get it from Sir Roger anyway, it's better just to tell him to keep the thing."

"Do you think it will work?"

"I do. And if you still feel bad about stiffing the shop owner, you could slide an envelope with the appropriate payment under his door."

Ditters was coming around. He had one amendment, though: "Why don't you give the Colt to Banbury? I think it would be better coming from you. He hates me."

Hathaway rolled this over in his mind. "You may be right. You know, I better mention this to Otto, too, so he doesn't contradict us. I'll find him and tell him the gun he took off you was supposed to be a gift for Banbury."

* * *

Ditters was cheerfully pitching rocks into the lake when Hathaway left and went inside. He was looking for Otto Pincher, the person in charge of confiscated pistols. After about five steps, he almost collided with Finch instead.

The assistant stroked his beard.

"I heard about your little escapade last night," he said. He paused meaningfully, as if working up to something that sickened him to say. "I wanted to, er, congratulate you on your engagement to Adrienne Banbury," he remarked gruffly, grabbing Hathaway's hand and giving it the mandatory shake.

This was hardly what Hathaway expected. Too civil.

"Um, thanks." Hathaway was dumbstruck. In the years they had known each other, he had come to expect an exchange of harsh words, idle threats, a bit more violent temperament and such from the likes of Finch. This approach definitely had a very un-Finch quality to it. It was almost as if Finch's understudy had stepped on in place of the true article.

"She's a wonderful girl, Hathaway," he added, echoing Ditters' words. Although the thought of her marrying Hathaway gnawed at Finch, his respect for her prevented him from acting on his best violent tendencies. "I have a lot of esteem for Miss Banbury," he said.

"As well you should, Finch."

"You better treat her right."

"You can be sure. She'll feel like a queen."

Finch doubted that. "I suppose you're better than that Dittersdorf weasel anyway."

"Thanks. Nice chatting with you …"

Finch gripped Hathaway's arm, holding him in place. "What about the Landers girl, the one you came here with?"

"Landers? Oh yeah. What about her?"

"You were seeing her, weren't you?"

"What? Well, yes."

"But that's all over now?" The old menacing Finch was beginning to resurface.

"Of course. Everything's off with me and Lesley. It's just Adrienne now."

Finch's face darkened. "Lesley? Who's Lesley?"

"What? Er, um." Hathaway's voice began to crack. "What did I say? Lesley?" He laughed nervously. "That's funny. Of course, I meant to say Grace … Brittany! I meant Brittany! Yes, Brittany Landers, that's it." Finch was moving toward him, and like any sensible man Hathaway was backing off.

Finch continued to push forward. "Who do you think you are, some kind of Don Juan? Lesley, Brittany, Grace … how many girls do you got stashed away? Wait!" His face lit up, as if some lofty thought had occurred to him. "It was you!" he said.

"What was me?"

"It was you on the train! Grace! You're the one who sent that girl Grace Bosworth the love letter. You're Snuggle Bear! Is that why she didn't show? You know that we can't even get in contact with her? What did you do to her? Did you toss her aside too?"

"No! I mean, I didn't send the note! I don't know Grace Bosworth."

"Oh yeah? That's not what a porter on the train said."

"What porter? What did a porter say?"

"When I was trying to find Grace, I bribed a porter, and he said you had dinner with her."

Hathaway frowned at the lack of chivalry guiding porters these days.

"Another porter said he saw you two return to your room."

"He said that? I mean, did you bribe him too?"

"No, I shook him by the collar until he told me. Why?"

"Just curious."

"Well, stop it! So what do you have to say now, weasel?"

"Um," said Hathaway, pressing himself up against the wall. "I hardly think you can go by the word of a blue-faced porter, Finch. I'm sure he was simply bargaining for oxygen. Perhaps it occurs to you now why prosecuting attorneys are prevented from strangling defense witnesses. The testimony would be slanted."

Finch, impatient with this discussion of the criminal justice system, said "Ha!"

"What was that, Finch?"

"I said 'Ha!' I should bash your brains in."

"I hardly think you should," Hathaway argued. "I have no doubt that you *could* bash my brains in, and certainly believe you *would* bash them in, but I'm not sure *should* enters into it. There seems no moral justification for the act."

"I'm going to bash your brains in and throw you in the lake."

Hathaway pondered this. "I'm not sure you want to do that, Finch. I can see you've given it some thought, and I don't want to discourage you, but the lake's too shallow. The authorities would spot me in a minute. Besides, bashing a fellow's brain takes a lot out of you. You may find that once you have bashed my brain and are posed with the option of dragging my corpse out to the lake that you'd just as soon put your feet up and call it a day. Now, as far as these crazy allegations—" Before Hathaway had a chance to recap the facts in such a way that all would be understood, Finch lunged at him.

Hathaway stumbled back to avoid the onslaught. Finch came scrambling after him, and the chase began.

The hunted skidded around the corner and hung a right through an open door.

He found Lady Banbury within, sipping tea. He stood panting at the door. Finch came barreling into the room behind him, virtually tearing this door off its hinges.

"Aha! Got you, you—" He saw Lady Banbury, and the sight of her made him choke on the words.

Hathaway poured himself some tea and took a seat. Finch continued to stare, his face cherry red. He attempted to pour himself some Earl Grey, but the sight of Hathaway sitting cheerfully by the side of his employer was too much for him. After rattling the silver service and teacups, giving one the momentary impression that an earthquake was coming through, he mumbled something under his breath, banged the teapot down, and marched out of the room.

Hathaway smiled at the hostess. He was happy to see that, after last night, she did not appear to be holding a grudge. He continued to smile. He was still smiling, in fact, when she looked up again. This time, she started suddenly and dropped her teacup.

Hathaway retrieved it for her.

"Mr. Hathaway?" she asked hesitantly, taking the china. "I understand that Adrienne has taken a fancy to you. I was not aware that you two knew each other."

"Me neither. I mean, yes."

"Is Mr. Dittersdorf terribly upset?"

"Ditters? Oh well, you know."

"Adrienne seems … pleased."

On the word "pleased," Otto Pincher came in.

Hathaway excused himself. "Hey, old buddy," he said, taking the bodyguard aside. "I need that pistol back—the one you took off Ditters. I'm giving it to Sir Roger."

"The antique? It was yours, then? Sure, Johnny. I put it in Sir Roger's cabinet."

After a brief discussion about single malt, Hathaway went to Sir Roger's office.

* * *

As always, the tycoon received his guest warmly.

"Mr. Hathaway? What a pleasant surprise. I was about to fax the announcement of my daughter's engagement to the newspaper."

Hathaway stepped into the office. "No hurry. They probably have their hands full covering the storm damage."

"You're probably right," said Sir Roger. "I hate using the machine anyway. Rotten hunk of junk. That's what's wrong with the world today, you know?"

"Fax machines?"

"Fax machines and all the rest of it! Computers, mobile phones. Rotten, all of them. Machines, machines, machines."

"Didn't you make your money in electronics?"

"What if I did? I'm no better than the rest, Mr. Hathaway. That's why I used some of that money to build what you're standing on."

"The floor?"

"Not just the floor, all of Rangeley. Rangeley is a tribute to old-world values and technology. You don't find any of that new junk in Rangeley Manor!"

"Except for a fax machine."

Sir Roger conceded this. "We're not savages. I hate technology, though. Do you know why I got into electronics?"

"I suppose …"

"Don't try and guess, Mr. Hathaway."

"No?"

"You won't guess it."

"No. No, I suppose not."

"I began my career in electronics to meet a girl."

"Lady Banbury?"

"She wasn't Lady Banbury then. 'Maggie,' I called her."

"Why would you call her that?"

"That was her name. We were young. Poor. I mean, my father owned half of Manchester, but that's not the point. It was a simpler time, Mr. Hathaway. She worked for Larson Electronics in New York. She was a secretary. I joined the firm as a salesman, and we fell in love. Sometimes I miss those days. They made sense. I had a purpose. I mean, later I liked running my company too, but now—well, now, I'm just a blob."

"A blob, Sir Roger?"

"A blob," said Sir Roger. "A blob with a wife who finds rich strangers more interesting than her husband, and a daughter who foists lunatics off on him in the guise of fiancés. But that's all changed now," the tycoon beamed. "With you. I must admit, I'm confused by this romance with Adrienne, but nonetheless I'm all for it."

Hathaway said "right" and nodded. He felt bad fooling his kindly host. Overshadowing this, though, was the belief that Sir Roger was getting a good son-in-law in Ditters—even if he didn't know it yet.

Hathaway could see how he would prefer the option standing before him now—the tall, well-dressed option, with the excellent taste in hats—but in the final analysis he was not the man for Adrienne. Sure, when Sir Roger discovered that he had been tricked and had not gotten the son-in-law as advertised, he'd pout for a couple of weeks, but someday, Hathaway was convinced, the tycoon would learn to love the little guy.

On that pleasing mental note, he said, "Actually, Sir Roger, I popped in to give you a gift."

"Something more?"

"Actually, it's from Ditters. An antique. Otto put it in your cabinet last night."

"Oh yes?"

After fumbling around with a set of keys, Sir Roger opened the cabinet. He stared at its contents and then proceeded to empty it onto his desk. When he had finished, they found themselves peering down at a handful of papers and a half-eaten apple.

Hathaway gaped. "That's not everything, is it?"

Any other host would have required some sort of inquiry. Call for a search of the premises, contact the police, or at least ring for Jackson in order to ask if he had gotten above himself in the last few hours and given in to a spell of kleptomania. After all, antiques do not break out of locked cabinets on their own. Houdini maybe, but definitely not antiques.

But Sir Roger made no fuss, and Hathaway eventually left, shaking his head.

* * *

Outside Sir Roger's office, he came across Warren. He put the Colt on the back burner. "Warren, I need to talk to you."

Warren blinked. "Actually, I need to talk to you too," he said.

"I'll go first. You need to give Sir Roger the Azure Star back. Chief Adwick's snooping around. I don't have time to go into it now, but the thing's stolen. If the chief finds you with it, he might implicate us in its theft. So give it back; just say it looks authentic to you."

Warren shifted his feet. "Actually, I don't have it anymore."

"You already gave it back?"

"Not exactly. I lost it."

"You lost it? You lost the Azure Star?"

"You see, last night I hid it on my balcony."

"You hid it on your balcony? You hid the Azure Star on your balcony?"

"That's what I said, isn't it? You see, I thought someone might be after it, after what happened on the train and all, so I made a little slit in one of the chair cushions on my balcony and stuck it in there."

"Your balcony has chairs?"

"Yeah. Three of them."

"My balcony doesn't have any chairs."

"Anyway, I came back at lunch today, and the Azure Star was gone. It seems the maid had removed the cushions from all the balconies and had them cleaned. Why they're doing that now, with the guests here, I couldn't tell you. Seems sloppy and irresponsible, if you ask me."

"The maid took the Azure Star?"

"She took the cushions. She was explaining it to me, and apparently they have this machine that steam cleans—"

"Warren, I'm not interested. What happened to the Azure Star?"

"I don't know. The cushions I have now are not mine. I asked her about the ones I had originally, and she said she didn't keep track of whose cushions were whose. They just redistribute them after they're cleaned. No one seems to know who has my cushions. Hathaway, you look upset."

"I am upset! If Sir Roger doesn't get his Azure Star back, he's likely to go to Chief Adwick. If he goes to Chief Adwick, Adwick will ask him where he got the Azure Star in the first place. And if Sir Roger answers this honestly, you and I can take a trip to Leavenworth, you for losing a priceless objet d'art, and me for transporting stolen goods."

Warren wasn't listening. "A trip sounds nice, Hathaway, but I'm not interested in that right now. Right now I need to go make my stupid speech. Are you coming?"

Hathaway was coming. Pausing to bang his forehead against the doorframe, he followed Warren downstairs to Sir Roger's museum.

14 — Violence at an Art Discussion

Adrienne and Lesley had already assembled in the museum in anticipation of Harold Konig's art discussion. They were standing near the archway by a small table, helping themselves to tea and cakes. In light of the intrigue surrounding the Azure Star, Hathaway and Warren were distressed to notice that Chief Adwick had staked out an area by the pottery display.

The officer nodded to the new arrivals. "Afternoon, Mr. Hathaway, Mr. Konig. I was just looking through the collection. A lot of valuable stuff here."

"Is there?" asked Hathaway. He glanced at Warren, noting the other's blank expression. "Say, I wonder where Sir Roger is hiding himself."

There was a stretch of silence during which the tycoon in question made his entrance. He was wearing a sweatshirt and shorts with knee-high black socks. Otto trailed behind.

"Excuse my attire," Sir Roger announced to the room. "I was exercising in my gym. Lady Banbury has me on a strict diet and workout plan." He mopped his head with a large towel. "Let's get on with it, shall we? Mr. Konig, I believe you were going to explain to us how you can tell a forgery from the real thing."

Warren dropped his tea cake. "What?"

The audience turned their stares to the resident art expert.

Warren stepped in front of a display of oil canvases. "Er, right. Um, yes, well, the thing of the thing is, art forgeries, or forgeries of art, as they are sometimes called, come in many shapes and forms. Most of the time the forgeries look a lot like some bit of art, but what happens is someone has taken some real art and … um … forged it. We call that person a forger. Anyone who buys the art, which is to say the forger sells it to them, that person, the buyer, we call him the 'forgee.' "

The audience stood silent, in awe of Warren's theories. There were skeptics among them, as there always are at truly groundbreaking moments. Adrienne verbalized these views. "I don't see what that tells us," she said. "What about the paintings behind you, Mr. Konig? Father paid through the nose for them. Can you tell if they're genuine or not?"

Warren wiped his forehead. When he spoke, his voice faltered. "These paintings? The ones right behind me?"

"Yes," said Sir Roger, taking an interest. "I purchased these six in Barcelona last spring. I'm sure you recognize the characteristic form and bold use of color as belonging to Gris. I never trusted the dealer, though. Tell me, am I—how did you put it?—'the forgee' in this case?"

Warren put his nose up to each of the canvases. Feeling the audience would probably expect a show, he slipped one of the frames off the wall. Holding it up to his ear, he shook it, like a child attempting to guess his Christmas present. Furrowing his brow, he turned it over and knocked on the back, nodding approvingly. Flipping it to the painted side, he eyed it carefully. Then he sniffed it.

Hathaway grimaced at the display, hoping Warren wouldn't get it into his head to taste one. Finally, the expert turned it upside down and methodically touched all four corners and the center of the canvas.

"Yep, she's genuine all right."

Sir Roger leapt to his feet. "Bravo! And you can tell it's real from all that?"

"Oh sure."

"Splendid. Tell me, Mr. Konig, now that we have determined their authenticity, for how much would you appraise the collection?"

Warren blinked. "About a thousand?"

"Oh dear," replied the tycoon.

"Did I say a thousand?" said Warren. "I meant a million."

"Oh my. My, my, my. I only paid eight thousand for each piece. Would you say a million for all six?"

"What? Oh no. Million each. Easy."

The audience continued to stare at the spectacle, speechless. Adrienne frowned contemptuously. Otto folded his arms. Hathaway shook his head. Lesley sipped tea.

Sir Roger positively beamed. "This is extraordinary. Now, moving on to objets d'art," he said, "how do you make your qualification there? Take, for example, those daggers from South America."

Warren stepped over and picked up a blade.

"No, Mr. Konig," said Sir Roger. "That's a butter knife, I think."

Warren nodded and returned the utensil to the tea table. From the exhibit, he reached for a long blade with a wooden handle. He pondered this quietly.

Fortunately, the room was spared another creative dissertation, as a matter requiring everyone's attention presented itself.

"Hey!" said a voice. "The door's locked!" The pronouncement came from Adwick, who, during Warren's speech, had attempted to slip out unnoticed. He stood at a large oak door, which normally led to the staircase.

"Locked?" asked Warren, happy to have the floor opened to a new subject. He stepped over and yanked the handle, rattling the foundation. "It won't budge," he observed. Warren Kingsley might have had his weaknesses, but door-pulling was not one of them. If he said a door wouldn't budge, it wouldn't budge.

Nevertheless, Sir Roger gave the handle a tug for good measure. "I don't see how it can be locked," he said, as Adwick threw his weight against it.

The chief stepped back. "It definitely won't budge."

"It's probably Jackson fooling about," suggested Sir Roger.

"Does your butler typically lock guests in the basement?"

"Not so in the past," admitted the tycoon, "but sometimes he gets this look in his eye—" He returned to the door. "I say, Jackson, are you there?" he called into the oak. He repeated the sentiment. "If I didn't know better," he said, "I'd say he was ignoring us."

* * *

On the other side of the door, the freelance burglar Barnet admired his handiwork: a thin strip of metal jammed at just the right spot. That should keep them busy, he thought. He legged it upstairs to the parlor.

Straightening his tuxedo, which was beginning to show the wear and tear of his activities, he stepped within and found the man he was looking for. The butler was standing by the wet bar, conversing with Mahrute.

"Hey, Mr. Jackson?" said Barnet.

The butler wheeled around and arched an eyebrow. "Sir?"

"I thought you'd want to know some of the guests are locked in the basement. I can hear them banging."

Jackson excused himself. Mahrute followed with a meditative look on his face. The instant they had gone, Barnet clasped his hands together and dashed down to Jackson's room. No chance on being disturbed now, he told himself.

Without wasting a moment, he began to rifle the premises for Azure Star #2.

* * *

In the museum, the residents had begun to grow antsy. Warren pounded and said "Hey!" And then, approaching the thing from his own angle, Chief Adwick pounded and said "Hey!"

During this commotion, Lesley turned to Hathaway and said she would try to find something to pry open the door. It seemed a sensible bet to him. She scooted off, and Hathaway stepped over to Adrienne and Sir Roger at the tea service. Adrienne held out her empty cup for her "fiancé" to fill.

Hathaway took the hint. You gotta keep up appearances.

"Brittany and I are going to look for another way out," he said, pouring. It was as these words were leaving his lips that Adrienne let out a shriek, causing him to fling the teapot down the hall.

Hathaway stared. He hadn't known Adrienne Banbury very long, so he had no real point of reference for determining how much shrieking in the middle of tea shaped her normal routine. Whether it was just a whim, a spur-of-the-moment shriek or something she had cultivated over the years, perhaps going back to her childhood and a younger brother who regularly made off with the last Pop-Tart, he couldn't say. So it was with reserved judgment that he approached the subject. "Something wrong?"

The room had shifted to a startled silence. All eyes now turned to the girl with the powerful set of lungs.

Adrienne was goggling at the catwalks above them. "A burglar!" she exclaimed. She pointed up at a distant figure crouching beside one of the display cases.

Nibu Nibudar sprang back from the railing, gripping Azure Star #3 in his hand. Having secured the object from the display case, he had been waiting for the gathering below to leave. Ordinarily, he would not have been averse to socializing, but he had not expected anyone in the museum at this hour and, as a result, had slipped out of his conductor duds.

The chief called up to him. "You there. Come out where we can see you."

Nibu did not comply. His hand quivering, he reached within his pocket and produced the Colt. He had found the revolver last night while searching for keys in Sir Roger's office. He had procured the gun, figuring it might come in handy in an emergency.

Pulling back the hammer, he fired a shot down into the corridor.

The bullet reflected off a pillar. The chief, bounding back, shouted, "Hit the deck!"

Hearing this, Otto grabbed Banbury by the sweatshirt. "Hit the deck, Sir Roger!"

The tycoon, clearly nonplussed, wrestled himself free. "Are you mad? Hit the deck? Hit it with what?"

Otto paused for no lengthy explanations. He shoved Sir Roger behind a statue of a shapely Venus and covered them both with his body.

Banbury probably would have had more to say on this, but at that point another loud bang echoed in the distance.

In the chaos that followed—the chief yelling "Sniper!"; Sir Roger occasionally stepping out from the statue, demanding to know what was happening; and Otto holding him back—Warren was the only one who had not moved from the spot.

The chief returned fire. Adrienne and Hathaway dove behind the statue next to Sir Roger. Hathaway would have happily remained anchored to Venus's ankle, had he not looked up and seen Warren planted in the middle of the room, right in the line of fire.

Hathaway shouted at him, but the bodyguard merely turned his head and blinked at him, like a helpless child lost in a supermarket. His client launched from the spot, just as another shot reflected off Venus's elbow. A second one winged by him as he tackled Warren. Together, they slid across the marble and landed in an undignified tangle under a table. Warren said, "Ow."

Shortly thereafter, Adwick ventured up the stairs and called down that the assailant had disappeared.

Hathaway rolled out from the table. A thought occurred to him. "Lesley!" he cried.

Warren watched as his client rushed from the scene.

* * *

Sprinting down a few halls, Hathaway slid around a corner near the Post-Impressionists and saw Lesley at the other end.

"Oh, John," she waved happily. "Did they get the door open?"

Huffing deeply but definitely with volumes he needed to express, it was all Hathaway could do to cough out, "Lesley."

Lesley tilted her head and grinned widely. "I can't hear you."

He made another attempt at speech, but all that came out was a gasped warning. It occurred to him that if he was going to participate in any more sprinting events, he would need Lady Banbury to put him on one of her workout plans.

Just then, the lights went out. Lesley called out John's name.

There was the sound of footsteps.

A gunshot echoed.

A shriek.

Blundering forward, Hathaway met with a soft form blundering toward him, and before he knew it, the soft form and he were tumbling end over end down a flight of steps.

The lights came back on, and he was relieved to note that the soft form in question was not the assassin, which would have been awkward, but was, in fact, Lesley.

They were sprawled out, face-to-face. Despite the fact that he was lying supine on a marble floor, probably shot, with every bone in his body undoubtedly broken, he did have one thing that would have brought a smile to any man's face: Lesley lying on top of him with her warm body pressed against his. All in all, he wasn't complaining.

He and Lesley appeared none the worse for wear, leading him to conclude that the shot had missed them both. In fact, it had been fired nowhere near them.

Lesley was looking down at him with large, grateful eyes. "You put your body between the bullet and me," she said in a soft voice.

"It's what any man would have done," he told her. Before he could ask if she was all right, she kissed him.

Time drifted by, and Hathaway happened to glance back up the stairs to the Post-Impressionist display. There, standing next to a colorful Glackens, was Finch, freshly arrived on the scene. Warren was standing next to Finch. Neither looked entirely pleased.

"Hathaway!" they said in stereo.

Hathaway jumped up. He helped Lesley to her feet. "Say! Finch! I didn't notice you there. Lucky you didn't wander in here a second ago. You missed quite a scene."

"Doesn't seem like I missed a thing!"

"What's that?" He followed Finch's stare to Lesley. "Oh right. This isn't what it looks like. I know that's what you were probably expecting me to say, but in this case it's, ah, not what it looks like. You see, there was an assassin, Finch."

Finch and Warren took a step closer.

"As I was saying, there was an assassin. Harold will tell you. Say, Harold, you look reasonably bullet-free. Fared the storm pretty well, I guess. But I cut you off, Harold. You were about to explain to Finch how this compromising scene is completely innocent. Harold?"

Warren gave Hathaway a haughty stare, indicating that he was planning to do nothing of the sort.

Lesley stepped up. "John saved my life!"

Warren looked at Hathaway sideways. "He did, did he?" He continued to stare. Hardly the amiable look one usually got from Warren. Typically Warren's face was vacant. Whether he was discussing the back nine, or pausing to tell a client that he saw someone slip arsenic in their martini and forgot to mention it, one got the blank visage. But this was far from blank; deeper thoughts were behind it. This was more along the lines of a Finchesque look.

"Yes, he did. Wasn't that brave of him, Harold?"

"I suppose."

"Isn't he wonderful?"

"I suppose."

How long this might have gone on, we may never know. Finch spoke now. "I was right, you letch. Even during an emergency you can't control yourself. Have you no decency, no shame?"

Hathaway sputtered, "No. I mean, yes. I mean, what?"

Lesley interrupted, "What's he talking about, John? Why does he care who you kiss?"

Finch fielded the question. "Because, little girl, this idiot is engaged to Sir Roger's daughter!"

Hathaway's eyes bulged. "No! I mean, not really!"

Lesley, ignoring the "little girl" comment, looked at Hathaway. Unable to speak, she turned away.

Chief Adwick, Mahrute and Otto came over to join them.

"He threw the circuit breaker and escaped out a window," said Otto. "It looks like he took something from Sir Roger's collection."

"We do have a clue," added Adwick, holding an object up for their inspection. "Do you know what this is?"

"Looks like a little metal cylindrical shell of some sort," said Hathaway.

"That's right."

"It is? It's a little metal cylindrical shell of some sort?"

"It's a shell, Mr. Hathaway, a shell casing to be precise. Do you know what it goes to? It's a pistol shell. And I have a pretty good idea who it belongs to."

"You do?"

"Yes. It belongs to the bastard who robbed the Travers gun shop yesterday. This shell goes to an antique revolver, just like the one that was stolen."

Hathaway, realizing Ditters' gun had fallen into the marauder's hands, tried to argue the other side. "You can't know it's from *that* revolver."

"I certainly can know. I talked to the shop owner after the crime took place, and he told me that he only has a few revolvers in stock that take this caliber. .455."

"Would that be the same .455 caliber used in the Webley?" asked Mahrute.

"Yes, sir. You obviously know your guns."

A sudden horror gripped Hathaway. All this talk of antique revolvers in front of Otto would fill in the blanks for the manor bodyguard.

Sure enough, a thought appeared to flash across the square face. "Antique revolver? Did you say antique revolver?"

"Yes," prompted the chief.

Otto looked over at Hathaway and then back at the chief. Either he was struck by a pang of uncertainty or he was relishing memories of good scotch, but he ended up shaking his head.

Hathaway jumped in at the lull. "Listen, Chief, how do you know this guy didn't get the revolver out of Sir Roger's collection? He has all sorts of weapons."

"None that take the .455," said Sir Roger, arriving on the scene.

The next few minutes got pretty technical, speculating on the facts of the case. Most of the conversation was devoted to further discussion of shell casings, the likes of which only J. Travers and customer could have really found fascinating. The chief stuck to his notion that the gun shop robber was behind it all—although Hathaway could have told him that the great criminal mind behind the Travers Gun Shop Caper was no doubt up to his elbows in pickles at the moment and hadn't set foot near the revolver since Otto took it off him.

It was at some point during these debates that Sir Roger spoke again. Having shared his thoughts on the history of the .455 caliber—noting that this had failed to grip the participants—he introduced a new topic. "Oh, I nearly forgot," he said, interrupting a disagreement between Hathaway and the chief on the subject of the height of the suspect. "You don't think this had anything to do with the shooting, do you?"

He pulled out a piece of paper and handed it to Adwick.

On it read the words:

you beTtEr watCH out OR you'RE dead!
D E a D!

"Otto gave me this letter this morning. Said it was a death threat that came in the mail yesterday. I didn't give it much thought. Besides, the letters were all cut out from newsprint. How am I supposed to take seriously something that's cut out from newsprint?"

Otto frowned thoughtfully, as Adwick studied the page.

* * *

Later that day, Hathaway went searching for Lesley in order to explain the misunderstanding in the museum. Strolling out to the lake, he found Mahrute instead.

"Hey, Mahrute, have you seen, uh, Brittany?"

"Miss Darlington and Mr. Kingsley are in a boat on the lake."

Miss Darlington. Hathaway should have known that Mahrute would pierce her identity.

He glared out at the rowboat. "Did she seem upset?"

"A little agitated, perhaps. She asked me to wish you the best with Miss Banbury."

"I have to talk to her. I couldn't say anything in the museum, but I'm not really engaged. I'm only doing it to do Ditters a good turn."

"I am happy to hear it." A long pause. "I discovered the whereabouts of Mr. Kingsley's cushion."

Hathaway turned from his stare.

He was confused. What did Warren's cushion have to do with anything?

"Oh, you mean the one with the Azure Star in it?"

"Indeed. Mr. Kingsley explained the situation to me, and feeling that the recovery of the antique was within all of our best interests, I took it upon myself to locate it."

"Do you have it with you?"

"No. I said I had located it, not retrieved it. I spoke to the maid, and she seems to think she moved a set of cushions to the balcony on Mr. Finch's room. She didn't give it much thought at the time, but one of the cushions had a tear in the bottom."

"As if something had been stuffed in it?"

"Precisely. Unfortunately, Mr. Finch's room is locked at the moment."

"Are you familiar with this Finch character, Mahrute? Also answers to the name Randal?"

"I believe Mr. Kingsley spoke briefly about him. He mentioned that you and Mr. Finch were old friends."

"Warren has a distorted view of humanity. Suffice it to say I know this Finch and this Finch despises me. Not that he's one of the first names on my Christmas card list either, mind you. How am I supposed to get the Star from a cushion on his balcony? For one thing, he thinks I have scorned Adrienne, for whom he has enormous respect. If I tap on his door inquiring after jeweled daggers, he's likely to beat me into the floorboards."

Mahrute nodded. "Grudge or not, I would imagine that no one could approach Mr. Finch along those lines without arousing some suspicion."

Hathaway muttered something in agreement and glanced back out at Lesley.

Out on the lake, Warren rowed the boat in circles. He had not fully grasped the double-oar principle.

"I think I have a thought, Mahrute. We can get the Azure Star easily, no questions asked. The way I see it is this. We knock on Finch's door. When Finch sticks his fat head out into the hall, I distract him while you slug him."

"I'm afraid not."

"Come on. What's a bit of slugging?"

"I'm sorry; the security organization to which I belong forbids their bodyguards from participating in any criminal activity."

"It's not a criminal activity. It's simply breaking into some guy's room and whacking his head off. I know you could do it. No, huh? Well, this is splendid. I have bodyguards coming out of my ears, and none of them can slug a simple assistant to a tycoon? This is a sad state of affairs; that's all I have to say."

In the middle of this standoff, Jackson appeared holding a silver salver in his good arm.

"Say, Jackson, how are you with slugging people?"

The butler apologized and said he hadn't slugged anyone for years. He did have a fax for Mr. Hathaway. As if that were any help.

"Who would be faxing me?" he asked Mahrute idly, after Jackson had left them.

"I couldn't say. If you will excuse me, I have been monitoring Mr. Kingsley's activities, and it appears he is dangerously close to falling into the lake."

Mahrute went off, and Hathaway decided to take his message inside. The sun had set, and he wanted to read it in better light. He found a cozy spot in the drawing room and looked it over. The fax was from Susan Hamilton, Uncle George's secretary.

> JOHNNY,
>
> GOV. LANDERS TOLD YOUR UNCLE THAT YOU ACTED LIKE A BUFFOON WITH HIS DAUGHTER BRITTANY. YOUR UNCLE'S PRETTY TICKED. SAYS HE'S GOING TO DISOWN YOU.
>
> —SUSAN HAMILTON
>
> P.S.: COLBY HUMNER TOLD ME TO TELL YOU NOT TO WORRY ABOUT THE "GREEN BERET." THE GUY LEFT FOR THE CARIBBEAN A COUPLE DAYS AGO. COLBY SAID YOU WOULD UNDERSTAND. HOPE YOU DO, BECAUSE I SURE DON'T.

Hathaway tapped the paper thoughtfully against the table. At least one chapter of his recent misadventures was over. Of course, it would have been nice to have had this information a little earlier—like before he had hired Warren, the assassin's best friend—but you can't have everything.

Outside in the hall, someone slammed down a phone. Presently, Chief Adwick entered the room.

"Mr. Hathaway, just the man I was looking for."

"Oh?"

"You probably already know that I've asked everyone to stay put for the next day or so until I can conduct my investigation of the shooting in the museum."

"I hadn't heard, but if the bridge is still out, I'm not going anywhere, Chief."

"Actually, they should have it repaired by tonight. There was something else you may want to know, though. When I spoke to my deputy, he told me that one of those suspects that attacked you on the train escaped yesterday."

Hathaway shot up in his chair. "They escaped?"

"Not both," said the chief, "just Nibu Nibudar."

"What's the matter—couldn't the other gorilla fashion a pistol from a bar of soap? Wait! You say Nibu escaped yesterday? Isn't that the same day they attacked me?"

"Yes. Apparently, Nibu got loose shortly after the assault."

"What happened? Wasn't there enough room in the squad car? Or did your deputy just think Nibu had an honest face and decide to start his own criminal rehabilitation program?"

The chief wasn't amused. "It was the damnedest thing. While I was questioning you, my deputies were taking the suspects back to the station. Both were still unconscious."

"Your deputies?"

"The suspects. It wasn't until they were back at the station that one of the deputies noticed that the Nibu guy wasn't the Nibu guy at all. It was some train porter."

More train porters. What these poor guys won't endure, thought Hathaway.

"The guy's fine," explained Adwick. "He woke up groggy. Said the last thing he remembers is walking down the hall and someone socking him over the head."

"Something very few train porters appreciate, I should imagine, but what about Nibu?"

"He switched clothes with the porter and disappeared on us, which really puts a hole in our case. I can already tell that the district attorney isn't going to like this."

Hathaway glared. "Damn the district attorney! The district attorney can screw himself. What about Nibu?"

"We don't know where he is now. He may have been the man in the museum today; we don't know. By the way, I still haven't questioned Miss Landers about that."

"She's out on the lake, if you want her."

"Good. And how about Warren Kingsley?"

Hathaway almost replied, "He's out on the lake too," but caught himself. "Um, who's Warren Kingsley?"

"I don't know. His name's on the guest list, but no one seems to know who he is."

"Maybe he didn't show?"

"Maybe. If you do see him, let me know, will you? I'd like to question him. See you at dinner."

Finishing his drink, Hathaway followed. With any luck, he would run into Finch on the way, and the latter could bash his brains in.

15 — Guests Revealed

In fact, Finch was not among the seated inhabitants. The table, made up of a select handful of guests, included Lesley and Warren, acting cool toward one another for a change; Adrienne looking sullen; Sir Roger chowing down; Lady Banbury attempting to engage Nibu, dressed as Richter again, in a conversation about Brahms' First Symphony; and finally Hathaway, meditating on the various twists and turns in the weekend. Ditters, trying to avoid Adwick, had not shown for supper. Adrienne had promised to bring him out a little plate of something once the coast was clear.

Dinner concluded, Hathaway left the meal pretty much as he had arrived, deep in thought. He headed for the drawing room. Spotting Finch on the way—an angry blur coming around the other corner—Hathaway's first thought was to turn and run.

Fortunately, he managed to duck behind some curtains in the foyer before the resident thug blew by. Standing quietly behind the drapes, it occurred to him that he was not alone.

It was not until a voice said "Is that you, Hathaway?" that it dawned on him that the man concealed in the linen was none other than Warren Kingsley, alias Harold Konig.

"Warren?" whispered Hathaway.

"Yes?"

"What are you doing?"

"Huh?"

"What are you doing? You're not hiding from Finch, are you?"

"No, I'm hiding from Chief Adwick. He's not with you, is he?"

Hathaway rolled his eyes, although the gesture was obscured in the brocade. "I'm alone. Why are you hiding from Chief Adwick?" He thought that was Ditters' job.

"Someone told me the chief's looking for Warren Kingsley."

"So?"

"So, he's questioning people in the shooting today. Warren might be a suspect."

"Warren, think about it. Warren Kingsley isn't a suspect in the shooting. You were one of the ones getting shot at, remember?"

For a moment, the drapes made no response. "But he's still looking for Warren Kingsley, and that's me."

"Warren."

"Yes?"

"He doesn't know you're Warren Kingsley. No one knows you're Warren Kingsley."

Again the fabric deliberated on this. An embroidered flower stirred. "Lesley does."

"Lesley?" Evidently, the actor playing the part of Harold Konig and the actress playing Brittany Landers had been conferring offstage.

"Brittany told me she's really Lesley Darlington."

"And you told her you're not Konig?"

"I figured it was the perfect time. Besides, I didn't know how much longer I could continue pretending to be an art expert. Do you know what she said to me when I told her who I was?"

"Not off the top of my head."

"She said I lied to her."

"Did she throw a hiking boot at you?"

"No. I don't think she had one on her. Anyway, I said that she lied to me, too, about being Brittany. She said it was totally different. How does that work, Hathaway? Thought I had her on that one."

Hathaway nodded knowingly.

"She said I could have protected her, if she knew I was a bodyguard. I might not have told her I was a bodyguard, but I never left her side."

"Unlike with some of your clients."

"Exactly. Anyway, now we're not speaking."

"She's not speaking to me either. She thinks I'm engaged to Adrienne."

Warren brooded quietly. "The last thing she said was if it weren't for John, she'd probably be dead thanks to me. Who's John?"

"I am."

"Oh. Do you really think the assassin in the museum was trying to kill her?"

"I don't know. If it was an assassin, he could have been after any of us, I guess."

"You don't really think he could have been after you?"

"You needn't sound so incredulous, Warren. I'll have you know that there have been plenty of assassins with the name John Hathaway on their A-list. As my bodyguard, this should concern you."

"Oh, it does, Hathaway; it does. Of course, if someone really wants to kill you, they can be pretty determined. Try blending in."

"Warren, I'm going to leave now."

"Okay. Bye, Hathaway."

Hathaway hesitated. The thoughts rolling around his bean were deep, brooding thoughts. He reviewed. Here he was, standing behind the curtains in a mansion, hiding like some cowardly tyke from a childhood bully. And what he wanted to know was why. He realized how often he avoided things—uncles, bill collectors, Green Berets. He was skillful at it too, but with skillful avoidance comes a certain emptiness.

"Warren, have you ever woken up one morning and realized that you were wasting your life?"

Warren gave the question some thought. "Nope," he replied.

"You're fortunate, then." Hathaway poked his head out. Holding a handful of the drapes, he paused. "Out of curiosity, would you have any moral objections to slugging someone for me?"

"Big guy?"

"About average."

"It's not that Otto, is it?"

"No. Finch."

"He's pretty big, too, isn't he?"

"Never mind. You wouldn't happen to know an easy way to get to a third-story balcony, would you?"

"Did you try the roof?"

"The roof?"

"Yes, jump down to it from the roof. That's exactly how an assassin got one of my clients in Palm Beach."

The roof. It couldn't be that simple. "How would I get to the roof?"

"From another third-story balcony," said Warren. "Like mine."

Hathaway considered this. "You have a room on the third floor?" he asked. Those were the nice rooms.

"They moved my room because I thought I saw a beetle in my other one. I hate bugs."

Hathaway shook his head. "So you think you can get to the roof from there?"

"Sure. Easy."

"Come on. I need your help," Hathaway said, emerging into the hall.

* * *

After breezing through the foyer and pausing because he thought he could hear voices in the curtains, Randal Finch went to get a snack in the kitchen. Halfway through his meal of crackers and salami, he remembered something he needed from his room.

* * *

Upstairs, in a long corridor in the northwest wing, Nibu poked his head out.

With the third Azure Star secure in his pocket, he was planning on asking the tycoon if the bridge had been repaired yet. Like the other impostors at Rangeley, his impersonation was beginning to wear thin, and the sooner he could make good his escape the better.

Surveying the hall, he removed a pair of headphones from his ears and placed them on the bureau back inside his room. A faint voice could be heard drifting out from the recorder: *You are a good assassin. You strike with catlike swiftness. You are the wind …*

Nibu closed the door and proceeded down the hall to Sir Roger's room. Knocking, he reached up to wipe the sweat from his brow, a drawback to wearing padding and a false beard in the heat. His beard felt loose. He went to press it firmly against his face, but it only peeled off and fell to the floor.

He whisked it off the rug in time to hear footsteps coming from both directions of the hall. Knowing that a clean-shaven Richter would hardly go over well with the residents, he slipped back into the bedroom. It was not until he had closed the door that he realized that it was not actually his bedroom.

* * *

From the north side of the hall came Otto Pincher. Since their conversation the evening before, Otto had kept his eye on "the maestro." Tracking him about the mansion, he had followed him to this spot.

He paused in the middle of the corridor, scouting the scene. Eventually, from the south side of the stage, plodded Finch. He hesitated in his tracks and focused a curious stare at the bodyguard.

Just to fill out the gathering, the door to the west opened and out popped Sir Roger, answering Nibu's pounding.

There was silence, as the three men looked between one another. Finally, Banbury slipped back behind his closed door, Otto left to pick up Richter's trail elsewhere, and Finch proceeded within his nearby bedroom.

Once inside, he clicked on a lamp and stood filing through a pile of papers on his desk. He heard someone sneeze behind him. Stepping over to investigate, he observed a pair of shoes connected to a ducked form under a table by the window. Before he could demand that this form show himself, Nibu decided the jig was up and launched out from the table, knocking Finch across the room.

Seconds after the crook had scrambled out the door, Finch stood, rubbing his head and mumbling under his breath. He noticed something by his foot. Upon closer inspection, he determined that it was some sort of ornate dagger.

***

In a room around the corner, Hathaway and Warren stepped out onto the bodyguard's balcony. Hathaway, a little annoyed that Warren had a much nicer room than he had, climbed onto the railing and got a boost to the roof.

After tossing his client about eighteen feet from where he would have liked to have been, Warren pulled himself up. "Say, Hathaway, what are you doing way over there? Finch's room is over this way," he said, mincing over to the right. Hathaway picked himself up and followed, mincing a bit himself, until he reached the spot where Warren was waiting.

The view from the roof was spectacular. It was a clear night, and Hathaway could see past the grounds out into the forest. He would have stopped to look around a little more but decided not to let his attention stray. When you're on a roof, any wrong step could mean plummeting into the night. This is especially true when the only person standing by to grab the back of your shirt is Warren Kingsley.

"Is that the balcony, Hathaway?"

Hathaway glanced down. "I think it is. Is that the cushion you hid the Star in?"

Warren nodded. Of course, all chair cushions looked the same to him.

"Okay," said Hathaway, "first I need you to tie these together."

"Are those my bedsheets?" asked Warren.

"Yeah. I borrowed them."

"What am I supposed to sleep on now?"

"Warren, tie them together!"

"Why?"

"Because, as I suspected, it's too far to jump, at least if you want any accuracy, and in this case accuracy certainly counts." He handed Warren the sheets and took another look around. "No, not like that."

"What?"

"You didn't tie them end to end. You tied them together in the middle."

"So?"

"So, that defeats the purpose. See, they're no longer than they were separate."

"You didn't tell me you wanted them long."

"That was the general idea, yes."

"How's that?"

"Ducky. Now, since I could never for a second lower you down, you will have to lower me down, okay?"

"K."

After insisting Warren use two hands, Hathaway began to climb down the bedsheets. It was only about twenty feet to the balcony, and all went splendidly at first, until Hathaway said something, and Warren let him drop like a falling piano.

By some miracle, he landed on the balcony below. He looked up and saw Warren's face sticking out over the edge of the roof. "What did you say, Hathaway?"

"Nothing. I was just going to say 'Don't let go.' " He picked himself up and went to the chairs. Examining the cushions, he found one with a small tear in the back. Slipping it open, he pulled the Azure Star out from the stuffing. "Warren, are you still there?"

"Still here, Hathaway," said the face protruding from the roof.

"Good. I'm going to toss this to you, so I can free up my hands for climbing. Ready? Catch!"

"What am I supposed to do with it?" asked the bodyguard, after he had fumbled the dagger into his grip.

"Give it to Mahrute. We'll give it to Sir Roger later." Hathaway brushed himself off. "Okay, I'm going to throw the sheet back up to you. Ready? Warren?"

Hathaway glanced up at the roof, but no smiling, square-jawed face appeared. He paged back through his instructions; they seemed so simple. Then he got it. He should have mentioned that he would need Warren to pull him up *before* he left to give the Star to Mahrute. Hathaway blamed himself, really.

He turned and peered through the balcony window. It started to rain again.

* * *

On the other side of the window, in a corner of the room where Hathaway hadn't noticed him, Finch was holding a dagger, his brow furrowed in thought. The dagger, dropped by Nibu in the scuffle, wasn't just any dagger; it had a gem-covered handle and a large blue stone in the bottom. Had he listened to his employer's ramblings, Finch would have known that the object he held was the Azure Star, the third in the series to date.

During his pondering, the balcony door slid open, and in crept Hathaway. The two men stood staring at each other. Their jaws dropped, and on the Finch side the dagger hit the floor with a clunk.

"What are you doing here, Hathaway?"

"How's that? Oh, you mean here. Right. Just strolling by, and thought I'd pop in."

"How'd you get in here? My door's locked."

"Is it? Good idea, Finch. With thieves and assassins running wild, you can never be too sure."

Finch blinked. Remembering the dagger lying behind him, he stepped back to conceal it. "I asked you how you got in here."

"Me? I came in through the window."

"Are you insane?"

"Sometimes I think so, yes. Anyway, this has been fun, but I have other persons to pop in on tonight, so I will get out of your hair now."

"Stop right there, Hathaway!" He hadn't meant to step so far forward. Before he could catch himself, he had revealed the object under his foot.

"Where'd you get that?" asked Hathaway.

Finch scooped it up. "This isn't what it looks like. Some guy dropped it. I came back and found him hiding under the table."

"How long ago?"

"About twenty minutes. Why?"

"No reason." Hathaway was trying to figure out how an ornate dagger he had given Warren three minutes ago could have wound up in Finch's room twenty minutes earlier.

"I think this came out of Sir Roger's collection," continued Finch. "Remember someone stole something from a display case this morning?"

"Yes, I know. I was there at the time." Hathaway paused. "You came in later, didn't you?"

"You don't think I stole it, do you?"

"I don't know, Finch. You used to steal chalk from the teacher's desk all the time."

"That was twenty years ago! I told you, someone dropped this … you don't believe me, do you?"

"You don't exactly have an honest face, Finch."

"But I'm telling you I'm not the thief! You're not going to tell anyone you saw me with this, are you? I mean, we're friends, right?"

"Friends?"

"I've always thought so, Hathaway."

"You have, have you?"

"Sure. I mean, you think I'm innocent, don't you?"

Hathaway was going to enjoy this. "Innocent? Is that what you asked me, Finch? You need a character witness? I have a gob to say about your character, Finch. You're a creep, a first-class one. You're also a thug, a hothead, an ass and several other things that any fair-minded individual would agree you indeed are but I can't at the moment think of. But rest assured, Finch, they're on the tip of my tongue. Bully, that's one of them. Now where was I? Oh yes—about this business of my trifling with Miss Banbury?"

"Oh, that. Obviously, I wronged you."

"Good. We understand each other, then. Because, I'm a fair man—"

"Extremely fair," Finch agreed.

"And I'm forgiving."

"Forgiving."

"Are you going to let me finish, Finch?"

"Of course, Hathaway, of course."

"Good. To recap, I'm fair and forgiving. You can be sure that no one will hear about any of this from me. Don't let it happen again, though. Give me the dagger. I'll make sure it gets back to its proper owner."

Part Four

16 — Trouble with a Tuba

Hathaway returned to his room pretty pleased with himself. He was so pleased, in fact, that he did not immediately notice that the power had gone out in the mansion. Standing in his darkened quarters snapping the light to no avail, he finally realized that the lights all down the hall were out. The lightning outside told the story.

Since he was only planning to sleep anyway, he blundered into his room, trying to find his bed by the light of the full moon. One can never be too cautious navigating a darkened room, however, for hardly had he traveled six feet when he stumbled on a corpse someone had left strewn in the middle of the floor. He caught his foot on this corpse and went ass over teakettle.

Looking up, in sync with a flash of lightning, he suddenly realized that the corpse was moving and, from what he could see in that glimpse, currently ransacking his suitcase.

All pretty presumptuous for a corpse.

Waiting for the mandatory crash of thunder, Hathaway shouted, "Hey!"

The figure, not a corpse but rather our friend Barnet, jumped and flung Hathaway's socks across the room.

Hathaway tackled him. One grabbed the other by the neck, then the latter snagged the former by the foot, and generally they spilled into furniture and made a nasty racket. Hathaway had just gotten the fellow where he wanted him when Barnet clobbered him over the head with a blunt, tuba-shaped object and escaped.

A minute later, Hathaway was still massaging the temples and wondering what the hell happened. The lights came on then, the result of someone's clever tinkering with the backup generator. The room, unsurprisingly, had a disheveled look. Something Hathaway noticed right off was a tuba lying in the middle of the floor. The strange thing was he didn't own a tuba, never had.

* * * *

Barnet raced down the dimly lit halls. The tuba, which he had brought along with him as part of his brilliant disguise, had actually proved an effective means of escape.

Back at his room, he shut the door and paused to find his bearings, not unlike Hathaway several rooms over. These bearings mostly sorted, he pulled out his phone and dialed a number.

A pleasant female voice answered on the other end. "Hello?"

"This is 'the Sniffer.' I searched Hathaway's room like you told me to, but he doesn't have it. Neither does Konig. The butler had it, but now it's gone. I quit." He hung up.

* * * *

On the other side of the line, Lady Margaret Banbury returned her cell phone to her nightstand and reflected on how difficult it was to get good thieves these days. She climbed out of bed, telling her half-conscious husband to go back to sleep.

* * * *

Sometime after that, Mahrute bumped into Lady Banbury coming out of her bedroom.

She stepped back and forced a smile. Although she had never quite understood who he was, that was no reason to be uncivil. "Good evening, Mr. Mahrute. We are both up late, I see. I was on my way to the kitchen. If you'll excuse me?"

Mahrute bowed. "Lady Banbury?"

"Yes, Mr. Mahrute?"

"I understand your husband is interested in a certain item. Something for his collection."

"How did you—yes, I suppose he is."

"Perhaps this is what he is looking for?" Without further ado, he produced an Azure Star, the fourth one and counting, and presented it to his very astonished hostess.

* * * *

By the time Hathaway arrived at Mahrute's room, the other had returned from his meeting with Lady Banbury and had put a selection of light jazz playing on his portable stereo.

Hathaway was beginning to think that the bodyguard's bodyguard was competing with Otto for least need of sleep. Then again, recently Hathaway could have placed himself in that category.

He apologized for disturbing him. "That's not more Beethoven you're listening to there, is it?"

"Bix Beiderbecke."

"Ah. Tuba player?"

"Cornet."

"Good. We can cross Bix off our list of suspects, then." He paused. "What's a cornet, Mahrute?"

"A small, trumpetlike instrument."

"Ah. I see why the intruder chose the tuba. Packs more of a punch. Sorry, I'm a bit shook up. I found someone ransacking my room."

"Indeed?"

"I think it was the same guy I saw outside Sir Roger's office yesterday. He had a tuba with him this time. He hit me over the head with it, in fact."

"We can conclude, then, that the suspect plays in the orchestra."

"The mansion has an orchestra?"

"The Bath Chamber Orchestra, they're guests here."

"So you think this guy got into the mansion by slipping into the tuba section? Who notices the tuba player being the general sentiment. I wonder if he was after the Azure Star. By the way, I dug the thing out of the chair cushion like you suggested. The thing is, not three seconds later, I came upon Randal Finch with another Star. It was like I was seeing double. Banbury had said something about counterfeits, and I was thinking maybe someone's circulating them around here. Oh, I almost forgot." He pulled out the newspaper clipping. "Last night I found this in Banbury's desk. Don't ask how. Anyway, this article claims the real Azure Star belongs to Boris Pefferu." He took out the Azure Star he had gotten from Finch. "I wish it had a better picture. You know, maybe if we compare this one to the one Warren gave you, we could figure out which one is the real one."

Mahrute looked mystified. "Mr. Kingsley?"

"Didn't Warren come by and give you the Azure Star?"

"No, he did not."

"Son of a …" Hathaway was about to follow up on this when Jackson passed by the open door and spun in.

"Mr. Hathaway, come with me. There has been an attempted murder."

"Of whom?"

"Mr. Konig."

* * * *

Once he realized Jackson meant Warren, the statement held more of an impact.

The funny thing was, even though Warren was a menace and a lunatic and generally a threat to the free world, democracy and everything they held dear, Hathaway found himself dismayed. Over the past few days, he had developed a sort of fondness for old Warren, despite his eccentricities, and resented the idea of someone bumping him off.

They followed Jackson to Dr. Powers' room, the guest who had sewn Jackson back together after the butler's winging. Inside, Warren was stretched out on a bed. Standing over him were Chief Adwick and Otto Pincher. The doctor stopped Hathaway and Mahrute at the door.

"He's doing fine," she said. "He was attacked with some sort of knife, but apparently the assailant's blade only brushed up against him. It's more of a flesh wound than anything. I gave him a painkiller, but it seems to have made him quite muddled."

"That's okay," Hathaway assured her. "He's usually quite muddled."

They stepped over to the patient.

"Hathaway!" said Warren cheerfully, sitting up and then looking like he wished he hadn't. "Hathaway," he whispered, "someone tried to knock me off."

"We heard."

Warren noticed his bodyguard. "Mahrute! I didn't see you there. Say, why the long face? It's okay. I'm not dead. Did you know someone tried to knock me off? Ouch! Who put this wall here? Say, Chief, you're still here, huh? What can I do for you? Did you know someone tried to knock me off?"

"Yes, sir," replied the chief. "Just tell us everything you remember."

"Remember," said Warren. "Remember about what?"

"Your assault."

"That's a lie, Chief! I didn't assault anyone."

"I meant the assault on you, Mr. Konig."

"Oh, that assault. Why didn't you say so? Try to be more clear in the future. Now then, the assault. Hathaway and I had just been on the roof. Now, why were we on the roof? I was helping him break into someone's room or something. No, that's not it. It's okay, Hathaway, I'll think of it. Wait! I think I was supposed to give something to Mahrute. Yes, it's all coming back to me now. I was on my way to Mahrute's. I had just turned the corner, and I had a notion that someone was following me. I looked back and caught a glimpse of a figure lurking in the shadows. Immediately I recognized this figure was up to no good. I'm trained to pick up on these things, you know. I had hardly uttered 'Say there, you in the shadows, who goes there?' when the lights went out. That's when the assassin leapt out and plunged a knife into my chest. I remember thinking at the time 'Well, this is no good.' Oh, hello, Lesley, I mean Brittany."

It was no hallucination. Lesley Darlington was indeed among them. "Warren, thank God you're okay!"

"Lesley, did you know someone tried to knock me off?"

"I just heard. You're so brave!"

"Oh, I know."

"You shouldn't have bothered trying to protect me like that. Standing outside my door and all that."

"No, I was just ..."

"But I'm glad you did," she said. "To think that there's an assassin loose in the house. You could have been killed."

"It was pretty awful," Warren agreed.

"Was he very large?"

"Pretty large. There may have been two; I can't remember."

At this point, the doctor stepped over and respectfully asked everyone to leave. "I'm afraid you'll have to leave too, miss," she said to Lesley. "My patient needs his rest."

Lesley promised to be back later. Otto and the chief followed her out, the latter mentioning that he had all that he needed.

Lesley smiled at Hathaway as she left. Even though she had essentially made up with Warren, she still had not developed the same feelings for him as she had for Hathaway. Though she hadn't mentioned it to him, and doubted that she ever would now, Hathaway had been to her the sort of warm, fun, considerate man she had been searching for her whole life. She missed his company.

He missed her too. He moved to go after her, so he could finally explain about Adrienne, but Warren interrupted his escape.

"It's true what they say, Hathaway; your life does flash before your eyes."

"Is that right?"

"It does." There was a pause. "Do you know why I became a bodyguard, Hathaway?"

"No, why did you?" Hathaway asked, even though it seemed pretty irrelevant.

"It was something my grandfather told me when I was very young. 'Warren,' he said, when I was very young, 'you have the appearance of heroism. No one cares that you don't have the stuff inside.' I've always remembered that."

"Inspirational," said Hathaway.

"He never told me that when you're a hero, people want you dead. Pretty blockheaded of him, I think."

"You need your rest, Warren. We'll be back to see you later."

Warren stood and followed them to the door. He reeled back, as if something concerning the floor had been too much for him. "My goodness I'm tall."

He stumbled forward. Hathaway noticed that his left arm was in a sling, à la Jackson and Adwick. It seemed like everyone in Rangeley would be bandaged before the weekend was through. "Hathaway, you can rest assured that I'm still on the job. It takes more than a little knife to scare Warren Kingsley."

"That's good to know," said Hathaway. He frowned. Considering Warren's rather sobering reputation, the prospect of him continuing in his duties with effectively one arm tied behind his back filled his former client with a definite uneasiness.

"Oh, speaking of which, I lost that dagger you gave me."

In all the excitement, Hathaway had forgotten about Azure Star #1. "You lost it?"

"I think the assassin made off with it. Actually, I think that's what he used to stab me. It was a lot sharper than it looked. Whoa, I'm dizzy."

Warren maneuvered back to rest, and Mahrute and Hathaway shuffled out. On their way, they heard a crash followed by a "Who moved my bed?"

* * * *

Nibu Nibudar dashed into his room and closed the door behind him. He pulled out the Azure Star and placed it on the table.

The last he had heard, the bridge was almost repaired. By the time he changed clothes, sneaked out to the garage to steal a car and drove there, it would be open. He grabbed his Richter outfit off a nearby chair.

* * * *

Hathaway was happy that Warren was alive, but he couldn't suppress a slight irritation at having the original Azure Star missing from their camp once again. He examined the dagger he had gotten from Finch.

He decided not to comment on Mahrute's pensiveness. He figured the idea of someone taking a slice out of a client was something Mahrute couldn't help mulling over a bit. Warren was used to clients going face down in the pudding at dinner, but it was a new thing to Mahrute.

They stepped into Hathaway's room. "I saw you speaking with the chief, Mahrute. Did he give you any valuable information?"

"He believes he has had a breakthrough in the case."

"No kidding? Well, lucky for me I have this case all worked out too."

"Indeed?"

"Open and shut is the way I see it. It seems to me—" Hathaway paused. "Did you hear a ruffling sound, Mahrute?"

"Yes."

"Sounds like it came from the wardrobe. There it goes again," he said, and the ruffling was followed by a bumping noise. With all due caution, Hathaway stepped over to investigate. He yanked the door open.

Obscured in his shirts was the happy couple, Adrienne and Ditters, huddled together and squinting as the light of the room filled their space.

"Hello, hello," said Hathaway. He was particularly pleased to find Adrienne like this. Catch her glaring at people lying on the back lawn now.

"Hiya, Hath," said Ditters, crawling out. Adrienne followed—glaring, as to be expected. "Good, he's gone," he observed, glancing around. "Hiya, Mahrute."

"Who's gone?" asked Hathaway.

"The chief."

"The chief was here?"

"Just a minute ago. We were waiting for you to come back. I went to the door to see what was keeping you and spotted the chief coming this way. That's when Adrienne and I hid in your closet. Hope you don't mind?"

"Not at all. But why would the chief come here? He knew I was talking to Warren."

"I think he searched the joint. We couldn't see him, of course, but it sounded like he was going over your room with a fine-tooth comb. Luckily, I held the wardrobe door shut. How'd you know we were in there, by the way?"

Hathaway explained about the ruffling noise, and Adrienne glowered.

"I told you someone would hear you," she said, slapping Ditters' shoulder.

"I thought you two were eloping?" Hathaway asked her.

"We were, but the chief mucked up the works. Otto locked the garage. Chief's orders, he said. No one's going anywhere until the assailant's found, he said."

"Damn inconvenient," Hathaway said.

"Yeah, and now it's only a matter of time before Father figures out that you and I aren't engaged."

"Are you sure you can't explain—"

"There is no reasoning with Father. I've tried it. When Walter and I were first engaged, I told him how responsible Walter was, what an impressive scholar he was in school …"

"No, he wasn't."

"No one," continued Adrienne, "could have painted a more impressive picture of Walter. But it was no use. He wouldn't listen."

In the silence that followed, Ditters broke in with a new topic. He asked Hathaway about the dagger he was holding. Hathaway ran through the finer points, handing it over so his friend could give it a look-see.

Adrienne was strolling back and forth. Suddenly, a notion occurred to her, and she slapped Ditters on the back again, sending the Azure Star winging across the room.

"I've got an idea! We don't have to elope!"

"Huh?" asked Ditters and Hathaway.

"Father does whatever Randal tells him, right? Randal was the one who originally advised against Walter. He said he was inappropriate, not good enough for me. Don't you see? All you have to do, Walter, is blackmail Randal about this dagger Hathaway found him with, and he'll recommend you."

"I don't know …"

Hathaway concurred. Seemed dangerous to him.

"It's perfect," she insisted.

"Adrienne," Ditters began. "Dear," he said, "if I blackmail Finch, he's likely to throw me through a window."

"Pah!" replied Adrienne, exasperated.

"Really, dear, it's his temper."

"If you don't have the backbone to do it, Walter, then fine! What about you, Hathaway? Would you blackmail Randal for Walter?"

"Sorry, I have the same aversion to crashing through windows."

"Neither one of you has any backbone! We wouldn't be in this mess, Walter, if you had stood up to Otto and forced him to let us leave."

"Stood up to Otto?! He's about eight feet tall!"

Adrienne let it go at *Pah!* again.

"Listen you two," said Hathaway, "you need to elope. Forget these stratagems. You can't elope until the chief takes off the locks, right? Well then, all we have to do is solve the crime wave at the mansion. Fortunately, I'm prepared to do just that."

"You?" asked Adrienne.

"Yes, me. At the moment, I have a delivery to make, but when I return, all will be revealed."

Adrienne looked unimpressed.

"Hide here until then." He turned to Mahrute. "Any idea where I can find Sir Roger at this hour?"

"I believe I heard Jackson mention Sir Roger was in his office."

"Thanks. While I'm gone, would you mind running a little errand? Check into the orchestra for me. See if you can round up the tuba player."

"I'll see what I can do," said Mahrute.

17 — Adrienne Throws a Jar

With the chief snooping around, Hathaway wanted to return the Azure Star to Sir Roger as soon as possible. Whether the one he'd found in Finch's room was counterfeit or not, at least Banbury would take it off his hands.

Reaching the office door, Hathaway knocked and proceeded in with a cheery hello. He would have gotten right to the point, but an obstacle presented itself. Sir Roger was already in conference with Chief Adwick.

After choking and gasping on his greeting, reflex took over, and Hathaway tossed the Azure Star out the window.

Sir Roger was the first to speak. "Mr. Hathaway. Always a pleasant surprise. Come in, come in."

Hathaway noticed the chief wearing a puzzled stare.

"Did you just throw something out the window, sir?" asked the officer.

Hathaway looked out the window. "Me? No. That window?"

"I thought I saw something fly out the window," the chief said to Sir Roger.

Hathaway raised his eyebrows in good cheer, as the chief stood by with a perplexed look. Things might have gotten a good deal thicker, but fortunately Jackson stepped in with a fax.

The chief read over the message. "Hot damn!" he said, snapping it in the air, and quickly excused himself.

Hathaway was still mulling over what possible news could have caused a dull man like Adwick to leave whistling a happy tune, but presently he came out of it. "Would you excuse me, Sir Roger? I need a breath of air. Back in a jiffy."

He found the Azure Star where he had flung it—on the moist grass. After he had retrieved it, he took a moment to wave to Sir Roger inside his office. As he stepped away from the window, he could see a man in a tuxedo jogging along the side of the mansion.

The tuba player! Hathaway dashed across the fog-covered lawn in pursuit.

The fleeing guest outdistanced him at first, but Hathaway was not a man to give in easily. He dug in, and at the turn where the greenhouse meets the mansion, he tackled him, knocking the intruder into a pile of clay pots.

Trying to suppress the need to say "Ha!" or "Ta-da!" or something to that effect, he looked down and realized he had accosted Kurt Richter once again. "I'm sorry, Maestro," he said, helping him to his feet. "I thought you were someone else."

"You surprised me, my friend. I, er, was just out for a walk."

Hathaway nodded approvingly. "Carry on. Don't mind me." Nibu stumbled off, dislodging some soil from his ear, and Hathaway made his way back to Sir Roger's office.

"I'm sorry about that, Sir Roger," he announced, realizing that he was speaking to an empty room. The tycoon had vanished.

Hathaway returned to his room. His audience had walked out on him there as well. He was beginning to get annoyed. After all, when a guy leaves two tense elopers in his bedchamber, he expects to find two tense elopers when he returns. He was about to continue his search elsewhere when he heard a sound from the wardrobe—a crunching noise this time. On a hunch, he went to the door.

He wouldn't have expected his wardrobe to have the sort of appeal that promotes return customers, but nonetheless, there they were, Adrienne and Ditters, back in the thick of it. The open jar of pickles explained the crunching noise.

"Is the coast clear, Hath?"

"I wasn't aware that it had become cloudy."

The couple emerged. Adrienne's demeanor had become sufficiently more disgruntled. Hathaway noticed this right off. Poor Ditters, however, lacking his brand of insight, was taken entirely off guard when his loving duck of a fiancée grabbed the pickle jar out of his hands and flung it through Hathaway's open window.

"Why did you do that?" asked Ditters.

"How can you eat pickles at a time like this?!"

"I just can. Why did you do that?" he demanded.

"Do you know, Walter, that if you put half the effort into the jobs my father gave you that you put into those rotten cucumbers, you'd be president of Banbury Enterprises by now."

"I really wanted to know how that batch turned out, Adrienne."

Adrienne huffed and spun around, and Hathaway decided now was the time to step in. "Ditters, Adrienne, the tension is building. I think we can all see that."

"If I have to climb into that closet one more time …" began Adrienne.

"What were you doing in there anyway?"

"Otto," said Ditters. "We couldn't let him see us together, or he'd tell Adrienne's father."

"What was Otto doing here?"

"I think he was searching your room."

"Of all the … him too? He must have been looking for the Colt. It's not important. I have a plan. Ah, Mahrute. I was about to enlighten the room with my plan."

"I am relieved that I made it back in time."

"What did you find out?"

"Your theory on the Bath Chamber Orchestra was quite correct, but unfortunately also quite late. The other members informed me that the man purporting to be the tuba player's 'replacement' has vanished."

Before the room could comment on this, Lesley Darlington knocked and entered. "John, I—" At the sight of Adrienne, she backed off. "Sorry, I didn't realize you had company."

Hathaway rushed after her. "Lesley, come back."

"No, no, you're with your fiancée."

Adrienne stuck her oar in. "We're not really engaged."

"What?"

Hathaway pulled Lesley in. "She's right. I have been trying to explain all day. It's a farce."

* * * *

For the next fifteen minutes, Hathaway pieced together the setup. Lesley, a quick study, understood immediately, even though Hathaway got confused at one point in the retelling, and for a second it sounded as if Sir Roger was engaged to Chief Adwick.

"I'm sorry, John. I should have listened to you before."

They were in the kitchen now, lit by the lamps connected to the backup generator. Hathaway and Lesley sat close together at a small table by the pantry. Mahrute made a pot of tea on the gas stove in the background,.

"The only woman I have any interest in is you, Lesley."

"I feel the same way about you."

Hathaway wondered if Lesley was calling him a woman, but let it go. "What about Warren?"

"Are you jealous?"

"Of Warren?"

"You needn't be, believe me. I mean, Warren's strong, handsome, impressive …"

"Yes, yes—"

"But you're those things too. And more. The more is the part that matters. I guess I let Harold—or, that is, Warren—hang around me because I liked the attention. We were playing games, him pretending to be Harold Konig and me pretending to be Brittany Landers. When I thought you were engaged to Adrienne, I tried to convince myself that he meant more to me. But he doesn't. I'm sorry I was so thick."

"No, I was thick."

"No, me."

"No, me."

During this lovable cross-talk act, the butler joined them.

Hathaway welcomed him. "It's good you arrived, Jackson. I wanted to ask you: That message you gave to Adwick, what did it say?"

Jackson stiffened. "I have no idea, Mr. Hathaway."

"Come on, Jackson. You read it, didn't you?"

"It was not addressed to me, sir."

"Jackson!"

"I might have glanced at it. If I recall correctly, it read: 'The woman posing as Brittany Landers at Rangeley is an impostor.' The words were scrawled below a photo from a newspaper depicting the young lady. The fax came from the police station."

Hathaway and Lesley stood in unison. "The chief is onto you!" he exclaimed.

Jackson interrupted. "Actually, sir, soon after receiving the fax, Chief Adwick also put a call into Congressman Hathaway."

"Uncle George?"

"I happened to be listening on the other line. Congressman Hathaway told the chief that he had no nephew. His exact words were: 'Don't listen to that idiot. He's no nephew of mine.' "

Hathaway slapped his forehead. "The old coot! Not you, Jackson. Uncle George is still ticked about how I treated Brittany Landers—the real Brittany Landers. Come on, Lesley, Mahrute; let's get out of here before the chief comes along. This way! What's that, Jackson? It's this way? Thanks!"

The trio rushed upstairs. They had come to the corridor leading to Hathaway's room when Hathaway suddenly leapt back, causing the rest of the regiment to spill about behind him.

"What is it, John?"

"The chief. The bastard just went into my room! Quick, back the other way," he said, skidding to a halt again. "Oh jeez, I forgot about Ditters!"

From behind the door, they heard a battle cry, followed by the sound of a body hitting the floor. They burst in to see Ditters standing over the body, the recently re-dented tuba slung over his shoulder.

"Hey guys, I think I nabbed that marauder. He was skulking through the door, and I beaned him with this. Hey, why are you all looking at me like that?"

He turned back to view his handiwork and gasped the gasp of a man who has just coldcocked the chief of the Baccup police.

18 — Ditters Nabs an Intruder

Ditters had yet to find speech when they stepped full in the room, and even then, not until Hathaway had carefully wrenched the tuba from his astonished grip.

"But he's supposed to be the marauder!" he managed to blurt out, while Mahrute knelt down to examine the khaki blob. "I thought he was the marauder. He had his back to me, and it was dark, and he looked different. He had his trench on, Hath; he didn't have his trench on before. How was I to know he wasn't the marauder? This is going to piss him off, isn't it?"

"It's hard to say."

"He looks irritated, doesn't he? Does he look irritated to you?"

Hathaway was about to say that a tuba to the base of the skull seldom pleases even the most amiable, when Mahrute spoke.

"He's not dead" was his inspirational pronouncement.

Hathaway put his arm around his friend's shoulder. "See, Ditters, things are looking up."

Ditters looked less than cheered.

"What's this? An accident?" The question came from Otto, a new addition.

"Otto! Accident? No, nothing too extraordinary," said Hathaway. "Ditters here just mistook the chief's head for a large moth and gave it a quick swat with his tuba. Mistake anyone could make."

"I thought the chief would come here," said Otto, indifferent to any explanations. If it had been Sir Roger's head Ditters had swatted, Otto might have objected. Chief Adwick's head did not interest him. "He said he was looking for you. You and Miss Landers. He said he was going to put you both under arrest."

"Arrest? For what?"

"He didn't say."

"Mahrute, what are we going to do?"

The bodyguard's bodyguard stood. "It does appear that things have gotten complex. Fortunately, the chief is not an issue for the moment."

He nodded toward the floorboards. Hathaway got the point.

"Suppose that does put a kink in his plans for raiding the mansion … Say, Ditters, where's Adrienne?"

"Who?" asked the tuba samurai, still peering down at the ruffled officer.

"Adrienne. Your fiancée."

"Oh right, Adrienne. She left."

"She left?"

"She left. You know how girls are. She got fed up waiting around and decided to do something about it. She went to chew the fat with Finch. She said she was going to demand that he talk to Sir Roger about the engagement on my behalf."

"What about me?"

"I think she's going to tell him you're a lout. You know, to get his sympathy. Oh, and she'll probably mention Lesley. She'll say that you were seeing Lesley behind her back, that sort of thing. She wants Finch mad."

Hathaway spent only a few seconds expressing his dismay, feeling that a crazed dash through the halls was of the utmost urgency. It only took him a minute to reach Finch's room, mostly due to the fact that he hurdled the furniture the whole way and only stopped for a quick apology when he spilled headlong into Jackson. When he finally got there and burst through the door, he was so out of breath that he could only stand there gasping for oxygen and gaping at the pair of them.

Adrienne was standing at a distance from Finch, obviously in the middle of a discussion of some sort. From the look on the man's face, he was far from tickled with the young woman's most recent point. "Hathaway!"

"Finch."

"Hathaway!"

"Finch, I can explain … if you just … if you just …" He paused for more air. "If you just let me explain," he said.

"Hathaway! I'm going to tear you limb from limb."

Faced with this onslaught, Hathaway sprang over the bed. Adrienne was standing there.

"Is this any way to treat your future husband's oldest pal?" he asked her. "Is this how you repay me?" he wondered, sidestepping a charging Finch and scooting around a chair.

Adrienne endeavored to explain. "Don't you see?" she whispered. "Knowing you were no good for me, Finch would have to recommend Walter. It's simple."

"Simple? Simple! He'll kill me!"

"Maybe so, but that will make Walter look all the more appealing."

Hathaway hardly had time to shudder at the woman's coolness, before he had other things to attend to, namely dodging Finch and launching from the room.

He had made it all the way to a small study when Finch grabbed him by the back of the neck and shoved him up against the wall. "Got you, Hathaway. No slipping away this time."

"Finch," Hathaway choked. "Finch, you can't let your temper get the best of you."

"Why not?

"Why not? You just can't; that's all."

"Well, I'm going to. How do you like that? I'm going to deal with you the way I should have in school. To think a girl as wonderful as Adrienne Banbury could have had any interest in you. You! And then you cheat on her with this Landers girl and who knows who else."

"What about Lady Banbury?"

"You were with Lady Banbury too!"

"No, no, no! I mean, what would she think about all this. I'm a guest, Finch. What will she say if she learns you have beaten me into the floorboards?"

"She won't have to say anything if I hide the body well enough."

"Finch—I'm not sure you're aware of it, Finch, but you're closing your grip around my throat. Are you forgetting that I saw you with the dagger from Sir Roger's collection? I could tell Sir Roger."

"Who's he going to believe? Me, his assistant, or you, the man who cheated on his daughter?"

Hathaway felt he had a point there.

"Say, Hathaway, are you in here?"

It was Warren. Even with his arm in a sling, his presence did not fail to intimidate Finch. It didn't exactly motivate him to remove his mitt from Hathaway's throat, but it definitely made him think twice about giving Hathaway a sharp jab in the eye with him still there.

Warren stepped over to them. "I've been looking all over for you, Hathaway. Do you have any idea where the doctor got to? I'm supposed to have another painkiller, and I can't find her anywhere. She's not here, I see. Thanks anyway."

"Warren!" It was too late. The man had left.

Finch turned back to Hathaway. He pulled back his fist only to be interrupted again. "Who the hell are you?" he asked.

"I am Mahrute."

"Well, piss off! I'm trying to beat Hathaway here black and blue."

"I'm afraid I cannot allow you to do that."

"Oh yeah?" said Finch.

"Yes."

"Oh yeah? And you're going to stop me?"

"If necessary."

Finch let go of Hathaway's collar. He looked Mahrute up and down with a snort. The idea that Mahrute was actually a master in hand-to-hand combat, and that these skills were well honed from his years as a security expert and before that as a member of Her Majesty's Secret Service, was not a thought that suggested itself to Finch. To the secretary's rude intellect, here was a harmless little duffer in a suit. Fortunately for the bully, the thought of brawling with the man seemed unjust, even to Finch. Grumbling under his breath, he stormed out.

Hathaway gasped his appreciation.

"You are most welcome," said Mahrute. "If you don't mind, I suggest we return to your room. We need to attend to the mishap with the chief."

Hathaway agreed. "You know, I don't know if you've noticed, but the Dittersdorf wave of destruction is really beginning to mount up."

"Sir?"

"Don't get me wrong; he's one of my closest friends. But after fracturing something in the chief not once but twice, and after winging the butler Jackson with a bullet from the Colt, I expect to find, having left him for a good five minutes, that Ditters has somehow managed to run the cook through with an aboriginal spear."

Fortunately, the cook must have been safely ensconced in the wine cellar in their absence and out of Ditters' reach, for when they got back to the room, the body count hadn't changed.

"The chief's still out like a light, I see," said Hathaway.

"Well!" announced Adrienne, coming in behind them. "Trying to deal with Finch was a waste of time. Do you know what he said to me? He said he has no intention of recommending Walter to Father. He had the nerve to say that Walter was not the man for me."

Lesley, stepping forward, tried to interject something.

Hathaway caressed her shoulder. "Half a second, honey."

"John, I think you should see this ..." She pulled him out into the hall and spun him around to face two uniformed officers. One of them advanced.

"Deputy Morrison, sir. This is Deputy Thomas."

"Deputies! Good Lord, you must be here for Chief Adwick?"

"As a matter of fact, we are," answered the second deputy. "The bridge is all repaired." The officer paused suspiciously. "Is something wrong?"

"Huh? Oh no, no. Not a thing, not a thing."

"Have you seen him?"

"Who?"

"The chief."

"The chief? As in Adwick? Me? Gosh, no. You, Lesley?"

"Me?" answered Lesley. "No, no, I haven't seen him. My goodness, I don't know when I saw him last. Been ages. John?"

"Huh? Oh yeah, ages. Too long, really. I was just saying before you got here—that chief, where has he been keeping himself?—"

"Hathaway," said Adrienne, coming out into the hall, "do you want me to tell you what Finch said or not?"

"Now's not a good time, Adrienne."

"He said he was going to be sure to tell Father what an imbecile you are, but he'd be damned if he's going to recommend that Dittersdorf worm. Those were his words. He said I could do better. He said he couldn't advise it, the jerk. And after all the trouble I went through getting his sympathy for my engagement to you. I should have blackmailed him."

"Johnny," a voice said behind them, making Hathaway jump until he realized it was only Otto. "The chief … Oh, hello. Deputies?"

"John Hathaway!" Adrienne shouted, causing him to spin around again. "What are you going to do about this mess with Walter and me?"

"*Me?*" asked Hathaway. "You're the one—"

"Excuse me," said yet another voice behind him. "Excuse me, Mr. Hathaway …"

"Sir Roger!"

"Yes," replied the tycoon, standing by draped in his bathrobe. "Say, my good fellow, I was looking for that Konig chap. Have you seen him?"

At that moment, Ditters came out into the hall. "Say, Hath, are you coming back … Yikes!" he exclaimed, seeing the deputies. Without missing a beat, he dove back into the room.

"Who was that?" asked a deputy.

"Huh?" said Hathaway.

"Who was that?" repeated the other deputy.

"Huh?"

"Walter Dittersdorf," offered Adrienne. "He works for Father." Banbury rolled his eyes.

"He looked familiar," said one of the two deputies.

"He has that kind of face," Hathaway explained. "Kind of a shy guy."

The deputies looked perplexed.

"Oh, Otto," said Adrienne, noticing the bodyguard, "that reminds me. Mother was looking for Kurt Richter. It seems he's missing."

Otto's eyes lit with fire. "Missing! Aha!"

"I don't know if it warrants an 'aha,' Otto. Just go look for him, would you? We can't have guests disappearing on us. It looks bad."

Hathaway was all for it. "Yes, Otto, take the deputies. Perhaps you'll run into the chief on the way."

"But the chief is in … yes, right. This way, gentlemen."

That left just Adrienne, Lesley and Sir Roger clustered around Hathaway. Hathaway addressed them. "Where was I? Oh, Sir Roger. Half a second," he said, and turning, almost collided with Lesley.

"John, Ditters wanted me to ask if the coast is clear."

"What coast?" asked Sir Roger. "Clear of what?"

"Tell him they're gone," said Hathaway.

"Say, John," Lesley remarked, over the sound of Sir Roger asking "Who's gone?" "John, shall we try to move the body?"

"Body? What body?" The question also came from Sir Roger.

Ditters peered out again. "Hath, are you sure they're gone?"

"Yes!"

"Finally. Good evening, Sir Roger."

"Dipperdorp," replied Banbury coolly.

Ditters looked to be calming down, and Hathaway turned to attend to whatever it was he was attending to when another unwanted addition boomed "Sir Roger!" behind Banbury, causing him to jump a foot in the air and come down holding his chest.

"Randal! Don't sneak up on me like that!"

"Sir Roger, I have something to tell you about your daughter's engagement."

"Not now, Randal, not now."

"Father," said Adrienne, springing into action, "before Randal speaks, there is something I want to tell you about Randal and your collection."

"About me?" asked Finch.

"Yes, about you!" she said.

"But I don't want to hear about anyone from anyone," whined Sir Roger.

Just to fill out the party, Warren now joined them. "Hathaway, I can't find the doctor anywhere, and my arm's sore."

Hathaway told him to put some ice on it. He squeezed past, and Sir Roger looked up.

"I say, Mr. Konig. I was looking for you. My word, what happened to your arm?"

"What, the sling? Someone tried to knock me off."

"That would explain it." He spotted Jackson in the back of the crowd. "Jackson, do you have that cocoa I asked for? Good, bring it over here. Now, then, Mr. Konig, you have the item I had you appraise?"

"Actually, I'm holding on to it," Hathaway interceded.

"Splendid, splendid. May I have it?" Sir Roger frowned as the butler slid by them. "Jackson, I meant to ask you before. What's that around your arm? It looks like the one Mr. Konig is wearing."

"It is only a sling, sir."

"A sling? Why a sling? Why does everyone have slings?"

"It was from an accident, sir."

"Accident? What accident?"

"It is what is called a 'flesh wound.' "

"Flesh wound? Flesh wound. You and Mr. Konig—my word, the conductor!"

The crowd spun around.

All the excitement was in reference to the entrance of Nibu alias Kurt Richter, who appeared to be in a stupor of some sort. He was being dragged in by the deputies and Otto.

"We found him on the back lawn. Someone must have hit him with something. From the looks of it, it might have been a jar of some sort."

Ditters, who had been leaning amiably against the doorframe up until this point, sprang around and crashed into Jackson with the tea service. The word "jar" touched off something in Adrienne, too, who at the end of the hall drew herself up.

"A jar?" Hathaway said.

"Yes, a jar of pickles, apparently."

"Good God!" exclaimed Ditters, and Adrienne's and Hathaway's sentiments were with him.

At this point, Hathaway managed to slip away, escaping the noisy confusion of Adrienne and Finch arguing with Sir Roger, Nibu (reliving the trauma) moaning something about "it appeared from out of the sky," and Jackson reassembling a silver tea service from memory. As he pulled himself from the scene, he could also hear Warren asking him to pick up some painkillers while he was out, and Sir Roger calling after him about the item they had discussed and whether he could have it, if it wasn't too much bother.

* * * *

The peace and tranquility of the wing of the mansion that housed the kitchen was a welcome change to the hubbub of the last few minutes.

On the way, Hathaway had time to think.

Things, it occurred to him, were beginning to unravel. He tried to maintain the proper attitude. After all, all he had to do was figure out the story behind the Azure Star, pick up some painkillers for the world's best bodyguard and grab some ice for the conductor's head. Then he would simply need to find a place to stow the chief's body, unlock the garage so Adrienne and Ditters could elope, solve the mystery of the tuxedo-wearing guest and at some point work things out with his uncle.

And, hell, it was early yet.

Sometimes, though, things fall into place. Arriving at the kitchen for the ice, he came along Item Six from his list.

There, poring through a closet for an umbrella, was Barnet. Although Rangeley Manor's freelance burglar had tendered his resignation and left to walk back to town, he had returned when the storm started getting heavy.

Hathaway wasted no time. Bounding up on the damp figure, he pushed him inside the closet and locked him in by slipping a chair under the doorknob. He had seen that in a movie once.

With a smile of satisfaction, he dashed back to his room.

That's gratitude for you, though, for as he rounded the corner, he couldn't help noticing that the halls were bare. He was happy to see there were at least a few diehards left in his room. Lesley, Mahrute and Ditters. Adrienne—whom he could have done without. And, of course, the chief, who seemed to have been out cold for what amounted to no small length of time now. Hathaway hesitated to ask if someone had given him another sharp whack while they were waiting.

Mahrute set Hathaway's mind at ease. "The chief has been as such for a half an hour now."

"Are you sure he's not dead?"

"Quite sure. He has made groaning noises for the past few minutes and even mumbled a request for backup and something to the effect of 'officer down'…"

"Ah. Anyway, Adrienne, Ditters," he said, turning to the couple, "do you recall my saying I had everything under control, my saying I had this case all wrapped up?" Adrienne glared; Ditters blinked. "I am now prepared to make good on it." Adrienne rolled her eyes, and Ditters looked to Mahrute. "Right," Hathaway concluded. "Meet me downstairs, and I'll explain everything."

"What about the deputies?" asked Ditters.

"Better wear a disguise." Ditters and Adrienne left, neither far from sullen, and Hathaway glanced back at Mahrute. "About time we sealed up this caper, huh?"

"Yes, if I may—"

"Not right now, Mahrute; the mind is racing. Where is everybody?"

"When they noticed you had gone, they all retired for the evening. You appear to have been the glue that held the gathering together."

"Well, wake them up, and bring them all down to the drawing room."

"I'm not certain the drawing room would accommodate every guest on the premises. Perhaps the library will do?"

"That's fine," Hathaway remarked. "Oh. And see if you can scrape me up a pipe and a smoking jacket, will you?"

Part Five

19 — Master Sleuth Reveals All

Despite any assumptions to the contrary, not many inhabitants of a stately mansion are at their most glamorous at one thirty in the morning. Looking over the lot of them, assembled reluctantly in the library, Hathaway understood firsthand what it meant when they said the crowd turned ugly. There were notable exceptions, of course: Lesley, attractively draped in a silken robe, the sort of girl who rolls out of bed ready for fashion-model work. And Lady Banbury, looking as collected as ever. Though one suspected L. Banbury could remain coifed and unrattled in a hurricane. As for the rest, disheveled and harassed seemed to cover it.

Heading the mob of disgruntled guests was Finch, wearing an offensive pair of yellow pajamas, rendered all the more offensive because they had to see Finch wearing them. Hathaway didn't miss the look in his eye, the kind of look one imagines a bear would give you if you wandered upon its sleeping cave in the dead of winter and gave it a swift kick in the ribs.

Fortunately, the large supply of witnesses kept any mauling plans Finch might have had in check.

Starting clockwise, there was also Sir Roger Banbury, asleep on the sofa. Standing over him was Otto Pincher, looking bright eyed despite the time. To his left was Adrienne, tapping her foot. Ditters was next to her. Hathaway took him aside.

"Ditters, you're not wearing a disguise."

"Yes, and where in the hell did you expect me to come up with one? Do you think I have false mustaches lying around my room or something?"

Hathaway mused on this. Had he known Nibu's methods, he might have suggested Ditters pop up and borrow something from his satchel. "No, I suppose not. One just takes these things for granted. Not to worry, though, I don't think the chief is going to join us, somehow."

"Oh yeah? Why's that?"

"Quick thinking on my part. I locked him in my room before I came down. Should he awake, he'll soon wish he brought a magazine, for proceeding beyond the bounds of my room will not be an option."

Ditters still looked uneasy. He nodded uncertainly, mentioning that on the first glimpse of a trench coat, he was for the great open spaces. Hathaway said not to worry; he had a plan.

He returned to the front of the room. Rounding out the crowd, on the other side of the sofa was Lesley. Next to her was Nibu, icepack applied to the brow. Lady Banbury was in the chair by the window, Jackson standing stiffly by her side. Over in the corner was Warren, who would have looked less foggy if he hadn't taken a good knock on the head trying to lean against a bookcase. (Apparently, he had forgotten that the arm needed for the procedure was currently in a sling.)

Mahrute and the deputies stood quietly behind Hathaway.

"Mr. Hathaway, is it?" said one of the deputies. "Mr. Hathaway, I'm not sure we should do all this without the chief." A young officer, he obviously adhered to a definite hierarchy.

Hathaway argued against it. "Do all what? What are we doing that requires the chief?"

"All this. You say you have the entire case worked out? According to what the chief told us on the phone, that would include attempted murder, grand theft, petty theft, assault, battery and threatening the life of a knight."

"Yes," replied Hathaway, "that's about the size of it."

"But—"

"Listen, Deputy Morrison—"

"He's Morrison. I'm Thomas."

"Oh. Thomas, then. I know the chief would like to be here, but he's obviously otherwise engaged. I'm sure he would want you,

Thomas, to head the case in his absence. I mean, he wouldn't have made you two deputies if he didn't have faith in your abilities."

"We're his nephews."

"Oh. Nephews, huh? There you are, then. You aren't only going to do a chief a good turn by taking over this case, but an uncle as well. You're probably his favorite nephews, am I right? I know from personal experience the tight bond between nephew and uncle. Imagine how proud he will be when he finds out you wrapped up this case yourselves."

"It may keep him from threatening to fire us every other week."

"That's the spirit."

The deputy strolled away, and Hathaway began.

"Hello," he said, turning to the crowd, "I suspect you're all wondering why I brought you here today …"

At this point, a disgruntled member of the audience—Adrienne—winged a volume of Charles Dickens at him and asked him to cut out the Hercule Poirot stuff.

"As I was saying," he went on, "I brought you here today, or rather tonight, to clear up the incidents around the mansion. Namely, these incidents include the gunfight in the museum earlier today; the theft of an antique, or rather several antiques; and the attack on Warren, I mean Harold." Hathaway paused. The tough part here was going to be keeping track of who was who.

"What about thc conductor?" called out Lady Banbury.

Hathaway stumbled. "The … what? Oh yes, someone beaned the conductor," he said, watching Adrienne. "Sorry, I didn't mean to exclude you, Conductor Richter. Oh, and I should mention the death threat Sir Roger got."

Presently there came a sound from the audience akin to an engine misfiring, and a second later Sir Roger snorted awake. "Gug, I say, where am I? Who are all these people, Mr. Hathaway?"

"Guests, Sir Roger. I asked everyone to join me so I can clear up the crime wave at Rangeley Manor."

"Oh yes. Quite. You think now is the time, my boy?"

"Now's the perfect time, Sir Roger. Now then. Let us begin with this." Pausing dramatically, Hathaway produced the Azure Star from his pocket.

Sir Roger and Finch cringed, and Lady Banbury arched an eyebrow.

"This is the antique someone stole out of Sir Roger's museum," Hathaway told them.

Sir Roger brightened. "Oh, I already had that one. It's a counterfeit."

Nibu dropped his pack of ice.

Hathaway dropped the Star. "This one is the counterfeit?" he asked.

"You didn't know that?" snapped Adrienne.

"No … but be that as it may, someone went to a lot of trouble to get this."

Nibu froze.

"How do you know?" asked Adrienne.

"I know because I have the suspect in custody," said Hathaway.

Upon this statement, a hush didn't exactly fall over the crowd, since they were already pretty quiet to begin with, but they definitely regarded Hathaway with interest.

He stepped over to a window and opened it. The sound of the rain pouring down did wonders to calm his nerves.

"When you say you have a suspect in custody, Mr. Hathaway," said Lady Banbury, "what exactly do you mean?"

"I mean I've locked up the guy responsible for all this."

"You believe this crime wave, as you put it, was the work of one man?"

"Oh yes. Right now, twiddling his thumbs in the kitchen, there sits a complex criminal. An assassin, a thief and, yes, a snappy dresser."

The crowd looked uncertain.

"Why don't we bring him in? Otto, would you mind fetching him from the kitchen? He'll be the guy dressed as an orchestra member pounding away at the pantry door."

Otto left, and Hathaway decided to elaborate. "You see, ladies and gentlemen, it was all about greed."

"What was, Mr. Hathaway?"

"The motive, Lady Banbury."

"What motive?" asked Adrienne, and he began to think if Hercule Poirot had been here, he would have plunked this member of the audience on the end of her nose with his walking stick.

"The motive, dear Adrienne, for all the crimes. Surely you do not wish me to list them for you again?"

"No, once was enough."

"Good. The motive, you see, was greed. It was all about this antique."

"I thought you said it was about greed?"

"I did. Now, I'm elaborating and saying it's about an antique. The desire to procure the object was strong enough that the criminal was willing to commit murder."

"So what you are saying, Mr. Hathaway—" interjected Lady Banbury, perpetuating the back-and-forth routine her daughter had begun. Hathaway could see them playing good cop/bad cop in a snap. "What you are saying is the culprit behind the theft of this antique is the same culprit behind the attack on Mr. Konig and all those present in my husband's museum earlier this afternoon?"

"Yes."

"You claim the antique was the motive for the unspeakable acts of violence around the mansion?"

"That's right."

"But how can that be if this is a counterfeit?"

"I was getting to that."

"But how can any one antique be the singular motive for the attack in the museum and on Mr. Konig? He didn't have the antique."

"In a way he did."

Lady Banbury set down her teacup abruptly. "How can that be?"

The thread of his monologue thoroughly snarled by now, Hathaway observed to himself that, had he known any master sleuths, he would have advised them to steer clear of Rangeley Manor. The lady of the house, he would have told them, will never give you a minute's rest. As soon as you think you have solved the mystery of the bludgeoned earl in the billiard room and have retired to bed on a job well done, you'll get a nudge in the middle of the night, and it'll be Lady Margaret Banbury asking you to clarify your point about the curious footprints of chalk dust found in the vicinity of the body. The hostess who graciously yielded the floor to the resident investigator and allowed him to solve the string of attempted homicides around the mansion undisturbed was the hostess of the past, Hathaway guessed.

Before he could continue, he noticed Otto Pincher standing at the entryway. "Otto. What kept you? Say, where's the thief?"

"I'm sorry, Johnny. I searched the kitchen, and I couldn't find anything."

It is a pretty cheesy moment for a detective when his suspect runs out on him. Without physical evidence, the audience gets unruly.

"You couldn't find anybody?" Hathaway asked, and Otto shook his head. "You're sure? Small guy?"

"Nobody was there, Johnny."

"But—but, I locked the door. How'd the bastard manage to get out?" Hathaway was about to voice his astonishment further, perhaps suggesting that some well-meaning but hopelessly misguided citizen had come along and given the guy premature parole, but before he could do any suggesting of the sort, a "Hey!" sounded from offstage.

The *Hey!* was the *Hey!* of Chief Adwick. (Ditters gasped and dove behind the couch.) The officer kept his focus on the speaker. "Hold it right there, Mr. Hathaway."

"Chief! This is a surprise! Your deputies were pretty worked up looking for you. Probably thought you fell down a mine shaft or something. Just goes to show you that you should never jump to conclusions. Did you say hold it right there?"

"I did."

"Something we need to discuss?"

"Just your arrest, sir."

"My arrest? Surely you got the wrong guy—"

"Oh no, I've got the right one. You coldcocked me, sir, and locked me in your room."

"I … uh …" said Hathaway, stumbling a bit over the words. He looked to the crowd, who had taken a sudden interest in the proceedings. "I mean to say, locked you in my room, of all the … Say! How'd you get out?"

"It wasn't easy with this sling," said the chief, stepping inside the room and seizing Hathaway by the arm, "but I managed to climb down your balcony. I then scrambled around the house until I found you all here. Never thought of that, did you, Mr. Hathaway? Never thought I'd use the balcony?"

Actually, Hathaway hadn't. With all his escapades jumping from balcony to balcony this weekend, it never even occurred to him.

"I am going to read you your rights now, sir. Besides assaulting an officer of the law and resisting arrest, I am charging you with attempted grand theft, attempted murder, attempted fraud and suspicion of transporting stolen property across state lines." Hathaway gaped, and the chief turned to Lesley. "I am also arresting you, Miss Darlington, on the same charges."

"Me!" exclaimed Lesley, standing.

"Yes, miss."

Lady Banbury stood as well. "You called her Miss Darlington."

"Yes, ma'am. This is not Brittany Landers. I found her passport in her room. Her name is Lesley Darlington."

"Oh dear," exclaimed the hostess.

"I have every reason to believe that you and Mr. Hathaway are known felons," said the chief, "traveling under aliases. You are here, from the best I can tell, to assassinate Sir Roger and loot his museum."

Hathaway tried to remain calm. He told the chief, calmly, that he had it all wrong. "You see, there is this thief in a tuxedo loose in the mansion. In fact, you wouldn't happen to have unlocked the kitchen pantry in your travels—"

"Hathaway!" It was Finch asserting himself. "Not only did you cheat on Adrienne Banbury, but you're also a thief," he snarled, wrenching Hathaway free from the chief's grip.

"Finch," Hathaway gurgled, "remember what I said about jumping to conclusions ..."

"You've disrupted this fine family long enough. I'm going to tear out your gizzard."

Before that moment, Hathaway had never really considered whether he had a gizzard or not, gizzards not being a subject he would have given too much hefty thought to normally. Be that as it may, if he did have a gizzard, or even if he was blessed with an extra gizzard or two, he'd rather not have any of them torn out by Finch in mixed company.

"Hold on now, Mr. Finch," instructed the chief. "There'll be none of that until he's had a fair trial." He re-seized his left arm.

"You can give him a fair trial without a gizzard," said Finch, nearly tearing the right arm out of its socket.

"Hey!"

"No," asserted Adwick. "And you'd do best not to interfere with police business."

"Screw your police business!"

"I won't have my suspects lynched, Mr. Finch. This is a matter concerning the security of Sir Roger."

"Screw the security of Sir Roger!"

"I have to question Mr. Hathaway."

"Question him without a gizzard!"

"I have to determine if he was meaning to go through with his threat on Sir Roger."

"What threat?" asked Finch, pausing only briefly from the business of sloshing Hathaway back and forth.

"What threat?" Hathaway agreed.

"Didn't I mention those? Add it to the list, Thomas. All evidence points to Mr. Hathaway concerning that death threat you told me about, Sir Roger."

Lady Banbury gasped.

"Death threat!" Hathaway exclaimed. "I didn't threaten Sir Roger."

"Oh, but I think you did," said the chief. "I've had you under round-the-clock surveillance, Mr. Hathaway, and you've been seen going into Sir Roger's office on more than one occasion. You see, folks, I think Mr. Hathaway, or whoever he is, is the ringleader of a much larger crime syndicate with which Miss Darlington, alias Miss Landers, and countless other thugs are affiliated. I believe their plan began simple enough. Steal a priceless art piece and coerce Sir Roger into buying it. They threatened his life to intimidate him. When he balked, they decided to make good on their threats. And, I can only assume, having completed this contemptible deed, they would have proceeded to plunder his museum like the ruthless thieves that they are."

"But that's ridiculous," said Hathaway.

"I say, Chief," interjected Sir Roger, and Hathaway was happy to see that he was still with them, "you're not saying Mr. Hathaway was planning to rob my museum?"

"That is precisely what I am saying, Mr. Banbury. He and Miss Darlington."

"Who's Miss Darlington?"

"I am," answered Lesley.

"Oh yes. Splendid. Well, I think you're wrong about Mr. Hathaway. He wasn't stealing anything from me; he was bringing me something."

"No doubt something he was planning to sell to you at an inflated return."

"I didn't think so. You weren't planning to sell it to me at an inflated return, were you, Mr. Hathaway?"

"No!"

"You see, Chief, Mr. Hathaway wasn't planning to sell me the parcel at an inflated return."

"Oh, but he was."

Hathaway realized that the officer had stumbled upon a snag. "Chief Adwick, if Lesley and I were planning to sell this stolen art piece, wouldn't one of us have it with us?"

"Yeah, you would. You're holding it right now."

"This?" he asked, holding up the dagger. "This came out of Sir Roger's museum."

"Aha! So you were the thief in the shadows! Add it to the list, Morrison."

The deputy jotted it down. Hathaway gave it another try:

"Chief, I was the one getting shot at."

"Yes, but your girlfriend had slipped away."

Lesley gasped.

Hathaway choked. "But that's absurd. I mean, if she shot at us then where's the gun? You have no evidence."

"But I do."

"But you don't."

"But I do. I found this!" A moment of fidgeting in his trench coat pockets, and the chief dramatically whipped out the elusive Colt.

"Where'd you get that?!"

"Your room, Mr. Hathaway."

"Oh, Hathaway," chimed in Warren, "I forgot to tell you. I put that in your room. I found it in the hall after I was attacked. The assassin dropped it."

Nibu sat quietly, enjoying this thoroughly.

"I knew you wanted it," said Warren, "so I left it on your bed."

Hathaway sighed. The rest of the audience whispered observations to one another.

"That looks like a gun from the antique shop in town," said Officer Morrison. "In fact, it looks like the same make and model of one that was recently stolen from there."

"I suspect it is the same gun," said the chief.

"Say," spoke up Sir Roger, "may I see that?"

The chief blinked at the tycoon. "It's evidence, sir."

Sir Roger clucked impatiently, and the chief yielded. "I also found this in your room, Mr. Hathaway," he said, pulling out another Azure Star loosely wrapped in brown paper.

"What the …" Hathaway's head was spinning.

"Excuse me, sir," Jackson said quietly. "I believe I can explain. That parcel came from Harold Konig. I figured he had sent it to himself for some reason, perhaps to avoid traveling with it, so for safekeeping I put it in his room. I don't know how it wound up in your quarters."

Hathaway turned to Warren. It sickened him to think that it had been in the bodyguard's room the whole time.

Warren frowned. "Oh yeah, I forgot to mention that. I found that in my room a couple hours ago. I thought it looked suspicious, so I put it in your room, Hathaway."

Hathaway shook his head and sighed.

The witnesses for the prosecution having said their bit, the chief went on, "I think everything's coming together here, Mr. Hathaway. You sent the death threat to intimidate Sir Roger into not going to the police. Then, seeing your plan fail, you attacked him in the museum. You attacked Mr. Konig, the art expert, perhaps because he was onto you—"

"I didn't attack Harold Konig!" Hathaway said. "Dammit, he's not even Harold Konig." Warren spilled a tray of drinks. "He's my bodyguard, Warren Kingsley."

Chief Adwick eyed the man, standing sheepishly in the back of the room. "Bodyguard, huh? Kingpins always travel with muscle, don't they?"

Otto stuck his oar in. "This is absurd. Johnny didn't do all of these things. He didn't send any death threats. And he didn't bludgeon the conductor."

"I wouldn't be so sure, Mr. Pincher. Bludgeon the conductor? Someone bludgeoned the conductor?"

"With a pickle jar."

"A pickle jar?" repeated the chief. "My word, the thief in the Travers Shop robbery left a pickle jar behind. We figured it was his calling card. But Mr. Hathaway wasn't the perp in that case," said the chief, and the former breathed a sigh of relief that John P. Hathaway was innocent of at least one crime against the citizenry of Maine. "Probably someone on his payroll, though. Short guy, apple cheeks. Now what's all this about coldcocking the conductor with a pickle jar?"

"A pickle jar?" Sir Roger remarked, looking up from the revolver. "That sounds like Dipperdorp to me."

In all the excitement, Ditters Dittersdorf had been trying to slip out of the room unnoticed. When the tycoon blurted this out, the pickleman was passing behind a floor lamp, and such was his agitation when he heard his name, or a close approximation thereof, that he jumped back and sent the lamp spronging apart.

The chief's glance fell on him. "You there!" he exclaimed. "You there! Now I recognize you. Those apple cheeks. The gun-shop robber, boys!"

"The one who broke your arm?"

"That's the one. Seize him! We'll get the whole gang before the night is done."

Ditters sprang over the sofa to avoid the lunge of Morrison, only to scramble into the path of Thomas. Lady Banbury was gasping again, and the crowd was on their feet.

Hathaway thought he'd better offer the voice of reason. "No," he said. "No, you see, it was an honest mistake. Ditters thought the pistol was pickles!"

It's funny the sort of thing that will make a room, pretty much agreed to be afire with chaos, freeze and ponder your remarks. When Hathaway said this, he was delighted to see that for once he had gotten the fickle crowd's attention.

"It's no good pleading insanity," said the chief. "It won't work."

And with that, the chaos erupted again. The only fortunate thing was, owing to some tricky footwork from Ditters, the chief was forced to enter the fold. In so doing, he left Hathaway unattended.

The prisoner backed off. He had hardly taken three steps when two hands grabbed him by the collar, and he heard Finch's voice growl, "Got you, Hathaway."

At times like these, Hathaway's first thought was to look to Mahrute, but for once the bodyguard's bodyguard had let him down. Instead of rushing to the side of his client's client, he appeared to be following the activities of the maestro Kurt Richter, which seemed a pretty irresponsible thing to do when a guy's in danger of having his gizzard torn out.

"Now, Finch, I know what you're thinking, and it's all wrong."

"Oh yeah?"

"You can't listen to the chief."

"No?"

"No, his perspective is distorted; comes from too many hours spent poring over mugshots, outlining corpses with chalk and asking suspects where they were on the night of the fifteenth. Makes a man cynical. Eventually, bitter pills like the chief start accusing men like myself of heading large crime syndicates. Natural progression, really."

"Is it?"

"Yes. But none of it's true."

"Oh yeah?"

"Not a word of it. True, things might not have worked out between me and Adrienne—not because I cheated on her with Lesley, but because Adrienne and I didn't see eye to eye on matters. As a matter of fact, I happen to have it on good authority that Adrienne thinks you're pretty special, Finch."

"Oh yeah?"

"Yeah. She told me so."

"Well, she told me I was a jerk."

"Ah. Well, you know how women are."

Hathaway had expected another *Oh yeah*, having given the guy his cue, but Finch opted not to go that route. He substituted the *Oh yeah* with his fist. He had just drawn it back when the chief returned to perform his constabulary duty.

"I said that was enough of that," he said, grabbing at Finch. The latter wasn't listening. He took a wild swing at Hathaway and struck the chief in the jaw.

The sight of Adwick staggering back and landing in an unconscious mound on the coffee table (poor guy, twice in one night) was enough to give the room pause.

Even Finch seemed to have forgotten the business of tearing out Hathaway's gizzard and was staring down at the remains with nothing short of chagrin.

One supposes that once you have been coshed with a tuba, your head hardens to the blows of the world. The crowd had hardly gathered around him before Adwick grumbled and came to. Mahrute and Otto helped him into a chair.

"Did somebody hit me?" he asked.

Chief Adwick was guessing how many fingers Otto was holding up when Mahrute took advantage of the silence and quietly cleared his throat. "Ladies and gentlemen, I believe I can explain everything."

Hathaway noticed that when Mahrute said it, everyone turned, ready to listen to him, unlike with Hathaway, whom they'd just as soon have thrown rotten vegetables at, had they thought ahead to slip any into their pajamas.

"I believe the answer rests in here," Mahrute said, holding up a small velvet case.

"Did somebody hit me?" asked Chief Adwick.

Mahrute opened the case.

"What is it?" asked someone from the crowd, as Mahrute placed the thing on a table, gleaming in the light of Ditters' broken lamp.

"I know what it is," boomed Banbury. "It's the Azure Star. The real one."

The new Azure Star (#4) rested next to Azure Star #3, the one from the museum. Mahrute placed Azure Star #2 next to it, the one Jackson had put in Hathaway's room.

"Finally, there is this one," said Mahrute. He removed another Star from his pocket, Azure Star #1 (the one Hathaway had brought), and rounded out the set.

Seeing the Azure Star in quadruplicate took Hathaway aback some at first. Of course, when it came to this *objet*, he never could appreciate what the big attraction was. "Mahrute, they're multiplying."

Nibu stood. He was feeling around his suit. "Where'd you get that?"

"I took the liberty of picking your pocket," said Mahrute.

Lady Banbury gaped. "You picked the conductor's pocket, Mr. Mahrute?"

"Not the conductor, Lady Banbury," Mahrute corrected, stepping across the room. Tearing off the false beard, he announced, "Nibu Nibudar."

20 — Master Sleuth Takes It in the Shorts

"Nibu!" said Hathaway with disgust.

"Who?" asked someone from the crowd again, obviously puzzled over recent developments. An audience, after all, likes to know the source of any ensuing suspense, and it tends to diminish the full wallop of any dramatic reveals if half of them missed what preceded the intermission.

"Nibu," he repeated, still disgusted, "the guy who tried to snuff out my life on the train."

"Oh," said the representative, but one could tell most of them still felt out of the loop.

"What is the meaning of this?" Lady Banbury cried. She was a hostess who resented having her guests held up to public ridicule.

"If you will pardon the presumption, Lady Banbury," said Mahrute, ever the diplomat, "I believe I can explain. This man, posing as Kurt Richter, is actually a known assassin."

"Oh. Continue, then," she agreed. Jackson refreshed her teacup.

Hathaway spoke again. "So Nibu followed us back here? You seem to know him, Mahrute?"

"I have never actually met Mr. Nibudar, but I am quite aware of his reputation."

Nibu stood glaring, rubbing his face.

"But what's his connection to the Azure Star?" Hathaway asked.

Mahrute tipped his head toward their antagonist. "Perhaps you would like to field that one, Mr. Nibudar?"

Nibu sneered. "I have retired from the assassin work," he explained. "I have become the high-profile thief. I learned of the Azure Star through one of my cases. Theodore Darlington."

"My brother!" Lesley squealed. "It was you who tried to kill him."

The audience really seemed boggled by this one. Even Hathaway, who felt he had a pretty good handle on the facts up until this point, admitted to being perplexed.

Lesley turned to the room. "My brother is Teddy Darlington. He works for the British Secret Service. The last time I saw him was a few weeks ago. He showed up at my house and told me that people were trying to kill him and that he was going to have to go into hiding for a while. You were the assassin sent to kill him?"

"Yes," Nibu replied, "my employer wanted him out of the way."

"Your employer?"

"Boris Pefferu."

Hathaway remembered the name from the article in Sir Roger's desk. "Boris Pefferu? He used to own the Azure Star."

"Yes, my friend, and young Darlington stole it."

"Teddy stole it?" asked Lesley.

"Actually," Mahrute added, "I believe he, too, had an employer. Theodore was working for Prince Dresdu, Boris Pefferu's rival."

"But I thought Boris Pefferu was dead." This was Sir Roger. "That's why I had no qualms about wanting his Azure Star for my collection."

Adrienne frowned. "Dresdu? Pefferu? What country is this anyway?"

"It is a former Soviet republic," said Mahrute. "The country is in turmoil. Pefferu's heirs and Prince Dresdu are vying for control."

"When Pefferu died," Nibu continued, "I decided to retrieve the Azure Star from young Teddy myself. Sort of freelance."

"You pushed Teddy through a window," said Lesley. "He broke his leg, you know?"

"I am sorry, miss."

"And all you wanted was this stupid dagger?"

"Yes, and your brother hid it well. I could not locate it. Nor could I find Theodore after that."

"I told you—he went into hiding. You'll never find him."

"Perhaps not. That is why I began to follow you, in case your brother gave you the Azure Star to keep."

"You broke into my house!"

"And trailed your activities until I learned that Congressman Hathaway had located the Azure Star."

"You started following me then?" Hathaway asked.

"Yes, my friend. I followed you all the way here." Nibu looked perplexed at the row of daggers on the table. "But now I see that there are four Azure Stars."

Mahrute had an explanation for that. "It would appear that when Sir Roger put out the word that he wanted the Azure Star, more than one found its way here. Mr. Hathaway brought the one his uncle had secured. Harold Konig sent a second one. The third, Sir Roger already owned. The fourth is mine."

Hathaway was stunned. "Yours, Mahrute?"

Mahrute answered with a nod.

"Well, which one is genuine?" wondered Sir Roger. "That's what I'd like to know."

Mahrute smiled. "They are all genuine, ladies and gentlemen."

Sir Roger goggled at the man. "But how is that possible? There is only one Azure Star."

"Yes, sir. It's a common misconception, but the Azure Star is not a dagger."

"It looks like a dagger to me."

Mahrute endeavored to clarify. "The Azure Star is actually a coat of arms, made up of five linked daggers. When linked at their handles, they appear to form a sun or star shape with five points."

"Five, Mahrute?" asked Hathaway.

"Yes. One is missing from our set here. Your brother, Miss Darlington, knew the only way he could win the will of the people, on the prince's behalf, was to secure the Azure Star from Boris Pefferu, whose family had stolen it centuries before."

"So that's why Teddy became an assistant to Pefferu? To help out the prince?"

"Yes, miss. As an assistant, Theodore could infiltrate the palace and find the Azure Star."

"But what's so important about the Azure Star?" Hathaway wanted to know.

"Since ancient times," said Mahrute, "the Azure Star has been a symbol of leadership in that country. Originally, an ancient king brought his knights together, four accomplished warriors each representing a corner of the kingdom. They connected their weapons with the king's and presented the shield to the country as a sign of peace. Legend had it that the one who has the Azure Star will rule."

Hathaway had it all pegged. "So, Nibu, you stole it because you wanted to rule?"

"No, my friend. I wanted it for the money. The gems."

"Then, sir," Mahrute interjected, "you have done all this for nothing. The Azure Star never had any gems of any value, which is part of the reason these pieces were appraised as counterfeits. The decorations are common stones, not valuable gems as some historians believe. The Star has always held nothing more than symbolic value."

Nibu stared. "They're worthless?" The assassin blinked at the row of daggers, leaving the floor open for a new speaker.

"This is some list of crimes you have racked up here," commented the chief, back among the living, and apparently with no grudge toward Finch. "You'll be going away for a lot of years for this, Mr. Nibudar. Now, how long have you and Mr. Hathaway been working together?" he asked, pen to pad.

Hathaway spouted more objections, but the chief wasn't listening.

"What happened, Mr. Nibudar? Did you two argue about how to split the loot?" Apparently, a tuba to the head, followed closely by a sock in the eye by Finch, had done the chief's powers of reasoning no amount of good. It was clear to everyone in the room that the officer was off his rocker.

"Hey," said one of the deputies, "did Hathaway throw the jar at Nibu?"

Adwick rolled his eyes. He was thinking angry thoughts about nephews. "Never mind that. It must have been the pickleman there," he said, indicating a very shocked Ditters. "We'll sort it out downtown."

"Hold the line," Hathaway jumped in. "Ditters didn't bean the conductor. You see, Adrienne was ticked off about holing up in the wardrobe with Ditters—"

"Adrienne attacked Nibu?" asked Lady Banbury, shocked.

"It was an accident," Hathaway explained.

"Adrienne, how could you?" said the indignant mother.

"But, Mother, he wasn't even the conductor. He's some assassin."

"That's not the point; a guest is a guest."

"Now, now," said the chief, "that's enough shouting, Lady Banbury. We'll sort this out downtown." The officer approached the assassin.

Nibu stepped back. "You appear to have Nibu right where you want him." He peered sideways at the chief and then back at the crowd of guests surrounding him. He looked at Mahrute. "A very clever man. But not too clever for Nibu. Ha!"

The *Ha!*, in case one might conclude otherwise, was not one of those hollow *Ha!'s* criminals announce to the master sleuth at the end of an investigation—the *Ha!* of resignation stated after the handcuffs are applied and they're carting the guy off. It was not a *Ha!* that said "Says you" or "See if I care, copper." This was a *Ha!* with some meaning. Nibu had gotten his hands on the Colt. (Evidently, Sir Roger had set the revolver down on an end table, as any easily distracted collector of antiquities is wont to do.)

Nibu swung around with the weapon. Wielding this gun had pretty much the same effect every time. Whether it was Ditters on the terrace or a known assassin threatening innocent bystanders, the general consensus was to dive for cover, and this they all did.

Nibu grinned. "Nibu not so helpless now, hey?"

All of a sudden, there was a whisking noise, and Otto was on the job. Standing between Mahrute and Nibu, he addressed Nibu boldly. "Funny thing about the pistol you are holding there, Mr. Nibudar. The last time you fired your gun was in the museum. But how many shots did you fire? And has anyone fooled with the gun since? You have got to stop and think about these things. You have got to ask yourself, 'Do I feel lucky?' Well, do you, you *Schwein*?"

Nibu blinked. His hand twitched. He pulled the trigger. *Click, click, click, click.*

Otto betrayed a manly smile. "Antiques are nice," he said, "when they work." Nibu was backing away toward the door. "Stop right there, Nibu; that's far enough. I said halt!" He dove at the assassin, and Nibu fought him off. Wrenching himself free of Otto's grip, Nibu whacked Otto on the forehead with the Colt and scampered off.

Otto lay there on the floor, out to the world. It was the first real sleep he'd had in weeks.

There was a quiet moment after this. The library began to come back to life, as guests removed themselves from behind sofas and bookcases. There was a notable sense of relief in the air.

Sir Roger looked down at the unconscious Otto. "Funny, the security agency said he was the best."

21 — Sir Roger Warms to a Fellow Collector

The moment of calm, the serenity experienced when the resident assassin finally calls it a night and shuffles off, was not long felt.

Lady Banbury was following Adrienne around the room, chiding the girl for the unladylike business of pitching pickle jars at guests; Ditters and Lesley were circling nervously; Warren was in the corner downing his fourth whisky; and Otto, now awake, had joined the chief and deputies in trying to track down Nibu. The four men were currently stomping around in the dimly lit halls overhead, occasionally calling out things like "Hey! Hold it there! Oh, sorry, Mr. Pincher" or "Hey! Got you, you *Schwein*. Oh, pardon me, Morrison, I thought you were Nibu."

All in all, it made for an unpleasant atmosphere for two in the morning. Somewhere in the proceedings, despite all the chaos, Sir Roger stopped Ditters mid-pace. His approach toward his future son-in-law was abnormally cheerful.

"Say there, my good fellow, did you really pinch this?"

He was referring to the Colt, which he had picked up off the floor and was currently submitting to a second look.

"Huh?" said Ditters. All the activity of the evening had knocked his aplomb on its ear. Add Sir Roger's jolly, mustached grin, and his agitation was not hard to fathom. "I mean, yes," he answered. "That is, I guess so."

"Golly, my boy, I didn't know you had it in you."

"Huh?"

"Taste, my boy, taste. I never would have imagined you'd have had the eye to pick out such a splendid piece. Makes one proud that they're teaching you young chaps the right things in school these days."

"Huh?"

"The revolver, my good fellow. I couldn't have chosen a better one myself."

"You couldn't?"

"No. Look at the lines. Craftsmanship. I didn't notice it at first, but I've been looking for this piece."

"Really?"

"Absolutely, absolutely. I had to check my guide," he went on, holding up a dusty volume, "in order to know for certain. Sure enough, this is one of the Colts used by British soldiers during WWII. The .455 caliber should have tipped me off immediately. As you know, the Colt normally takes a .44 or .45. This one is different. During a gun shortage, some British soldiers were actually issued these, refitted so they fired the same caliber as their Webleys. Can you imagine using an old cowboy revolver when everyone else is running around with automatic weapons? Yes, sir, I've been looking for one of these for years."

Ditters brightened. "I've always loved antiques, you know?"

"Really? You shouldn't have stolen it, though."

"No, no."

"Stealing, I've always said, is the wrong way to go about these things. But I can see how you young fellows get above yourselves sometimes; was like that myself when I was your age."

Ditters had an idea. "Sir Roger, why don't you take it?"

"Me? You mean for my collection? That's downright generous of you. Yes, generous. I'll send a check to the shop owner in the morning. You know, this weekend has been the most fun I've had in a long time. And I even got a new gun out of it."

"I think the shop owner had a leather holster that goes with it."

"Did he? Very observant of you to notice. You're obviously a man of great complexity, Mr. Dittersdorf. How anyone could tell with that vacant look on your face, I'll never know, but you're obviously a man of great depths," said Banbury, pausing for a moment to mull something over. "What I can't understand is why you would want to marry a nag like my daughter."

Across the room, Hathaway stepped over to Mahrute, who was standing in a far-off corner looking out at the rain. "You've done it again, Mahrute."

"Pardon?"

"Saved the day. Did the good deed."

"Oh yes. Thank you for saying so."

"I don't mind telling you, though, I'd feel better if I knew what became of that tuxedo-wearing thief. Nagging feeling we missed a loose end there."

"Yes. Would you wait here?" Mahrute returned an instant later with Lady Banbury in tow.

Hathaway was puzzled. For an older woman, Lady Banbury was definitely pleasant enough to look at, and if you wanted to know what it was like to be married to an eccentric tycoon, she was your expert. But as far as Hathaway was concerned, the conversation could have stridden along rather well without her. "What would make this moment perfect is our hostess" he did not recall announcing.

"You'll pardon me," said Mahrute, "but I wanted to check with Lady Banbury before I continued."

"Check with her?" asked Hathaway. "Why would you have to check with her?"

"I had reason to believe that Lady Banbury may have fostered mixed feelings about my disclosure of the facts."

"Disclosure? Facts?"

"About the prowler."

"The prowler? You mean, the thief! You saw him, Lady Banbury?"

"I hired him," she replied.

One hates to gape at one's hostess, but at times it is unavoidable. "I'm sorry, Lady Banbury," he said; "it's been one of those long evenings, and it sounded like you said you hired the man who's been skulking around the premises for the last three days."

"I did. I hired him to steal the Azure Star. You see, Mr. Konig's assistant called a few days ago, before you arrived. It was lucky, I guess, that I happened to pick up the phone, for that is something I usually leave to the help. At any rate, the girl wanted me to tell her employer that she had found the paperwork on the Azure Star purchase, an antique he was delivering to my husband a few days from then. As soon as I learned this, I knew I had to do something. I'm sure you question my methods, Mr. Hathaway."

"No, no. A bit offbeat, perhaps?"

"You see, I really could not bear to have it around the house. We had countless arguments about it. Besides being a fine example of Roger's distorted taste in collectibles, it had an intrigue surrounding it I did not like. Not only had he already bought one, which he later became convinced was a counterfeit, he informed me that once he found the genuine one, he planned to display it in our foyer. I couldn't have that. Of course, I feel awful about everything that has occurred. If Roger ever finds out, I'm not sure I could face him. You will understand, then, that when I happened along the kitchen and found my employee locked in the pantry, I had no choice but to set him free?"

"Absolutely."

"You see, Mr. Mahrute had come to me and explained that he had the Azure Star and was planning to work out a deal to buy it from Roger. All I needed then was to get rid of my hired thief. I know how it made you look."

"Don't give it a thought."

Lady Banbury left after this, and once more Hathaway turned to Mahrute. "You never can tell, eh, Mahrute? No matter who she is, a woman can always surprise you."

Mahrute nodded.

At this point, Ditters appeared before them. "I have decided to leg it," he said.

"Leg it?"

"Yes, you know, shove off. Take to the open road. Shake the dust …"

"Yes, yes. You still think Sir Roger won't approve your engagement to Adrienne?"

"Adrienne? No. Actually, now that I've given him the Colt, he and I couldn't be friendlier. It's the chief."

"Maybe you should give him a pistol."

"Hilarious. Listen, I don't have time for this. I'm leaving. You should come too."

"Now, now, Ditters, you jump the gun. We need to reason with him. He'll back off."

"He won't back off with me. I robbed the pistol shop, broke his arm and hit him with a tuba."

"True," Hathaway agreed, recalling that Ditters had been having quite a bit of excitement lately. "But how are you going to make good your escape? Your jeep's still locked up."

"I'll figure something out."

Hathaway might have argued a more practical route, but just then Lesley joined them. "Now what, John?"

"I don't know. My friend here suggests we all go on the lam."

"Yes, and I'd better get going on it," Ditters said. "I feel the element of the law breathing down my neck, and frankly, I could do without it. Besides, I want to say goodbye to Betty."

"Betty?"

"The girl from the neighborhood."

"Oh right, the peach. Incidentally, if you're wondering what became of Adrienne, she stepped out into the hall."

"Huh? Oh thanks."

"Shall I pack?" asked Lesley, after Ditters had meandered off.

"It might be a good idea. I'll be right up. I want to talk to Warren." Hathaway found the bodyguard draining another drink by the wet bar.

"This gin tastes funny," he said.

"It's scotch."

"Oh. That would account for it. Have you seen Lesley, Hathaway?"

"She just left."

"Ah. Do you remember what she said to me earlier?"

"Not particularly."

"She said I was brave."

"Girls can make mistakes."

"I feel brave, Hathaway. My arm hurts like the dickens, but I feel brave."

"Well, all those whiskies—they'd boost most men's morale. Actually, the amount you've put away would kill most men, but that's another issue."

"What's that, Hathaway? My mind wandered."

"Not important."

"I was thinking about that Nibu guy. Remember him?"

"Vaguely."

"Boy, did he blend in. I thought I was good. Funny, though, he wasn't after me, after all. I don't know what I was afraid of."

"Were you afraid of him?"

"Oh yes. Assassins have always scared me, but now I'm not afraid anymore."

Hathaway was delighted. Could it be that Warren had become a decent sort, a bodyguard willing to give life and limb for client and country?

Warren was still vocalizing his thoughts:

"And do you know what else? Pretending to be Harold Konig made me realize that I don't want to be famous. Being famous is a pain. I always figured, because of my size and muscles, becoming a famous bodyguard was a natural. But, you know what, I'm not sure I like it. When you're a bodyguard, people try to kill you. What fun is that? I need a job with less pressure."

Before Hathaway could get Warren to clarify this, Sir Roger was back among them. He addressed Warren. "I wanted to ask you, young fellow, are you *the* Warren Kingsley?"

"I think so," said Warren.

"I say, then, this is splendid. You're the best, I hear."

"That's true. Ask Hathaway."

"I already have a bodyguard, but he's far too overbearing. Of course, in your business I guess you have to be, considering that you're in the line of fire and all that."

"Line of fire?"

"Stepping in front of the bullet, becoming a human shield. You'd think a young fellow like you could find a better way to spend his time."

"Funny you should say that, Sir Roger. Hathaway and I were just discussing that, and personally, I've come to the conclusion that bodyguards should take it easy. Most of us work too hard to protect our clients from assassins. My policy has always been to avoid them."

"Avoid assassins, you say?"

"Yes," agreed the bodyguard. "Avoid them altogether."

"I never thought about it that way. Yes, I can see what you mean. Are you free to start work for me, Mr. Kingsley?"

The room had pretty much cleared out now, and Hathaway decided to get some rest. He had hardly made it to the stairs when an exhausted chief and two deputies came around the corner.

Adwick hollered to Mahrute, "We can't find that damn Nibu anywhere! You didn't see him come this way, did you?"

"No, sir."

"Damn! We thought we saw him heading back toward the library."

"The library?" asked Hathaway. "Warren and Sir Roger are still in there!"

The urgency of the statement was lost on them, all except Mahrute. They dashed to the scene only to find Warren gazing out at the grounds.

Sir Roger was nowhere in sight, and Hathaway figured with Warren on the job, the geezer could have been carried off by wolves, and the former would have been none the wiser.

"Warren," said Hathaway, "have you seen Nibu?"

"Of course I've seen him; we all did, remember?"

"No, no, have you seen him again? Did he return?"

"Return what?"

Hathaway failed to suppress a yelp of frustration. "Where's Sir Roger?"

"Have we moved on from the subject of Nibu?"

"Yes, yes, where's Sir Roger?"

"I don't know. He was here a second ago. Say, is that his foot?" (In the history of personal security, how many bodyguards have uttered those very words?)

Rushing over to the foot in question, they were relieved to discover that it was still connected to its host body, the latter of which was sprawled out behind a sofa. It appeared that Warren had broken his record. A dead client in just under five minutes.

"Sir Roger," whispered Hathaway.

"Sir Roger," whispered Adwick, Deputies One and Two, and Mahrute.

The corpse sprang to life, kicking out an entire lower shelf of books.

"Who's there?" he shuddered. "Who's that? Why are you all staring at me?"

"Mr. Banbury, you're alive, sir," said Adwick.

"Of course, I'm alive, you dolt. What did you expect? I was taking a nap. It's late."

"You were napping here, sir?"

"I must have dozed off."

"We're glad you're all right. Did you see Nibu by chance?"

"Are you still talking about Nibu?" asked Warren. "Didn't I tell you, I thought I saw him run across the lawn?"

"When?"

"Just now."

They all emerged from behind the sofa, all except Sir Roger, who was currently filling the room with the sounds of contented snoring.

"I'll head him off," said Adwick. "He's probably trying to get to the garage."

"What should we do?" asked a deputy.

"What should you do?" Chief Adwick's gaze fell on Hathaway. "Arrest that man, that's what. You should have done it an hour ago. After you've finished with that, collect those Azure Stars. We'll need them for evidence." The officer hurried off.

The deputies exchanged looks.

"Did he mean to arrest Mr. Hathaway or Mr. Kingsley?" one asked the other.

It was true the chief had not been very accurate with his pointing finger, having indicated the hatrack between Warren and Hathaway more than anything else.

Mahrute cleared his throat. "If I may, Deputy Morrison, I would suggest that you clarify his orders."

"But, er, what if one of them escapes while we're gone? You know, the one we're supposed to arrest."

"Yes, sir, that would be most unfortunate. I could, of course, watch them for you."

"Okay," replied Morrison hesitantly.

"We'll be right back, though," said Thomas, and the pair left.

Hathaway shook his head. "Let's not wait around here too long. Allow them to put two and two—"

"Hey!" said a new voice.

Hathaway furrowed his brow. The trouble with the sort of establishment where people regularly pop in unannounced and startle the bejeebers out of you is not so much the shock of the encounter, but keeping track of them all. After all, when someone sneaks up behind you and shouts "Hey!" you cannot simply tell yourself, "This must be my archenemy Moriarty paying me another visit." Because the place was littered with Moriartys. It could be Chief Adwick returning, because if you want a job done right, you do it yourself. It could be Finch, here for his hourly throttling of Hathaway. It could be Nibu, preparing to knife him where he stood. It could even be the thief we know as Barnet, back because he hadn't ticked off Hathaway enough this weekend and would do this one on a pro bono basis.

Hathaway turned. "Oh, it's you, Finch."

"Hathaway!"

"Yeah, it's me. Listen, this really isn't a good time."

"We have unfinished business, Hathaway. I still haven't bashed your brains in. And no police chief or bodyguard is gonna stop me this time either."

Hathaway was growing tired of his old schoolmate. "Piss off, Finch. I'm not in the mood to have my brains bashed in."

"Hathaway, you giant wimp, I'm going to rip your ..."

From the bedroom upstairs, where Lady Banbury was retiring after a trying day; to the kitchen where Chief Adwick and deputies searched for Nibu; to as far out as the greenhouse where the burglar Barnet legged it into the directionless night, a loud thump echoed out from the library.

In the years they had known one another, Randal Finch and John Hathaway had never actually come to blows. From Finch's successful campaign of intimidation and Hathaway's successful campaign of avoidance, there was no reason to. Hathaway decided to change this policy. Wheeling around and focusing an unamused glare at Finch, just as he would have eyed a bug he was preparing to swat with a rolled-up newspaper, John Hathaway punched Randal Finch in the face.

It was the last thing the oaf expected. He was not used to people standing up to him.

The punch sent him stumbling back. Landing on a coffee table, a piece of furniture that was not used to people dropping on it, Finch crushed it in an explosion of wood—the thud heard by Lady Banbury, Chief Adwick and even Barnet, from their positions across the estate.

Leaning up and holding his mouth, Finch whined, "You hit me, Hathaway."

At this point, a throat being cleared sounded from the doorway. "Excuse me, sirs," said the butler Jackson. "I don't know if this means anything, but Mr. Dittersdorf is gone."

The room pondered these words. They hardly had time to absorb them before Adrienne strolled in, followed by Adwick and the boys.

"What's going on here?" she asked. "Do you know what hour it is?"

"Mr. Dittersdorf has escaped, miss," replied Jackson.

This hadn't been the answer she expected. Typically, when you say, "Do you know what hour it is?" the other party replies with a rough estimate of the time—or, if the one responding takes into account the rhetorical edge to the speaker's voice, they answer, "Golly, no. Sorry." Seldom does one reply that your fiancé has fled the state.

In the moments that followed, during which Adrienne stood blinking at the butler, she appeared almost soft—vulnerable, even. Either that, or she was preparing to rip Jackson's head off; it was hard to tell with her. Whichever the case, Jackson decided not to chance it and left immediately thereafter.

For the next thirty seconds, Adrienne stared out the window across the lawn, her brow furrowed and her chest heaving. "Father was right," she said finally, more to the window than any of them. "Ditters Dittersdorf sucks!"

Hathaway might have pointed out that, in the current standing of things, Roger Banbury would be the last person to speak so harshly about a fellow collector, but he didn't feel it was his place to mention it.

"Did you hear that?" asked Chief Adwick to Morrison and Thomas.

"Yeah," said Morrison. "Sir Roger didn't like that pickleman much either."

"No, you nitwit, what the butler said. Quick, to the squad car! We may be able to catch him still!" In their haste to cop Ditters, none of them noticed Hathaway.

The room was surprisingly quiet after this. Adrienne noticed Finch covered in bits of wood and exhibiting a fat lip.

"You coming, Randal?" she asked wearily. "I hid my luggage in the shrubbery. I need someone to help me collect it."

Finch didn't know how to react. A second ago, he had no other focus beyond Hathaway. But now Hathaway seemed a distant memory. Adrienne Banbury wanted his help. "Wait up," he said.

Oddly enough, it was Hathaway who commented on their departure. "You know, Mahrute, one often says it, but never before has it seemed more appropriate: those two deserve each other." He shivered. "And now, perhaps we should take off before the chief returns. I'm sure I can work out everything with the officer, but I would prefer to do it on the phone from another state."

22 — The Unusual Usefulness of an Umbrella

"Any idea how to make good our escape, Mahrute?" Hathaway asked, taking the stairs.

"I am sure Mr. Dittersdorf would agree to give us a lift."

"What do you mean?"

This question was still hanging in the air, as they arrived at the room and found Ditters sitting on Hathaway's bed.

Next to him was an unidentified young woman with a cheerful face and curvy figure.

"Surprised?" asked Ditters.

Lesley was waiting by the window. She beamed at Hathaway when he came in.

Hathaway, pausing to bask in her glow, turned to Ditters. "I thought you took off?"

"That was Mahrute's idea," said Ditters. "Mahrute thought it up. Good one, Mahrute."

"Thank you, Mr. Dittersdorf."

"Did it work like you said?"

"Perfectly."

"Did what work?" asked Hathaway.

"On my suggestion, Mr. Dittersdorf informed Mr. Jackson that he was leaving. The purpose of this was to mislead Chief Adwick and his deputies."

"Mislead them?"

"I had hoped that upon discovering that Mr. Dittersdorf had left the premises, the chief would immediately attempt to find the young gentleman, and in so doing he would unlock the garage. Due to the rain, the deputies had placed the squad vehicle inside it."

"So the chief races off into the night on a wild-goose chase, and we stand here and have a good laugh." Hathaway nodded at the quiet charm of the scheme. He then turned and smiled cordially at the girl with the cheerful face.

"This is Betty," Ditters explained. "She's going to join us, if it's all right with you. I went to say goodbye to her and suddenly realized I didn't want to say goodbye, if you know what I mean."

Hathaway shook her hand. "What about Adrienne?" he asked discreetly.

"Adrienne is not the girl for me, Hath. Did you ever notice she has a stern streak?"

"Maybe slightly," said Hathaway.

"She's nothing like Betty. Betty's a peach."

Betty, a shy girl, giggled and nudged Ditters. "You're embarrassing me, Ditty."

"I'm going to do a lot more than embarrass you, Betty Adwick!" said Ditters, tickling her.

Hathaway was aghast. Not just at this wanton display of tickling, but at her name. "Adwick?! You don't mean Chief—"

"Daddy's going to be pissed," said Betty, sitting upright again.

Hathaway had no response to this. "Anyway," he remarked, "should we leave now, Mahrute?"

"I would not advise it yet. We will want to give the chief ample distance."

"Right." A short pause. "This is amazing, Mahrute. First you solve *The Mysterious Affair of the Azure Star*, and now this. By the way, how do you know so much?"

"About the Azure Star? I thought I had mentioned that. I was commissioned by Prince Dresdu to recover the Azure Star."

"So working for Warren was a ruse?"

"Not completely. I heard of Sir Roger's desire to find the Azure Star after I was already in the employ of Mr. Kingsley. When your friend Mr. Humner told Mr. Kingsley of your trip here, I merely did my part to encourage Mr. Kingsley to accept the commission."

Lesley, taking advantage of the break in the conversation, asked, "Do you really know Teddy, Mr. Mahrute?"

"Yes, miss, and you'll be happy to know that he is safe. When Prince Dresdu resumes the reins of the country, your brother will have a place in his cabinet."

"And you think the Azure Star will get him his throne?" Hathaway wondered.

"Oh yes. Although the parliament is thinking of dissolving the monarchy. Even still, Dresdu will have won the will of the people."

"You never explained—how did the daggers become scattered in the first place? Who unlinked them?"

"Theodore had help securing the Star from the mansion. In order to slip the object out without notice, they disassembled it. Each of the five men took a prong of the Azure Star. Unfortunately, the other four men were not as successful as Mr. Darlington in keeping their daggers safe. All four daggers were lost, some sold to collectors like Sir Roger Banbury."

"And they all wound up here. But we're missing one."

"That would be Mr. Darlington's."

"So Teddy did have one?" asked Lesley.

"To be precise, you do, miss."

"Me?"

"Yes, miss. Is your umbrella handy?"

Lesley retrieved the item off her packed luggage. She handed it to Mahrute.

"Your brother was concerned that the opposition would find him. In order to keep the Azure Star safe, he hid it here."

Mahrute opened the umbrella's handle to reveal a hollowed-out center. The fifth Azure Star slid out.

"He did not expect you would become Nibu's target."

Hathaway looked over the assortment of daggers.

"Are we just going to take these?"

Mahrute nodded. "Sir Roger has been amply compensated. I had feared he would not part with the object, but seeing how much trouble it had caused, he agreed to sell. He told me that on second thought the thing looked rather garish to him."

And on that happy note, they left for the open road.

*****

They met no one on their way to the garage, although one could still detect the far-off sound of Otto Pincher, the security guard who never slept, patrolling the premises.

They reached the garage, finding it precisely as they had hoped, unlocked and open.

Ditters wasted no time venturing within the darkened void.

The area surrounding the garage was also dark, with only the moonlight and its faint reflection off the lake to light it.

At least the rain had stopped.

Despite the lack of lighting, Ditters managed to pull out the jeep fairly quickly, and never once required the help of a search-and-rescue team.

It only took him about two minutes to pass into the darkness, trip over a garden rake, tell this garden rake where to get off, bump into what sounded like some sort of shelving, forge on, have a minor disagreement with a tin can or two and cause a cat to come screeching out from its poorly chosen nightly resting spot—before, eventually, his friends could hear the distinctive roar of an engine coming alive.

This was followed by the sight of the headlight beams and the vehicle itself, ready for the journey of a lifetime.

"Hop in," said Ditters.

Mahrute didn't hop exactly but certainly found his way into the back seat neatly. Next, it was Lesley's turn, but she hesitated.

"Oh rats, I forgot something."

For an instant, Hathaway thought it was the Adrienne-Ditters elopement all over again—the detail of a forgotten piece of luggage being precisely what made the activity a bummer of an outing. The difference here, however, was Hathaway's patience with Adrienne was shorter than it would be with Lesley. The Adriennes of this world forget luggage, he was convinced, for the express purpose of wreaking havoc on their men, whereas the Lesleys simply let the luggage slip their minds, and who can fault them for that?

"I'll retrieve it," he said. "What did you forget?"

"A book of Byron's verse. It has a flower pressed in it. Warren picked it for me on one of our walks. It's a nice book. My father gave it to me."

"Ah," Hathaway remarked, interested to learn what his bodyguard had been up to in his off-hours. Apparently, if you've looked everywhere else, the world's best can be found up to his kneecaps in daffodils.

"Oh, and I also forgot my umbrella," she said.

"It looks like the rain has stopped actually."

"Yes, I know, but it belongs to Teddy. Even though we got the Azure Star out of it, I would like to have it. Thank you ever so much."

"Right-o."

Dashing off, he stumbled over the aforementioned cat. The feline had settled beneath his ankles during the conversation, the thought never occurring to the little guy that Hathaway's position in the parking lot in the middle of the night was merely temporary.

Back inside, he found very little had changed. He could still hear Otto skulking about, and room lights were still occasionally coming on or off, indicating the movement of the last of the guests.

Retrieving the Byron and the umbrella, he rushed back down the stairs, not particularly watching where he was going. No sooner had he answered the question nagging at him for the past few minutes, as to whether Byron was the one who had the line about beauty or if that was Keats—deciding it was Keats—than he realized he had stumbled into unknown regions. He paused to assess the situation.

It's rather disconcerting when you expect to pop out into the crisp night air where your friends are waiting, clustered around an olive jeep—but discover instead that you have misplaced the friends, the olive jeep and the entire outside for that matter, and find that the air is downright musty.

Mansions are not the friendliest places in the middle of the night, but Hathaway stood coolly by, getting his bearings.

The high ceilings and the spotty glimmer of knickknacks in the moonlight gave the place away right off. He had somehow wandered into Sir Roger's museum. Evidently, he had taken one flight of stairs too many on his way down.

He was just turning to retrace his steps when he was struck sharply in the abdomen by a blunt object. He doubled over, gripping his stomach.

Nibu stepped out from the shadows, wielding a hefty sword.

"We meet again" was his greeting. "Do not concern yourself; I only hit you with the hilt of the sword."

"Damn considerate of you," said Hathaway, slinking over against the wall.

"Thank you. I don't stab men in back. Not proper. Enough of this chitchat. Nibu kill you now."

"Wait!"

"What?" snapped Nibu, sword raised above his head. "What do you want now?"

"You're not going to kill an unarmed man, are you?"

"I don't mind."

"Ah well, killing unarmed men, Nibu—it's improper."

"I don't think that."

"No? Ah. Well, as long as you've given it plenty of thought," he declared, and grabbing on to a nearby podium, dashed a bust of Alexander the Great in Nibu's path.

Scattered podiums do not slow down trained assassins for long. Hathaway hardly had time to scramble away before Nibu came running madly after him. With nothing else to defend himself with, he blocked Nibu's assault with Lesley's umbrella.

They dueled across the hall.

"Ha!" Nibu shouted, swinging his sword wildly.

"Ha!" said Hathaway, flourishing the now tattered umbrella. They were standing near Sir Roger's sword collection. Hathaway managed to grab a real sword in time to meet Nibu's hacking blows. They clanged their blades together and maneuvered into a wider part of the hall. Here, more moonlight was coming through the windows, so they could see what they were doing—all in all, an environment more conducive to swordplay.

"Nibu," said Hathaway, getting a feel for his blade, "this strikes me as a bit over the top."

"How do you mean this?" asked Nibu, advancing.

Hathaway backed up a bit. "Consider the facts. I mean, knives, guns, now swords—you can't do it all in one day. Look, we both have swords; let's just call it a stalemate."

"I don't think so," said Nibu, jabbing.

"But why not? Besides, I thought you had retired from the assassin game?"

"I came out of retirement for you."

"But I don't even have the Star. Why kill me?"

"Principle."

"Look, you can't subscribe to this personal vendetta stuff. Too much pro bono work can really cut into your income."

"Enough!" Nibu cried, smashing a row of porcelain statuettes. "You talk too much." Nibu lunged at him, and Hathaway figured the reasoning period was over.

"I have to warn you, Nibu," he said, taking a defensive position, "when I was at school, in England, I was considered quite a force to be reckoned with when it came to fencing. My instructor, Mr. Nelson, said I had immense promise."

Nibu stepped forward. "I was trained by Pefferu's son. I was the only one of his 'promising students' he did not kill with his blade." And on that pronouncement, he brought his sword down on Hathaway's.

The next few minutes, without indulging in a play-by-play analysis of the match, involved a lot of quick action on Hathaway's part to avoid having his head lopped off or his gizzard cut out. At one point, they had been clanging the sabers together pretty well when Hathaway found that someone had put a wall where they shouldn't have and, thanks to them, he now had his back to it.

Seeing as how jumping atop a table always seems to be the thing to do in these situations, he jumped atop a table, just before Nibu brought his sword down splintering the wood. Having gotten all he could out of the table maneuver, Hathaway leapt to safety

Nibu spun around. "Hathaway fights well for a young punk."

Hathaway took this personally. "I'll have you know, Nibu, that the Hathaways were bettering their enemies with the blade for centuries before the Nibus had the wherewithal to jab each other with pointy sticks." Hathaway didn't know the historical foundation, of course, but Nibu hadn't asked for footnotes.

Actually, he hadn't liked the comment at all and decided to take it out on Hathaway's left ankler region.

Hathaway blocked amply and fought the assassin off. "You really seem to enjoy your work," he said, impressed by the other's fierceness. "I don't work much myself, but I'm always interested to meet people who can't get enough of it. Something I don't understand, though," he continued, the two of them having entered a long, narrow hall with glass cases displaying what Lady Banbury would have called fine examples of Roger's distorted taste in collectibles, "is why you quit being an assassin. I mean, why the career change? If you don't mind my asking?"

"I do not mind. It is not a good job. Actually, my friend, I have a tendency to botch the hit. My assignments tend to survive my attempt on their lives. Take, for instance, young Teddy."

"Surely a few of your hits hit the mark?"

"No. None. The only part I did well was the disguises."

Hathaway was properly sympathetic. He did find himself pondering what a brilliant career Nibu and Warren could have had together, though. A bodyguard with no surviving clients and an assassin who has had no successful hits. If they had just switched clientele, they would have had the most successful caseloads on the record books.

"Oh well," he said, and the fight carried on. They fought their way up a flight of stairs, still exchanging blows. Hathaway was wondering if one was allowed a rest in these things when Nibu freed the sword from Hathaway's grip.

It was quite a parlor trick. There they were, clanging away, Nibu on a lower stair, Hathaway on the landing. They locked swords. Hathaway swung his clockwise to free it, Nibu swung his counterclockwise with it, and when the blades arrived back around, Hathaway was one blade short. One minute sword, next minute no sword.

Retracing the maneuver, Hathaway saw that the blade in question had sailed out of his hands and was now lying out of reach at the bottom of the stairs.

"Don't suppose you'd mind if I nip down there and retrieve that?" he asked.

"I don't think so."

Hathaway said right and backed off. Suddenly, his ankles brushed against something—the cat from the garage. To bring the reader up to speed on its movements, he had followed Hathaway down to the basement, perhaps to ask if he had seen any mice around. Hathaway felt his foot slip, his balance teetered, the cat let out a screech and bounded for regions unknown, and before Hathaway could grab the railing, he fell backward down the steps, landing disheveled at the foot of the staircase.

It had been what they call a "fortunate fall," however, because it placed him only a few feet from his weapon. He leapt up and chased after it, but in the disorder of the moment, he accidentally kicked the sword across the floor and sent it sliding under another staircase.

Glancing back to see Nibu charging after him, Hathaway dashed up the new staircase and out onto the catwalks.

Nibu followed.

Hathaway backed off from the approaching assassin. He looked over the railing. Quite a jump. His back bumped against the wall. Nibu cornered him. The assassin went to hack his opponent to pieces, but, consistent with a perfect career, he managed to jab his sword into a bookcase. He pulled and pulled at it, but like an unworthy knight trying to free Excalibur, he couldn't extricate it.

In the split second Nibu was distracted, Hathaway seized the opportunity and shoved him off the catwalk. Nibu pitched over the railing and landed in a heap below.

Hathaway was no expert, but it couldn't have done the assassin much good.

A moment later, Mahrute arrived at his side. "Are you okay, Mr. Hathaway?"

"Fine, just fine." Hathaway peered over the railing. "I wonder where he landed."

They found Nibu mumbling half consciously, balled up on an antique curio table.

Otto joined them. "You found Nibu! Say, did you throw him off the balcony?"

"Something like that. Anyway, he's all yours, Otto."

"You aren't staying, Johnny?"

"Not with the chief prowling about."

"Oh right. By the way, I apologize about all that."

Hathaway looked blank, so Otto clarified:

"The chief blaming you for the death threat to Sir Roger. You see, actually, it was I who sent it."

Hathaway had been helping Nibu off the table. Hearing this, he let the assassin drop with a splat to the cement. "You sent it? Why would you threaten Sir Roger?"

"I was not really threatening him. I wanted him to think someone was after him, so he would appreciate me more. You gave me the idea, Johnny, when you said you hired a bodyguard because you received death threats. Anyway, sorry. Of course, the death threat didn't do any good. Sir Roger fired me five minutes ago."

Hathaway had suspected he might. "Well, you shouldn't have too much trouble getting work as a bodyguard. I mean, look at Warren."

"Actually, I was thinking of going into law enforcement. I think I can do more good there."

"I wish you luck. Let this bozo be your first prisoner," he said, handing over Nibu. "Take it easy, Otto."

"You too, Johnny." The future officer of the law paused. "Hey, you guys sure made a helluva mess," he muttered.

*****

"What took you so long?" asked Ditters, once they had arrived back at the garage.

"We met up with a little snag," said Hathaway. "But you'll be happy to know," he told Lesley, as they climbed in the back, "that the Nibu threat has been eliminated."

"Really, John? You really caught him?" Few things perk up a girl more than hearing that you have foiled the plans of her would-be assassin.

"If Otto has the appropriate book, he is throwing it at the guy as we speak. Speaking of which, here's your Byron."

"You're wonderful, John, just wonderful. How can I ever thank you?"

"We'll think of something, I'm sure. Oh, here's your umbrella. I wouldn't open it in any rainstorms."

"He's just so brave," sighed Lesley, "brave and wonderful, just wonderful."

"I hate to interrupt," said Ditters at the wheel, seated next to Betty, "but if I have to hear much more of how 'brave and wonderful' John is, I may have to drive into a tree. And on that topic, does anyone know where we're going?"

*****

The next evening, Hathaway, Mahrute and Lesley were sitting in the dining car of a train, on their way home. The cover of night had enveloped the landscape, and Hathaway was looking out the window at the passing scenery.

It had been exactly one day since the Hathaway Gang escaped Rangeley Manor.

"A most pleasant evening," Mahrute observed.

Hathaway nodded. "Quite a jaunt this has been. Remind me never to visit the state of Maine again. Not only did I miss out on a week of gambling, I think I lost my trilby in our travels through New England."

"I'm sorry, Mr. Hathaway."

"I'll buy you a new hat, John," Lesley told him. "I saw a fedora in London that would look great on you."

"Regarding your purchasing power," Mahrute went on, "I owe you both money for the safe return of the Azure Star."

"Oh, Mahrute, you don't have to pay us," said Lesley.

"It is my duty, miss. Any cash I do not use will be returned to my government."

"Well, if it would make you feel better," Hathaway agreed, "slip us a few bills."

"It would. I was instructed to pay five hundred."

"That's a tidy profit; though I have to tell you I wouldn't give you fifty bucks for the thing."

"I mean, of course, five hundred thousand."

Hathaway spilled his single malt. "Thousand! Five hundred thousand?"

"Yes. Each."

"I'm astounded," said Hathaway, astounded. "I thought your government was strapped?"

"The finances were never an issue. The royalty has always been more than well off. It is the morale boost they require, a boost I am now able to give them."

"I really must meet this royalty sometime. I mean, they must be fun at parties."

Lesley was speechless. "I don't know how to thank you," she managed to say.

Hathaway looked pensive. "The Azure Star really belonged to my uncle, you know. He bought it."

"The reward is for the safe return of the Azure Star," Mahrute insisted. "You are the ones who returned it. Not your uncle. Sir Roger told me he wanted you to have the reward."

The tycoon's gesture moved Hathaway. "I assume your government will pay you, Mahrute?"

"Yes, they are quite generous."

"Well then, we're all set for a good long time."

"Yes. Although it has never been my intention to stop working."

"That's funny; it was never my intention to start working," said Hathaway, leaning back.

*****

Life at Rangeley Manor shuffled on.

Ditters Dittersdorf and Betty Adwick—its defectors—headed for the countryside to start a cucumber farm, heavily financed by Sir Roger Banbury. (Although he had never mentioned it before, he always did appreciate a good pickle.)

Adrienne told her father that she probably wanted to marry Finch now, and she was also considering running for Congress, which Sir Roger would also heavily finance.

Warren became the manor bodyguard, a less overbearing variation of his predecessor. In his easy existence, devoid of responsibility, he filled his afternoons in the parlor, where he was served by the ever-efficient Jackson. As the bodyguard to a client who was happiest when left alone, Warren had time to devote to writing *Warren Kingsley: A Bodyguard's Memoirs*.

Lady Banbury contacted the real Kurt Richter, who agreed to the Bath Chamber Orchestra gig, assuming Sir Roger could supplement its funds a bit. She also straightened out the charges against Hathaway and Lesley with the authorities. Considering her standing in the community, the police made no arguments. To make up with her husband, she bought him a large decorated shield dating back to the Battle of Hastings.

Otto Pincher inquired in town about becoming Baccup's new sheriff, in light of the fact that Chief Adwick had handed in his resignation and taken early retirement.

Nibu Nibudar went to jail. Tired of his life as an assassin and a thief, he decided to study up to become a lawyer.

Bu, who had been released due to lack of evidence, promised to be his first client.

Barnet realized that he liked wearing formal attire and applied for a job as a maître d'.

The real Harold Konig arrived and reviewed Sir Roger's art collection, appraising his canvases at a slightly lower figure than Warren's estimate.

Sir Roger wrote checks for his family through the next week and then took a holiday.

He didn't mention where.

Further Reading

If you enjoyed *Five Star Detour*, check out *Double Cover*, a look back at Warren and Mahrute's first job together. See how the two bodyguards met and get a little more insight into what makes Warren the man that he is.

www.ingramcontent.com/pod-product-compliance
Lightning Source LLC
Chambersburg PA
CBHW020609310726
48979CB00008B/1405/J

9780991232406